FLIGHT

a novel

HARRY HASKELL

ACADEMY

CHICAGO

Copyright © 2017 by Harry Haskell
All rights reserved
First edition
Published by Academy Chicago Publishers
An imprint of Chicago Review Press Incorporated
814 North Franklin Street
Chicago, Illinois 60610

ISBN 978-1-61373-637-1

Library of Congress Cataloging-in-Publication Data

Names: Haskell, Harry, author.
Title: Maiden flight : a novel / Harry Haskell.
Description: Chicago, Illinois : Chicago Review Press, 2016. | Description
   based on print version record and CIP data provided by publisher; resource
   not viewed.
Identifiers: LCCN 2016021905 (print) | LCCN 2016010850 (ebook) | ISBN
   9781613736395 (adobe pdf) | ISBN 9781613736401 (epub) |
ISBN 9781613736388
   (kindle) | ISBN 9781613736371 (paperback)
Subjects: LCSH: Haskell, Katharine Wright, 1874–1929—Fiction. | Haskell,
   Henry Joseph, 1874–1952—Fiction. | Wright, Orville, 1871–1948—Fiction. |
   Dayton (Ohio)—Fiction. | Kansas City (Mo.)—Fiction. | BISAC: FICTION /
   Historical. | GSAFD: Biographical fiction. | Historical fiction. | Love
   stories.
Classification: LCC PS3608.A78997 (print) | LCC PS3608.A78997 M35 2016
   (ebook) | DDC 813/.6—dc23
LC record available at https://lccn.loc.gov/2016021905

Cover design: Andrew Brozyna, AJB Design, Inc.
Cover images: (front cover) Close-up view of airplane, including the pilot
and passenger seats, Library of Congress LC-DIG-ppprs-00691; (back cover)
Katharine and Orville Wright, with unidentified companions, at Tempelhof
Field, Berlin, 1909, Courtesy of Special Collections and Archives, Wright
State University.
Typesetting: Nord Compo
Interior images: (p. 1) Katharine Wright, ca. 1925, (p. 85) Harry Haskell at
Hawthorne Hill, and (p. 161) Orville Wright, November 1926, Courtesy of
Special Collections and Archives, Wright State University.

Printed in the United States of America
5 4 3 2 1

For Lucy Linnea Haskell,
Katharine's "kindred spirit"

Contents

Prologue

It's an old, familiar tale: a woman of a certain age, secure in a stable, emotionally undemanding relationship with a man she admires, is suddenly swept off her feet by a grand passion. Racked with doubt and remorse, she first denies her feelings, then tries to reason them away. Only after months of procrastination and soul searching does she accept the unavoidable necessity of choosing between love and duty.

The story is familiar, but the woman at the center of this book was far from ordinary. Katharine Wright was the younger sister of Wilbur and Orville Wright, the inventors of the airplane. Smart, vivacious, confident, and down to earth, she made friends wherever she went. Katharine's outgoing personality made her an indispensable asset to her world-famous brothers, who were widely perceived as aloof and socially awkward, especially where women were concerned.

Katharine was remarkable in other ways as well. Born in 1874, she struggled to balance the conventional strictures of Victorian domesticity against the emerging feminist sensibility of the modern era. Both as the "Wright sister" and as the second female trustee of Oberlin College, she embodied, in a very public and prominent way, the worldly, independent, and self-fulfilled New Woman of the early twentieth century.

To be sure, none of this would matter greatly if Katharine had not also been an exceptionally gifted, sensitive, intellectually curious, and articulate woman, equally alive to the complexity of her own emotions and to the forces of change, both social and technological, that were inexorably transforming the insular, family-centered world of her youth. An international celebrity in her own right, she slipped easily into her appointed role as her brothers' ambassador, charming captains of science and industry and crowned heads of Europe with her unaffected midwestern ways.

Katharine spent the first five decades of her life as a caregiver, dutifully filling the shoes of her mother, who died when Katharine was fifteen; serving as nurse, companion, and secretary to her affectionate but domineering father; and enthusiastically propelling her older brothers along the path to fame and fortune. After Wilbur died in 1912, she and Orville lived together in a relationship so easy and intimate that strangers often mistook them for husband and wife.

A lifelong bachelor whose shyness bordered on the pathological, Orville came to depend on his spinster sister's tireless support and fiercely protective loyalty. The diamond ring that he gave Katharine when she graduated from Oberlin in 1898 symbolized an emotional bond that transcended the usual closeness between brother and sister. Their quasi-marital union was reinforced by the tragedy of Wilbur's premature death. For years afterward, it seemed unthinkable to them both that it would ever be sundered.

Enter Harry Haskell, an old college friend of Katharine's from Kansas City and one of a handful of newspapermen whom she and Orville admitted into their inner circle. Over the years, he had become a trusted ally in Orville's battles to defend the Wright patents and the brothers' reputation as the fathers of human flight. When Harry's wife succumbed to cancer, Katharine instinctively offered consolation and understanding, and before either of them fully realized what was happening, their budding friendship had blossomed into romance.

So it was that two not-so-proper Victorians, both in their early fifties, both the products of strict religious upbringings, and both generously endowed with what Katharine was fond of calling "human nature," found themselves head over heels in love and conducting a clandestine affair under Orville's unsuspecting nose—indeed, under the very roof of his imposing, double-porticoed mansion in Dayton, Ohio.

Imagine, if you will, hearing Katharine, Harry, and Orville recount their experiences in their own words. This is what I have tried to do in the pages ahead, by weaving their three first-person "memoirs" (as explained in my author's note) into a single richly textured narrative. As the title suggests, *Maiden Flight* is first and foremost Katharine's book—the story of a bright, brave, passionate woman who followed her heart and suffered the unhappy consequences. She, Orville, and Harry are as alive to me as if I knew them in the flesh. It is my hope that this book will help bring them to life for others.

It is the end of February 1929. Katharine and Orville Wright have been estranged for more than two years. Not a word has passed

*between them since she became Harry Haskell's wife in Novem-
ber 1926 and moved from Dayton to Kansas City. Family and
friends have tried to mend the breach, to no avail. Harry blames
himself for tearing Katharine away from her old interests and asso-
ciations so late in life. For her part, Katharine is struggling to conceal
her grief from Harry, even as she fears that her brother's stony silence
has cast a pall over their marriage. Orville, meanwhile, has taken
refuge in denial. Unable to forgive his sister for deserting him, he
has steeled himself to forget her.*

*Of the millions of people around the world to whom the Wright
family name is synonymous with the miracle of human flight, only
a small coterie of intimates are privy to the tragic rift between sister
and brother. The final act of their domestic drama is about to begin.
On this bleak midwinter day, the three protagonists are cocooned
in reverie, each reliving the two eventful decades since fate brought
them together. It all started, Katharine recalls, in early 1909 . . .*

Devotion

Katharine

What I remember best about that winter in Pau is the bitter cold. If you ask me, all that talk of "sunny southern France" is a delusion and a snare. Orv and I practically froze in our beds! Will had sworn up and down that the Gassion was the best hotel in town, but I never was so uncomfortable in my whole life, not even in the icy grip of an Ohio winter—and that is no picnic, I assure you! Luckily, I came prepared for the worst. When Will took me up in the flying machine for the first time, I was all trussed up like a turkey, with my overcoat bound snug around my ankles and a long scarf looped over my hat to keep it tethered down.

Sure enough, as soon as we got up in the air, my chills and aches vanished in a trice. It was one thing to listen to the boys talk about airplanes—back home in Dayton I used to complain that we didn't hear anything *but* "flying machine" from morning till night—and something else again to go up in one myself. All those years I had stood on the ground watching Will and Orv make their practice flights over Huffman Prairie and fancied how it would feel to "do the bird act," as Orv put it. Now at last I knew, and I was so proud of them I could have burst wide open.

It was Orv who was grounded that day for a change. Only a few weeks had passed since he had his terrific smashup at Fort Myer while he was demonstrating the Wright flyer for the US Army. I'll never forget how his chin trembled and tears filled his eyes when I came into the hospital room and saw how badly he had been hurt. Dear, brave Little Brother! Wild horses couldn't have kept me from rushing to his bedside in Virginia. Then Will's letter arrived, inviting—no, *summoning*—us to come join him in France. That was just what the doctor ordered. Orv was still hobbling around on crutches, but Will needed our help getting the machines ready for the exhibition races in the spring, and we had never let him down yet.

The four months I spent in Europe with the boys in 1909 were a fairy tale from start to finish. My very own first flight lasted about seven minutes—but it might have been a lifetime for all I knew. The whole thing was like a dream that words can hardly begin to describe. All I could think to write to Pop the next day was, "Them *is* fine!" Pau sure is a beautiful place when the weather is nice. Will and I could make out the snowcapped peaks of the Pyrenees glimmering in the distance as we swooped and soared above the farm fields. Never in all my thirty-four years on earth had I seen such a heart-stopping sight. And not until I fell in love, many years later, would I feel like such a giddy young thing again.

"Omnia vincit amor," the Roman poet says—"Love conquers all." The ancients knew a thing or two when they gave the god of love his wings, the better to sweep us mortals off our feet! As nervy as I was up there in Will's flying machine that day at Pau, I knew in my heart of hearts that he would bring me back down to earth safe and sound. I always had perfect confidence in Will and Orv, ever since we were little children. Come to think of it, I always felt perfectly safe with Harry too.

We met up with him in Washington in the summer of '09, not long after we got back from Europe. The reporters were all hounding the boys for interviews, and it was my thankless job to keep them at bay. Ha ha! When Harry sent up his card, though, I insisted on making an exception. I had watched him come up in the world since our college days, from editor of the *Oberlin Review* to Washington correspondent of the *Kansas City Star*. There always was something special about Harry. His mind soaked up everything like a sponge, and his character was as solid as a rock. Even at Oberlin, I recognized the strength and dependability that came out so strongly when there was a call for them. It pleased me to see that he had become exactly the kind of man I thought he would.

Even so, when he presented himself that day at our hotel room, I had to pinch myself to make sure I was awake. He looked as if he had stepped straight out of his college yearbook photograph. To think that he was not only a husband and father but also a member in good standing of the Washington press corps. I felt easy with Harry on the spot, but Will and Orv could be as prickly as porcupines. Newspapermen had a way of setting them on edge. One of the national magazines had just published a story claiming that since neither of the boys had a college education, sister Kate had had to step in and help with the mathematical calculations for the flying machine.

It was sheer bosh and nonsense, of course, and no one who knew me would have credited it for a moment. I got good marks in math in school, but when it comes to higher mathematics, I have no head for figures—not one speck! Those reporters were simply determined to make a silk purse out of a sow's ear. Why, the *American Magazine* even offered me seven hundred and fifty dollars—half of my teacher's salary at the high school—for a series of articles to be called "The Sister's Story." I had a good mind to take the money and run—until I woke up and came to my senses. Not that it kept me from ribbing the boys about it, mind you. It did no harm to let them know they weren't the only pebbles on the beach!

All that bunk about my mathematical ability got under Orv's skin, right enough. He may not be a natural-born scholar, as Will was, or have a bona fide college degree, like me. But he is no slouch at engineering, trigonometry, geometry, and other subjects that make my head swim. I could see how het up he was over those tall tales the newspapermen had been spinning. So the minute Harry stepped through the door, I popped right up out of my chair and exclaimed, "We read that piece in *Hampton's* on the train last night, and I told the boys there was at least one person outside the family who would know it wasn't so!"

Harry

It seems just yesterday that the Wrights invited me up to their rooms in the old Raleigh Hotel. It was 1909, as I recall, the end of June. The *Star* had sent me to Washington six months earlier, and already I was beginning to feel like an old hand on the capital beat. I must have interviewed dozens of important people for the paper, but the Wright brothers were in a class by themselves. Orville's crash at Fort Myer and the death of Lieutenant Selfridge had been front-page news around the world. And Wilbur's daring demonstration flights in Europe had made him an international hero. *L'homme oiseau*, the French dubbed him—"the bird man."

As keen as I was to meet the world's most famous aviators, the prospect of renewing my friendship with their charming sister was an even bigger draw. A few weeks earlier I had stood in the crowd in the East Room of the White House watching President Taft give Wilbur and Orville their gold medals from the Aero Club of America. I was near enough to touch Katharine, almost, but they whisked her away, and I couldn't even speak to her. She was wearing a high-necked white gown, a large plumed hat, and the old-fashioned pince-nez eyeglasses that I remembered so well. The dark, silky hair that she was so proud of in college had turned snow-white. She used to pull it back in a tight bun, schoolmarm style. Somehow it seemed only natural that she had taken up teaching as a career.

Katharine and I were both raised in religious households— my parents were Congregationalist missionaries in the Near East, her father a bishop in the Church of the United Brethren—and our families shared a generally progressive outlook on issues like woman suffrage and coeducation. As a youngster, I was disposed to look on girls as a demoralizing influence in the classroom, but Katharine taught me the error of my ways. She was different from the other Oberlin girls—quick, alert, intelligent, easy to talk to, and a good listener. She was always bragging about her two older brothers—"the boys," she called them—who had a bicycle shop back home in Dayton. There was no doubt in her mind that they would amount to something someday.

We met in the fall of 1894, my junior year. Katharine was a freshman living at Mrs. Morrison's boardinghouse, where I took my meals. In those days, all incoming students were required to take a course known as Math Review. Each pupil was given a tablet that carried problems in algebra and geometry at the top of each page. They were supposed to work these problems three times a week and turn them in to the professor. Now, Katharine was an able scholar of languages, history, philosophy, and the natural sciences. But she had no feeling whatsoever for mathematics. She soon discovered that it was a favorite subject of mine, and before long I was detained after breakfast three times a week to give aid and advice. So much for the old canard about Katharine supplying math help to her older brothers!

The more we saw of each other at Oberlin, the more I grew to admire Katharine's sharp wit and strength of character. But any deeper feelings that might have grown up between us had no chance to develop, as my college girlfriend, Isabel Cummings, and I had decided to get married as soon as I was able to support her by my writing. As it turned out, Katharine was already spoken for at the time herself, though her engagement was a closely held secret. To the best of my knowledge, not even her own family was in on it. Long afterward she told me her fiancé's name and how she had finally broken it off with him when she discovered she wasn't really in love. After graduating in '96, I settled down in Kansas City, Katharine returned to Dayton two years later, and that was that—or so I thought.

Then Wilbur and Orville made their historic flight at Kitty Hawk. Incredible as it seems today, some of the best minds in the country simply ignored one of the great inventions of all time. There was a common saying that man would fly only when the law of gravity was repealed. Eminent scientists had demonstrated the absurdity of the whole idea. On the eve of the first flight, a noted American astronomer even published an article proving that human flight in a heavier-than-air machine was mathematically impossible. I was no expert, but from what Katharine had told me I found it impossible to believe that her brothers had fabricated the story out of whole cloth. As a family, the Wrights are proud, not to say clannish, but I never knew them to stretch the truth or go in for what Katharine calls "personal advertising."

The brief AP dispatch, datelined December 18, 1903, stirred up a nest of happy memories. When I read about the successful flight at Kitty Hawk on the front page of the *Star*, my first thought was of how proud Katharine must be to see Wilbur and Orville make good. At Oberlin she had spoken about the boys so often, and with such warmth and affection, that I almost felt I knew them. The popular image of the two stiff-necked "mechanics" from the Buckeye State just didn't add up in my mind. Katharine always had been so sociable and vivacious, the kind of woman who lit up a room with her presence. It wasn't easy to picture *her* as Wilbur and Orville's kid sister.

When I finally caught up with the three of them in Washington, I realized that my fellow newspapermen were all wet. The Wright brothers had earned the reputation of being "fierce" with reporters, but as far as I was concerned they couldn't have been more approachable and down to earth, Orville in particular. With his neatly trimmed mustache, starched white collar, and well-tailored three-piece suit, he might have passed for a bank manager or a small-town businessman. Not in my wildest dreams would I have taken him for what he actually was: a scientific supergenius with one of the most brilliant inventive and imaginative minds in human history.

Orville

The Wright brothers, they call us—as if Will and I were the only male pups in the litter! Do those fool reporters never bother to get their facts straight? There were *four* of us boys, not counting the twin who died in infancy, may he rest in peace. Reuch and Lorin were the original Wright brothers. They left home a good while before Will and I opened our first bicycle shop over on West Third Street. Reuch and I were a full ten years apart, and so unlike each other in temper and outlook that you'd never guess we had the same blood in our veins. He married young and struck out for Kansas City, where he and Lulu brought their four children into the world.

Reuch was a restless man, a loner, and about as stubborn as a Missouri mule. More than once Will and I tried to help him out when he was hard up, but it was no use. As Kate said, a person couldn't do anything to please Reuch; he was just naturally suspicious of everything and everybody. Lorin and he were as different as night and day. Easygoing and easy to please, that's Lorin for you—not that he can't be as ornery as the next fellow when it suits him. Runs in the family, you might say. Lorin tried his luck out west for a spell too. After Mother passed away, he came back to

Dayton and settled down with Netta to raise a family in the old neighborhood, down the way from the house we grew up in on Hawthorn Street.

And then there was Kate—Sterchens, we called her, or Swes for short. She was the baby, born August 19, 1874, three years to the day after me. There was always a special bond between us. As children we shared birthdays, toys, playmates—pretty near everything, in fact. It was Kate who held the family together after Mother died; maybe that's why I always seemed to feel like a little boy around her. When I had the accident at Fort Myer, she dropped everything and camped out beside my hospital bed for seven weeks, like my guardian angel. I said to her, "Sterchens, you watch and don't let them hurt my leg!" I didn't trust those army doctors within an inch of my life. Kate had always looked after us at home when we were ill, and I knew I could depend on her. As Mr. Chanute said, she was devotion itself in those days.

Growing up, Will and I knew all of Kate's schoolmates, and our friends were her friends too. She and I threw some swell house parties in the old days. How Father used to fret and fume when he caught on we'd been playing bridge behind his back. In his book, card games, dancing, and such were Satan's work. Once the Wright Company got off the ground, there never seemed to be enough time for such diversions. Will and I were on the move pretty much nonstop. Wherever we happened to be, though, we could always count on Kate to keep us up on the news from home. One Halloween she wrote about how she and her friends had dressed up in sheets and pillowcases and told one another's fortunes in verse. I can still recite hers, word for word:

You'll early leave this earthly sphere,
But not by death! O! No!
You'll guide an airship without fear,
Win fame and a rich beau.

Oh, Swes, Swes, how could you do it? How could you run off and leave me to rattle around this big, empty house alone? We were so happy together, just the two of us, happy and settled and fixed for life. The idea of you falling in love never seriously crossed my mind. I didn't think of you as appealing to other men, not in that way. In hindsight, I should have read the handwriting on the wall the minute you introduced us to Harry that day in Washington. The way you sprang up to greet him—it was like you were a schoolgirl again, all flustered and excited and beaming with pride.

Katharine

I was proud to have Will and Orv meet Harry and know that he was a friend of mine. They liked him right away. They liked most of my friends, if it comes to that—newspapermen excepted! And who can blame them? The way the papers mangled the story of the first flight was simply scandalous. When Lorin hand-carried Orv's telegram from Kitty Hawk to the city editor of the *Dayton Journal*, all Mr. High-and-Mighty had to say was, "Fifty-seven seconds, huh? If it'd been fifty-seven *minutes* it might have been a news item." I wanted to scream! Harry wasn't like that at all. He didn't come on gangbusters or set himself up on a pedestal. The boys knew instinctively that they could trust him. And seeing how quickly Will and Orv took to Harry made me like him all the more.

Some way we hadn't had much to do with each other since Oberlin. It was Harry who let our correspondence drop after he and Isabel were married, but I would have stopped writing regardless. I just didn't feel comfortable keeping up a regular correspondence with a married man. I've always thought it is not right to make any wife even a little bit uneasy. Anyhow, the letters he wrote me in those years were all lost in the big Dayton flood of 1913. The fine edition of Robert Louis Stevenson's *Vailima Letters* that he gave me at commencement in 1898—that was spoiled too. I tried to replace it later but couldn't get it in the original binding. I wonder if Harry kept the book I gave *him* for graduation—someday I'll have to ask him. I doubt it meant half as much to him as the Stevenson did to me.

My college roommate told me about visiting Harry one time in Kansas City. Such pride he takes in showing off his library! I can just picture him pulling the books off the shelves, one by one, and reading his favorite passages to Margaret. Books are one of the things that brought us together—books and a sense of common values, the solid, old-fashioned values that Oberlin stood for in our day. Harry loved the old Oberlin as much as I did. We fussed and fussed about every subject under the sun: poetry, philosophy, religion, literature, history—even mathematics! I'll never forget winning that twenty-five-dollar prize for my essay on the Monroe Doctrine in my sophomore year. I was so proud and happy when Harry—a respected upperclassman, if you please—walked me home from chapel after the ceremony. His praise was the sweetest of all. Yes, I always cared a lot for Harry's opinion of me. I made no bones of that!

I'm the only one in our family with a college diploma—not that it does me any credit to crow about it. Reuch and Lorin attended a Brethren school in Indiana, but they weren't cut out for book learning, I guess, and soon drifted away. Will had a first-class head on his shoulders—he would have gone to Yale if it hadn't been for his ice hockey accident. As for Orv, he was clever enough at brain work—when he wasn't working in his print shop, fixing bicycles, or just plain horsing around. A regular practical joker Little Brother was—and still is, from what I hear. One time his sixth-grade teacher sent him home for doing something wicked and told him not to come back without a written apology from our parents. Bubbo couldn't face telling them the truth, so he played hooky the rest of the year. I thought he'd catch it for sure, but to my amazement Pop didn't come down hard on him. As a matter of fact, I think he admired Orv's independent streak.

Father respected independence in us women as well—up to a point, anyway. He put me through Oberlin so I could earn my living as a schoolteacher and not have to depend on him in his old age. Then, after I came home and started teaching at the high school, he deeded the Hawthorn Street house over to me so I would never have to worry about having a roof over my head. All those years I spent living with him and the boys, as housekeeper, mother, sister, and daughter all rolled into one, I knew I could make my own way in the world if it ever came to that.

Considering he was born before the Civil War, Pop's views on the woman question were surprisingly advanced. He never for one minute doubted that women were entitled to the vote just the same as men. His convictions on that point were unshakable. One time, before the last war, he and Orv marched side by side in a suffrage parade through downtown Dayton. Pop was eighty-six years old—and was I ever proud to be his "Tochter" that day! In other ways, though, he was no different from most men of his generation. When he went away from home on church business, he used to write practically every day, reminding me to do this, that, or the other thing. He was a regular fountain of advice about cultivating modest feminine manners, keeping my temper under control, and everything.

The fact is, I s'pose, Pop was well-nigh helpless without a woman by his side. Mother used to do everything for him. He told me once that he never published an important editorial in the church newspaper without reading it to her first. If it wasn't clear to Mother, he said, there was no use expecting anyone else to understand it. They were as devoted to each other as any two people I ever knew. Pop said the light of our home went out when Mother died. I was only a girl of fifteen, but no one had to tell me that I was expected to step into her shoes. One letter Pop wrote nearly did me in, it pulled my heartstrings so: "But for you, we should feel like we had no home. I often think of something or see or hear of something that Mother would know and care something about, but she is not here, and there is no one knows or cares anything about it."

Mother was called Susan Catharine—such a beautiful name! Sometimes Pop got muddled and spelled my name with a C instead of a K—but I didn't take it to heart. It was his refusing to treat me like a grown woman that got my dander up. Even after I came home from college, he fussed and brooded over me like a mother hen. He insisted on knowing where I was going of an evening, who I was going out with, when I'd be home—and *everything*! After the boys went off to Europe in '07, every peculiarity he ever had came out in full blossom. I couldn't even leave the house in broad daylight without being lectured. I told Will and Orv that it was a pathetic state of affairs when going out for the cream was treasured up as the chief diversion of the evening.

Men! I've always lived with them and don't look on them as such a wonderful treat. Yet everyone knows the world has always been managed by men to promote that very idea. Women are dependent on the opinion of men in a way that men wouldn't tolerate for a second if our roles were reversed. Once in a great while a woman can break through and make a place for herself, but she has to be very exceptional. Even Pop had his blind spots when it came to dealing with my "sect." I'll never forget the letter he sent me in Pau, warning about the danger of going up in a hot-air balloon. "It does not make so much difference about *you*, but *Wilbur* ought to keep out of all balloon rides." Well sir, Orv and I went up in a balloon just the same, and we both lived to tell the tale. Nuff said!

It was a different story with the boys. From the time I was a little girl in flannel petticoats, they treated me as a reasonable human being and their equal in every way that mattered. They even paid me good wages to be their social manager and general dogsbody overseas. The one thing they just couldn't seem to get into their heads was how hard it was to give up my job after Bubbo had his accident. I never did anything so well as the teaching I did at the high school. Some way, teaching Latin and history to those children made me feel useful and needed. What's more, I had grown accustomed to having my own money to spend as I liked—not as much as Will and Orv had, mind you, but enough to ensure I would never be a burden to them or Pop.

It's not as if I didn't feel lucky to be working with the boys. I loved every minute of it—the travel, the adventure, the interesting people we met. But the flying machine was their baby, as Will liked to say, not mine. After they started building airplanes and hired a regular secretary to look after the business, there was less and less real work to keep me occupied. It wasn't until Will died that it weighed in on me that I was horribly dissatisfied with my life. As far as I'm concerned, there is no excuse for doing nothing but fritter away my time. If a man did that, I'd have my own opinion of him, you can be sure! But nobody would have understood if I hadn't played nurse to Orv in Virginia or stayed home to take care of him and Pop after Will was gone.

Little Brother positively refused to hear of my going back to teaching, no matter how hard I tried to make him see what it meant to me. When you come right down to it, he depended on me just as much as Father ever did—maybe more. I was the only one who could assure him that everything was being done for him. Some way, he was more like a lover than a brother to me. One of the girls in Dayton told Orv that I was the only woman who could ever suit him—and I 'spect she was right!

Orville

The day Kate came into this world was the day my problems all began. It was my third birthday, and they brought me upstairs in the old house to take a gander at my new baby sister. I saw then that I was getting into a peck of trouble, and I've never got out since.

As far back as I can remember, Kate and I were as close as hand and glove. The time I came down with typhoid fever, she insisted on staying home from college and nursing me back to health. And after the accident at Fort Myer, she was the only person I could bear to have near me. The moment she walked into my hospital room, smiling as if nothing much was the matter, I knew my injuries couldn't be so bad after all. The army doctors had dreaded her coming and were relieved that she wasn't hysterical. Little did they know *I* was the one would have gone off my head if it hadn't been for Swes. For weeks she stayed by my bedside from the middle of the afternoon until seven in the morning. Yes, Kate was the most loyal sister a man could ask for.

It was the same with Will. Pop always said he and I were as inseparable as twins. From the time we were little we lived together, played together, worked together, even thought together. Practically everything we achieved was the result of conversations, suggestions, and arguments between us. It made no difference which one of us invented what, we always took credit jointly. Why, Ullam even blamed himself for the smashup at Fort Myer. He claimed it never would have happened if he had been there to keep visitors from distracting me while I worked. We had an unspoken pact, Will and I—and Kate too—that we would always look out for one another, come hell or high water.

We'd still be looking out for one another too, if it hadn't been for the rotten seafood my brother ate in Boston. Will was so worn down by the pressures of work that when the fever grabbed hold of him, his body plumb gave out. May 30, 1912, it was—the darkest day of my life. It felt as if part of me had died with him. I had just purchased a new family car, and for weeks on end Pop, Kate, and I drove around in a fog, hardly exchanging a word. The worst thing of all was coming out here to Oakwood to check up on the new house. Will and I had bought the lot in February, and the workmen had started to lay the foundation. When I stood over the cellar hole and thought of Will lying in his grave up on the hill, I about gave up the ghost right then and there.

Like everything we did, Hawthorn Hill was meant to be a family project. But Will had too many other fish to fry to give it his full attention, so Swes and I ended up planning the house together, inside and out. We told the architect what we wanted in each room and even made a special expedition to Grand Rapids to shop for furniture. Naturally, it made no difference that my signature was on all the checks; the new place was always going to be more Kate's than mine. Matter of fact, the first set of drawings the architect showed us was labeled "Residence for Miss Katharine Wright." I had a good laugh when I showed them to Father. "We can't fool anybody," I said. "Everyone knows who will own the house."

It was Kate who insisted that we had outgrown the house on Hawthorn Street and needed a bigger place. Now that Will and I were respectable businessmen, she said, we had to have a home fit for entertaining—so there was nothing for it but to pull up stakes and move. Not that there was a whole lot left to move after the Miami River got through with us in the spring of '13. About all we managed to salvage from the old house were a few books and several small pieces of furniture. We might have saved almost everything had we had more notice of the flood, but Kate and I overslept and had to be out of the house within half an hour.

When the three of us finally moved out here to Oakwood a year or so later, we felt we had landed in the lap of luxury. We had lived practically on top of each other in the old house, so having room to spare took some getting used to. Father had the entire east wing pretty much to himself, except on rare occasions when the corner guest room was occupied. Kate took the bedroom across the hallway from his, overlooking the front drive, between my room and Will's. She called Will's room the "blue room," on account of the blue wallpaper, but to me it will always be Will's room, for all that he never slept in it. It's almost as if he were still with us.

Harry

Shortly after the war broke out in Europe, in the fall of 1914, I was pleasantly surprised to find a letter from Katharine in my mailbox, written on her new Hawthorn Hill stationery. She was up in arms over news reports that Wilbur and Orville had modeled their original flyer on a machine built by Samuel P. Langley, the former secretary of the Smithsonian Institution. The source of this preposterous claim was Glenn Curtiss, one of the Wrights' principal competitors in the airplane industry. Sometime before Wilbur died, Curtiss had gotten hold of a Wright flyer, purportedly "for scientific purposes," built his own airplane based upon it, and begun giving exhibition flights.

Langley had conducted his last experiment a mere nine days before the Wrights made their first flight at Kitty Hawk. The aerodrome, as the Langley machine was called, was an ignominious flop. No sooner did it leave the houseboat from which it had been launched than it plunged straight into the Potomac River. Langley, being a reputable scientist, was quick to congratulate the Wrights for succeeding where he had failed. Curtiss, however, had no such scruples. Ten years later he saw an opportunity to get around the patent restrictions that Orville was fighting to enforce in the courts. If he could prove that a machine that could fly had been built *before* the Wrights made their first flight, he hoped for a construction of the laws that would invalidate their patents.

With that goal in mind, Curtiss persuaded one of his friends at the Smithsonian to lend him the original aerodrome, an odd, bat-like affair that had been put on exhibition as a curiosity. Early in 1914 he transported it to Hammondsport, New York, where he rebuilt it, saving only about 20 percent of the original machine, and installed a new motor. With the reconstructed plane he was able to make some short hops, though not to stay in the air for any length of time. To any unbiased observer, it was obvious that the exercise was a publicity stunt, pure and simple. Ultimately, Curtiss's ploy failed and the Wright patents were upheld by the courts.

But the controversy didn't stop there. Certain high-ranking Smithsonian officials pursued Curtiss's campaign of misrepresentation for their own ends. For years afterward the institution's annual reports perpetuated the myth that the rebuilt Langley aerodrome had flown "without change." The officials undoubtedly hoped that the glory of sponsoring the first successful flight would bolster the Smithsonian's applications to Congress for larger appropriations. Katharine was so outraged by their unprincipled behavior that she was unable to sleep for weeks. At last, out of sheer exasperation, she enlisted me and one or two other trusted friends to help set the record straight.

Orville's impulse, characteristically, was to let the cosmic process take its course and settle things. He calmly observed that the Langley machine had *not* flown and that no sensible person would believe it had. At length, however, he gave in to Katharine's pleas and allowed her to distribute the statement we had drafted to various periodicals. The response was disappointingly predictable. To a man, the editors courteously apologized for any seeming implication that the Wrights were not the real inventors of the airplane. All felt that the outbreak of war in Europe made it an unsuitable time to print anything on the subject, especially so long after the events in question, but they promised to keep the statement on file for future use.

So that was that. Little did the Wrights know that their battle with the Smithsonian was only beginning.

In the summer of 1917, shortly after America entered the war, I contacted Orville in the course of my work as chief editorial writer for the *Star*. I wanted his help in getting the lowdown on the Wilson administration's ham-fisted war preparedness program, which our editorial page had been criticizing pretty vigorously. Knowing that Orville was serving as an advisor to the government on aeronautical matters, I requested an introduction to his friend Edward Deeds, the Dayton industrialist who had been put in charge of wartime aircraft procurement. Orville wrote back at once, enclosing a note to Colonel Deeds in which he described me as "a very good friend of Katharine and myself" and advised that he shouldn't hesitate to talk to me in confidence.

On my way back from seeing Deeds in Washington, I stopped off in Dayton to interview Orville for the paper. The opportunity to observe the world's foremost aeronautical engineer at work was too good to pass up. Katharine's "little brother" had changed hardly at all since our first meeting in Washington eight years earlier. His dress and appearance were as fastidious as ever, his manner modest and welcoming. Deliberate, well organized, and clear-thinking, he gave the impression of complete independence in thought and action. It was plain to see why his counsel was so eagerly sought by his fellow scientists and government officials alike.

At his scientific laboratory on Dayton's old West Side, Orville explained that he was conducting two lines of research, both potentially important to the war effort. One was the measurement of the air resistance of curved surfaces, a continuation of the pioneering work that he and Wilbur had done on the tables developed by the great German engineer Otto Lilienthal. The other was the development of a stabilizer to make the control of the airplane more nearly automatic. Listening to Orville expound on these arcane technical subjects, as patiently and methodically as he could to a layman, I began to grasp why he had proven such a formidable witness for the prosecution in the patent lawsuits against Curtiss.

That evening, Orville, Katharine, and I were conversing on the veranda at Hawthorn Hill, passing the time before dinner, when suddenly it came to me that I was sitting in their late father's favorite rocking chair. Bishop Wright had died upstairs in his sleep a few weeks earlier, at the ripe old age of eighty-eight. His spirit lived on in each of his offspring, but it was Orville who most clearly bore the stamp of his upright and steadfast character. I recognized the type from my own missionary father, who died in 1914 after decades of service in the Balkans. My brother Ed said that Father would as calmly have gone to the stake for his convictions as any martyr who ever burned. The words we had inscribed on his gravestone in Oberlin, SOLDIER OF THE CROSS, seemed equally apt for the Bishop, whose lonely crusade against the forces of darkness in the church had consumed so much of his and his children's lives.

Like the Bishop, my father was a man of stern and unquestion-
ing faith. This was borne home to me as a student at Oberlin, when
religious difficulties began to pile up on me and give me distress. I
wrote to Father in Bulgaria about some of these difficulties, including my questioning of miracles and my doubt of the doctrine of
atonement, which was one of the foundations of the theology of the
day. He wrote back a rather curt letter telling me that I should pay
no attention to such things, as the faith as delivered to the saints
was quite adequate and it was rather wicked to question it. Needless to say, I never took up the matter of religion with him again.

Katharine and Orville dutifully kept the Sabbath out of respect
for the Bishop's memory. But they had not been regular church-
goers for years, and religion played little apparent part in their
daily lives. Although they had never openly turned their backs
on their father's Old Testament creed, I sensed that deep down
neither of them had any more use for the old-time religion than
I did. Katharine's self-sacrificing devotion to the Bishop was one
of her most estimable virtues. Plainly, her loyalty to Orville ran
no less deep. As we sat together on that balmy summer evening,
rocking and talking, it struck me that they looked and acted for all
the world like a contented married couple.

From then to the end of the war, Orville furnished me with a
steady stream of valuable intelligence. He was convinced that the
government's forty-million-dollar aircraft production program
had been badly mismanaged and that the country would have to
depend upon men from civilian life, such as Colonel Deeds, to
push it through. As fate would have it, a special Justice Department
investigation issued a report that came down hard on Orville's
friend. Charles Evans Hughes, the chief investigator, went so far

as to recommend that Deeds be court-martialed for giving out misleading statements concerning the early shipments of airplanes and disclosing sensitive information to his former business associates in Dayton.

Confidentially, Orville allowed that there might be something to the first charge, although he was disposed to believe that Deeds had acted innocently and not from any criminal intent. He surmised that his friend had been misled through his own enthusiasm and the overenthusiastic reports of his subordinates. As to the second allegation, I had a hunch that Deeds had awarded a contract to his friends not only because he felt they could handle it but also because he saw no reason why they shouldn't get rich out of government contracts at the same time everybody else was. Businessmen generally seemed to regard the war as an opportunity to get theirs—and they got.

The sordid spectacle of wartime profiteering and incompetence left a sour taste in my mouth. But I will always be grateful to the government's aircraft program for one thing: it gave me an opportunity to renew my acquaintance with the Wrights.

Katharine

It did my heart good to see Harry and Orv hit it off that summer at Hawthorn Hill. They were so much alike that it seemed only natural they should become friends. I couldn't forget how sympathetic Harry had been when I wrote to him before the war, and how readily he had sprung to Orv's defense in our scrap with Glenn Curtiss. At the same time, I couldn't help noticing that he asked *me* to get Orv's reaction to the Hughes report, instead of going straight to the horse's mouth. If I hadn't known better, I might have suspected him of cooking up an excuse to write to me!

From then on he bent over backward to keep in touch with us both. One time—it was in 1919, I think—Orv and I drove out to Kansas to attend a family wedding. Bubbo had taken a road trip out west earlier that summer with Colonel Deeds and some other men. Their route took them through Kansas City while Harry and Isabel were away in Colorado on vacation. When Harry got home and discovered they had missed each other, he kicked up a fuss and insisted we make amends by stopping over on our way back to Kansas in October. Bubbo replied that we would be only too happy to "afflict" the Haskells with our presence—and so we did!

Harry and Isabel lived in a pleasant suburban neighborhood, not far from my brother Reuch and his family. While Harry took Orv downtown to meet his colleagues at the *Star*, Isabel and I stayed home and talked a mile a minute—real, honest-to-goodness *conversation* it was too, not the empty-headed small talk that so many of my sect go in for. Isabel was as smart as a whip. Though I hadn't known her well in college, I always enjoyed her company. Only later did we learn that the poor, dear creature was dying of cancer. Harry had managed to keep her condition a secret from both Isabel and their son, but young Henry seemed to sense that something was troubling his father. I remember how he sat right up against Harry all evening long, holding hands, as if it were the most natural thing in the world for a high school–age boy to do.

I had always had a happy life and didn't want to be married, frankly. But seeing how devoted Harry and Isabel were to each other, and how their son doted on them both, got me to thinking good and hard about what I had missed. Young Henry would be heading off to college soon, and I knew what a wrench it would be for his parents to let him go, his father especially. Imagine— at Oberlin I didn't think Harry had much feeling! I would have banked on his intellectual strength and character, but I never dreamed he cared much for companionship of any sort. How my dear old friend has changed, I said to myself. Surely it must have been married life that had developed those strong feelings in him.

When Orv and I returned to Kansas City a year later, Isabel and Harry had built a new house for themselves in a lovely residential district that put me in mind of our neighborhood in Oakwood. The move had put such a strain on Isabel's nervous system that she had contracted a severe case of hives. I was nearly undone when Harry took me upstairs to see her. She was frail and drawn, a pale shadow of the vital, energetic woman I had laughed and joked with a mere twelve months earlier. Harry clung by her side, petting and kissing her all the while. He looked terribly worn down himself, poor dear. Yet in spite of all the hard things that had come to them, neither of them uttered a word of complaint.

The Haskells' house—*our* house I s'pose I must call it now— was a white Dutch colonial with green shutters, set on a gently sloping corner lot. A pretty dry-laid stone wall edged the property, overhung by graceful elm trees and shrubbery. Harry and Isabel had planned and furnished the house together, just the way Orv and I had done at Hawthorn Hill. There were bright, floral-pattern curtains in the windows, oriental carpets covering the hardwood floors, and built-in bookcases downstairs and up, filled to over- flowing with Harry's precious books. Isabel was an avid reader too, though she was less bookish by nature than Harry. They seemed an ideal couple, perfectly matched and happy as larks—but of course

I knew it couldn't last, what with Isabel's failing health, and the whole thing made me unspeakably sad.

Orv was giving me no end of worries himself at that very time. For years he had been suffering from acute pain in his left hip. We suspected that his injuries had been poorly treated by the army doctors at Fort Myer in 1908. The pain became so intense that we had to bring in two nurses to help me care for him at home. Little Brother was pretty much flat on his back—he hadn't even felt up to driving out to Kansas City for Reuch's funeral that spring. Finally, one of Harry's doctor friends referred us to a specialist at the Mayo Clinic, and we headed straight up to Minnesota after leaving the Haskells. The new X-rays showed that Orv's sacroiliac joint had been injured in the accident and was mechanically irritating the sciatic nerve. The doctor fitted him with a tight belt to make the joint work as it should—and, lo and behold, it did the trick! Orv went home and started running up and down the stairs without any pain at all.

What with Orv's and Harry's problems, piled on top of poor Reuch's passing, my spirits had taken a terrific beating. Then something marvelous and utterly unexpected happened—almost a miracle, really. Just when I most needed a sympathetic shoulder to cry on, who should come into our lives but Stef! Orv invited him to Dayton to compare notes on their scientific work. I remember the first time we laid eyes on him in the fall of 1919. Stef looked every inch the dashing Arctic explorer, with his dark, wavy hair, high forehead, and broad, sensitive mouth. Orv and I were spellbound by the vivid accounts of his adventures in the far north. Both of us sized him up right away as being absolutely truthful—and *very* interesting.

A few months later, Stef—everyone calls him that because his real name, Vilhjalmur Stefansson, is such a mouthful—came back to Dayton to give a lecture. That was another day I'll not soon forget! As Stef was winding down his talk, the color abruptly drained out of his face, just as if somebody had pulled the plug. Orv and I looked at each other in alarm, and without saying a word I slipped onto the podium and escorted Stef out front to Orv's waiting car. It didn't take long for the doctor to find out what was the matter—our distinguished speaker had the Spanish influenza! Naturally, Stef was ordered to stay off his feet for several days, and while he convalesced at Hawthorn Hill, we put the long hours to good use by getting better acquainted.

By the time Stef felt well enough to go home to New York, Orv and he had become firm mutual admirers. As for me, I found Stef a lovely character, full of whims and "insistent ideas," and yet so gentle and considerate—as well as interesting and absolutely genuine and truthful. I was a woman of years—forty-five years, to be precise—and some experience and observation. I thought I had known just about every emotion that life had to offer. But something was stirring deep down inside me, something strange and unsettling and yet inexpressibly warm—unlike anything I had ever felt before.

Orville

It was a funny thing about Stef and Harry: one day it seemed we were just getting acquainted, and the next I knew they were old family friends. Didn't Will always say that Kate and I had a way of stepping right into the affections of nice people we met? If you want my honest opinion, Swes makes friends far too easily for her own good—mine too, I might add. A great deal of trouble could have been avoided for us both if she had only learned to exercise more caution in her relations with men. Granted, I was the one who invited Stef and Harry to Hawthorn Hill in the first place, but it didn't take long for me to cotton that they weren't beating a path to our door merely for the pleasure of *my* company.

For a man who has no technical training in aeronautics and engineering, Stef is singularly well informed. Many's the night we've sat up for hours on end discussing our scientific work. If the truth be told, I do most of the talking—but Stef never seems to begrudge giving me the floor for a change. What he and Kate found to talk about while I was away at the lab is anyone's guess. Swes doesn't have a scientific bone in her body, and as for Stef—well, I never pegged him as a ladies' man. Though, now I think of it, there has been talk about him and that lady novelist whose name I never can remember—Fannie Hurst, that's it. There's probably nothing in it, but you never can tell. The way that Greenwich Village outfit carries on, it's a wonder they get a lick of real, honest-to-goodness work done.

Not that I've ever known Stef to be at a loss for words. Harry always said he was as good a writer as he is a speaker. I remember the first time he came up to our summer place in Canada. He brought along the manuscript of *The Friendly Arctic* for Kate and me to look at, and we both had about the same reaction: if the book kept on as it promised, she told him, it was sure to be a "hammer." I don't see how Stef does it. He thinks nothing of turning out a new book every year or two. It's easy for a man like that to say I should write up the story of the invention of the aeroplane. Stef and Harry aren't far wrong when they argue that it's the only way to settle my dispute with the Smithsonian for good and always. But I'm an engineer, not a writer, and that's all there is to say.

Every time I think of those self-styled aeronautical "experts" in Washington, my blood starts to boil. It's as clear as the nose on my face that Will and I built the first man-carrying flying machine. We have the evidence to prove it—notebooks, photographs, eyewitnesses. The whole world knows that Langley's aerodrome never could have stayed up in the air—the Smithsonian people are just too proud and stubborn to admit it. The press agent gang are no better. If it weren't for men like Harry Haskell, Arthur Page, and Earl Findley, I don't believe a one of them would lift a finger to check their facts. I had to smile that time Harry sent me a couple of wildly inaccurate clippings from the *Star* about the Langley machine. It amuses me to see how responsible he and my other reporter friends feel for letting those stories slip into their papers.

Harry, Stef, Kate, Mr. Page—they're all in this together. It's a conspiracy, that's what it is—a conspiracy to get me to sit down against my will and write the book. God knows, I'd sooner turn it over to one of them and be done with it if I could. But I'm the only one who can do the job right. Nobody else knows the full story— what the problem of flying consisted of, what the state of the art was when Will and I tackled it, what we originated, what we used that others originated, to whom we owed most, how we came to succeed in actually flying, and so forth and so on.

Book or no book, though, you can be sure the Smithsonian won't give in without a fight. One time I was in Washington for a committee meeting and Langley's successor, Dr. Walcott, took me to see the rebuilt aerodrome. Although he took unusual pains to be courteous, I felt obliged to point out that the machine on display in the museum was not the same as the one Curtiss flew at Hammondsport in 1914. Walcott stood most of the time looking down at his hands, which he kept in nervous motion. He asked me to send him photos and details of the changes that Curtiss had made. He certainly was very uneasy about the matter, which I considered a hopeful sign. But that was a long time ago, and the Smithsonian hasn't backed down yet.

In my opinion, Griff Brewer said the last word on the subject way back in 1921. In his address to the Royal Aeronautical Society in London, he stated categorically that it was untrue to suggest that Langley's machine of 1903 had ever flown or ever could fly—and he had the facts to prove it. Everyone who understood anything at all about aeronautics was bound to be convinced by Griff's presentation. Harry agreed that he had turned out a bulletproof case, no matter what dust throwing the other side might resort to. Stef and Harry swung into action drumming up publicity for Griff's talk in the *New York Times* and other papers, while another friend of ours at Johns Hopkins brought it to the attention of the scientific journals.

Kate said Harry was on the job every minute, working like a horse to make sure our side of the story got out. And Stef talked Griff's paper up to everyone he saw. We have him to thank for that fine piece in the *New Republic* and the corker of an editorial that Mr. Page published in the *World's Work*. Then *Nature* weighed in with a tendentious article that was clearly inspired by the urgent appeals of the Smithsonian people. For years they had been quietly spreading their propaganda, putting us in the position where an answer to it would have looked like an unprovoked attack on Langley. Now the editor of *Nature* deliberately brought this point into the issue by asserting that Langley had done all the *scientific* work, while Will and I merely contributed the *mechanical device* that brought his scientific knowledge into practical use!

We saw then that we were in for a long, hard struggle—much to Kate's gratification, no doubt. She used to marvel at my calmness, but I saw no point in getting all worked up over the Smithsonian's mendacity. What did she expect, after all? Human nature is much the same in all times and places. Didn't Father teach us that the natural state of mankind is depravity? Speaking as a man of science, I see no reason to question the validity of that hypothesis.

All the same, nothing would give me greater pleasure than to force Walcott and his cronies to eat their words. I recollect coming across one of the Smithsonian's misleading pronouncements one time and calling out to Sterchens, "The conflict deepens. On ye braves!" It felt almost like the good old days, when Father and Will confronted his false accusers in the church: the Wright family against the world!

Katharine

Orv was like a new man after we got back from the Mayo Clinic that fall. He worked from morning to night and drove his automobile all around town without experiencing any pain whatsoever. We were having some ups and downs in the course of the fight with the Smithsonian, but that was to be expected. The main thing was that we were making some important points. There had always been an impression that the Langley machine antedated the Wright flyer by many years. People were coming to realize that the two machines were contemporaneous. The public now knew for the first time that Curtiss had made changes in the Langley machine. We hadn't convinced some of them that the changes were important, but in time I was confident that we would get all the facts out in the open.

Stef was one zealous missionary for our cause. He never lost interest or quit, even when Orv was in the doldrums. A good, everlasting friend he was to us both—but how I would have hated to have him for an enemy! Stef always insisted that it was the cause of truth he was trying to serve, but he couldn't make me believe that there wasn't a lot of personal devotion mixed up with it. His attitude toward Orv was almost touching. One day, out of a clear blue sky, he declared to me that he admired Little Brother more than any living man he knew. Then he paused, just to make sure he meant what he had said. "Yes," he added presently, "I mean just that."

Stef reminds me of the boys in his precise way of expressing himself. If only writing came half as easily to Orv as it does to him. Stef's account of his exploits in *The Friendly Arctic* is simply entrancing. He is a born storyteller—even if he does believe a few too many of his own tall tales! Little Brother has a way with words himself. He can write as clearly and interestingly as anyone I know, and on his own subject no one can touch him. But, gracious me, how he does hate to put words on paper! He has almost an inhibited will when it comes to writing letters and speeches and such. He doesn't even care to *receive* letters. At our summer place on Lambert Island he doesn't take a bit of interest in his mail. He is always afraid there will be some letters for him!

Orv's story of the invention of the airplane would make a great and immediate impression. It would carry conviction too, because there would be no careless statements in it. You never saw anything to equal Bubbo's ability to get things exactly straight. It is a joy to see him go after an opponent in an argument. He simply won't get off the track, no matter how alluring this side issue or that one may be. His memory has never been much good on the book he has just read or the play he has seen, but it is like a steel trap on the facts in aeronautical science and history.

Everyone agrees that the book ought to have been written ages ago. Orv himself has long seen the necessity of doing the job, but his bad back and his natural aversion to writing always held him back. Harry told me once that if he hadn't known the Wright brothers and did not have personal confidence in them, even his faith would have been shaken by that boneheaded editorial in *Nature*. He argued up and down that it was essential for Orv to get his story out before the article became part of the standard literature on the subject—and he expected *me* to take Little Brother in hand, if you please!

I finally did get Orv to send Griff Brewer some suggestions for an article on Langley's work. And I felt sure he would agree to collaborate with Burton Hendrick on a series of articles for Arthur Page's magazine, the *World's Work*. We met Mr. Hendrick at the Pages' country house on Long Island, and afterward Orv told our host that if the book finally had to be turned over to someone else, Mr. Hendrick would be his choice. Of course, nothing came of it in the end. I've about given up hope that Orv will ever get around to writing the book. At bottom, he feels just as I do—that it is ridiculous for a man to have to howl and howl to call attention to

what he has done, when it is as plain as day to anybody with eyes
to see. Orv has no time for personal advertising, that's all, and I
respect him for it.

Harry was such a trump through the whole business. What a
blessed relief it was to find one modest person among writers! The
more I saw of him, the more I admired him and wanted to be his
friend. He and Isabel had both been so fine and brave. I wished
with all my heart that Orv and I could do something besides sit
at home and worry about them. I valued Harry's friendship more
every year because I saw clearly what a priceless possession it was.
As Stef so nicely put it, "Understanding another human being is a
delicate task." Harry has always understood me. Even in college,
he was a kind of safety valve. I knew he would make allowance for
my explosive nature and my foibles and no harm would be done,
no matter how silly I was. Yes, a warm, steady friendship is about
as good a thing as there is in this often disappointing world.

When I think of a good friendship, the two things I always
associate with it are steadiness and serenity. Yet those are the very
two things that I *can't* put into my friendship with Stef. He is a
poet when it comes to human relations, and he has such exquisite,
delicate ideas. Almost without realizing it, I allowed him to become
a big part of my life in those years—so much that it scared me just
a little bit. For a time I almost couldn't bear the joy our friendship
gave me. It felt like a miracle, and the preciousness grew on me
continually, in the most substantial, wholesome way. It was one
of the best things that had ever come into my life, and by what a
queer chance! To be able to have such a feeling about anyone is
a blessed thing.

It did my heart good to bring Harry and Stef together and see them become fast friends. I never had any inkling that they might be rivals as well—at least, not until the time their paths nearly crossed at Hawthorn Hill. Stef was on a lecture tour in Ohio and sent me a telegram from Cleveland a few days before Christmas. It was just a quick note letting us know about his itinerary, but the first sentence brought me up short: "This is the day Haskell should be with you and I can get no nearer than the Portage Hotel at Akron." Was my imagination playing tricks, or did I detect a whiff of jealousy in Stef's words?

Harry

The Wrights had sung Stef's praises so loudly that Isabel and I jumped at the chance to meet him when he breezed through Kansas City in the fall of 1920. We got in our invitation just ahead of the Honorable Richard Sutton, my safari-loving dermatologist friend. In some ways, Stef could be Doctor Dick's twin brother. No doubt Arctic explorers and big-game hunters are cast in the same mold—aviators too, from what I've seen. Certainly Stef made no secret of his high regard for Orville. At one time, there was talk of his collaborating with Griff Brewer on a general history of flight, or even with Orville himself on "the book." But the idea was quietly shelved after Katharine pointed out that Stef was hardly qualified to voice an opinion on aeronautical subjects.

Stef is a vivid and engaging writer, and Orville evidently respects his competence in scientific matters. If anyone could have gotten Katharine's brother to stop procrastinating and get on with the job that needed to be done, it was Stef. On the other hand, the

Wrights are hardly wild about the racy Greenwich Village crowd that Stef runs with in New York. A cheap bunch of self-styled intellectuals, Katharine calls them—and that's just for starters. As a matter of fact, I was surprised that she took such a shine to Stef. As a rule, she has no time for the East Coast smart set. Whenever its baleful influence slips into my writing, she accuses me of aping Henry Mencken and Sinclair Lewis.

I must admit there is some truth to the charge. Sometimes I do wish I were as clever as the "Sage of Baltimore." My old chief at the *Star*, William Rockhill Nelson, would have snapped Mencken up in a trice and set him loose on our fair city, Kiwanized, Chamber-of-Commerced, Heart-of-Americaed as it is. The Old Man was no mean hell-raiser in his own right. Some of the sparkle went out of the *Star* after Colonel Nelson died in 1915. For a time I was tempted to pull up stakes and try my luck in Washington or New York. Katharine was all in favor. She thought a change of scene would do me good. But that was before the staff bought the paper and made me editor. Now I feel about Kansas City the way Katharine feels about Dayton: it will always be my home, the place I was meant to be.

On the whole, I've been happy at the *Star*, and the paper has been good to me. Yet one can't help having second thoughts. Things might have worked out quite differently, after all. What if I hadn't happened to show up at the *Star* on the very day the assistant telegraph editor resigned? What if I had taken one of the other jobs on offer in St. Louis, Denver, or New York? For that matter, what if Isabel and I hadn't become engaged in my senior year at Oberlin? What if I had been free to ask Katharine for her hand instead? I know now that she was always in my heart, "airy and true," like her namesake in the Stevenson poem:

We see you as we see a face
That trembles in a forest place
Upon the mirror of a pool
For ever quiet, clear and cool.

Stevenson is a special bond between Katharine and me. I was so taken with his descriptions of the South Seas in the *Vailima Letters* when it first came out that I sent her a copy for graduation. And when I finally got up the courage to say I loved her, it was Stevenson's words that came out of my mouth: "Home is the sailor, home from the sea, and the hunter home from the hill." That's just how we felt—that our real home was in each other's hearts, no matter how far we roamed.

But what am I saying? After all, my feelings for Isabel were no less real and sincere. When I first got to know her at Oberlin, she was so bright and cheerful and quick as a flash about seeing things. She was the very soul of sympathy. What young man could resist falling in love with such a charmer? Isabel was my idea of a thoroughly modern woman. She reminded me of Shaw's Candida or Ibsen's Nora. It was she who introduced me to plays, dancing, card playing—all the guilty pleasures that my parents had forbidden under their roof. I recall Father's indignation when some limb of Satan left a deck of cards lying on our front porch. Undoubtedly it was intended as a personal affront, and it went to the mark. Father took satisfaction in tearing up the cards into little bits to show what he thought of them.

I guess I was pretty much "all head" in those days, as Katharine often reminds me. Isabel was just the opposite—full of laughter and the sheer joy of living. She had the great gift of making routine household tasks seem fun. We used to gather in the kitchen after dinner, singing at the top of our lungs while she washed the dishes and Henry and I dried them. It was on her account that I joined the Unitarian Church after Father died. Isabel understood why I had lost faith in the stern Old Testament God my parents worshipped. She had the patience and fortitude of a saint. All through her long illness, even when she could barely raise herself out of bed, she never uttered a word of complaint or reproach.

Watching Isabel waste away year after year, helpless to relieve her suffering, was enough to crush any man's faith. In Charles Darwin's letters, I came across his suggestion that there was so much cruelty and evil in the world as to militate against the probability of any beneficent personality behind it. That had long been my opinion, but I hadn't had the realization of it until my own experience with Isabel. Certainly I would hate to be responsible for a universe so full of capricious cruelty as ours. It must be the weight of inherited fear come down from the stone-ax days that makes us assume a beneficent first cause is engaged in the torture we see around us and bids us kiss his hand.

Take Katharine's "little brother," for instance. If there were an ounce of justice in the world, Orville wouldn't have been forced to spend the best years of his life fighting to vindicate himself and Wilbur. The Smithsonian long ago would have admitted that the Langley business was a fraud and a cheat. The Wright flyer would be hanging in Washington today instead of London. But it seems to be human nature to hate to admit we have been wrong. Not even

Darwin was immune to envy. At one time it looked as if Alfred Russel Wallace's sketch on natural selection might take from him the credit of years of hard work. Somewhere in his letters Darwin writes, "I thought I had sufficient greatness of soul not to mind about priority. But I am ashamed to say I was mistaken."

I have often recalled Darwin's words in connection with Orville's ordeal. There is one crucial difference, though: Wallace was on the square; Curtiss and the Smithsonian were not.

Orville

"We learn much by tribulation," Father once wrote, "and by adversity our hearts are made better." By those lights, my heart must be as stout as an ox's by now. Fifteen long years of scrapping with Curtiss and the Smithsonian have taught me how Father felt when he locked horns with his fellow Brethren. He had right on his side, the same as I do. Yet it took years to reclaim his good name after Reverend Keiter and those other bandits hounded him out of the church. We were at Kitty Hawk when he lost his case in 1902. An infamous outrage, Will called it. He vowed then and there to make the members of the committee who had convicted Father sign a written retraction.

Father never could have won that fight on his own. It was Will who pored over the ledger books, week after week, and showed how Keiter had fiddled the accounts. My brother could outsmart and outlawyer the best of them. I remember one of our patent hearings when the judge asked him to explain how something or other worked. Will calmly strode over to the blackboard and drew a simple figure that anyone could understand. After the trial,

Curtiss's lawyer complained that if it hadn't been for Will and his "damned string and chalk," they would have won the case. Ullam had more brains in his little finger than most men do in their heads. But it was Curtiss and his diabolical scheming that did him in, as sure as the typhoid.

My fondest wish after Will and Father passed away was to live in peace and quiet at Hawthorn Hill. With the profits from the sale of the Wright Company, and Carrie to keep house for us, Kate and I had everything we needed. If only those two women weren't so darned headstrong. Even this place was scarcely big enough to hold them both. And neither Carrie nor Kate has ever had a good word to say about Miss Beck. So my secretary is bossy and high-handed, is she? I daresay she is. But I never knew a woman to be more competent, efficient, and dedicated to her work. I hardly see how I could have managed without her these past few years. Just knowing she's sitting outside the laboratory door gives me the peace of mind I need to concentrate on my work.

And another thing: Miss Beck never badgers me about the book. Everyone else harps on about it every chance they get. To hear them tell it, you'd think I had a sacred duty to write the blasted thing. For pity's sake, can't they see I'm not a writer? Thank goodness for Georgian Bay. There, at least, I can put their infernal nagging behind me. Kate and I used to hole up on Lambert Island for weeks on end, just the two of us, without a care in the world. People up there take us as they find us. It's a simple life—no dressing up, no dinner parties, no worrying about appearances. Something always needs fixing—the boathouse, the dock, the water pump, the outboard motor. Yes sir, tinkering is the life for me. When you come right down to it, machines are a whole lot simpler than human beings. More reliable too.

Swes looked forward to going up to the bay as much as I did. Yet even when we had the island all to ourselves, there she would sit hour after hour at the big table in the main cabin, writing those interminable letters to her friends. If you ask me, she might just as well have stayed home in Dayton and saved herself the postage. Hawthorn Hill is a regular open house. Family, friends, tradesmen, reporters, even total strangers—everyone seems to feel they can drop in unannounced practically any day of the week. Sometimes my home feels more like a hotel than a man's castle. I ask you, why did we go to the trouble of moving out of the city in the first place if it wasn't to get away from all that?

It was Kate that visitors generally came to see, of course. She was the gregarious one. I was just the man of the house, doing my best to keep my head down and stay out of trouble. You might say we complemented each other in that way. No wonder people used to take us for husband and wife. It was a good life we had too, a comfortable life. How was I to know that Kate wasn't as contented as I was? Oh, she talked about becoming a schoolteacher again, but she had no reason to go back to work. With the money Will left her, she had an income of her own and could do whatever she set her mind to. Anyhow, running this house is a big enough job. I gave her a liberal allowance, a housekeeper, a cook. What more could any reasonable woman ask for?

As for marriage, I took it for granted it was out of the question for both of us at our time of life. A few years ago, mind you, I might have allowed my head to be turned. I met some mighty attractive young ladies when I was a frisky pup. There was no lack of temptation—or opportunity either—in Washington and Paris. Ullam and Swes got pretty worked up about that, as I recall. They made up their minds that I was easy prey for female predators and needed their protection. But they had no call to worry. Whenever the reporters tried to catch me out by inquiring why there was no Mrs. Wright, I would firmly set them straight. "You can't have a wife and a flying machine too," I said. That generally satisfied their curiosity.

Not all of us are cut out for the married life, after all. Stef, for instance—you can hardly imagine *him* being tied down to a wife and home, now can you? With Harry it's a different story. I saw right off the bat that he was the kind of man who needed a wife to come home to at night. Kate and I often observed that Isabel and he seemed to be made for each other. A sad, sad business that was, to be sure. There is no getting over the loss of someone you love more than life itself. I learned that lesson when Will died. At least he didn't suffer long before he passed away. Isabel and Harry weren't so fortunate. The way he looked for a while during her final illness, it was nip and tuck which of them would wear out first.

Katharine

The last time we saw Isabel was a few months before she died, in the late winter of 1923. She was pretty much skin and bones by that time, and all but blind. Orv and I had given her Stef's new book, *Hunters of the Great North*, for Christmas, and Harry had been reading it aloud to her. They both seemed wonderfully courageous to me—but Harry has never gone in for heroics. Isabel and he were simply trying to do the best they could, he told me. Beneath his brave exterior, I could see that he was taking it very, very hard. In fact, I thought he might be on the edge of a breakdown. For the first time he couldn't keep the tears out of his eyes when he was alone with me. As the Bible says, "The heart knoweth its own bitterness." Was there ever anything truer? I have thought about that a good deal since I left my family and friends behind in Ohio and Little Brother shut me out of his life. We do, all of us, have to live alone, mostly.

Since Isabel had always been interested in Stef, I took the opportunity to tell her about the time I met Fannie Hurst at one of his artistic shindigs in New York. Such a clever woman Miss Hurst is. I don't care for her novels myself—if you ask me, she can't hold a candle to Dorothy Canfield or Hamlin Garland—but I can understand why Stef finds them amusing. He has decidedly unconventional tastes—in both books *and* people! Orv and I hadn't had the pleasure of his company much since he retired from active exploration. Bubbo hated to see Stef become a full-time lecturer—he said it would inevitably lead him into the use of professional tricks for creating interest. If only Stef weren't such an incorrigible go-getter. In my opinion, he would be well advised to stop talking and writing and *do* something!

I had no idea how reckless Stef's ambition was until the Wrangel Island episode flared up in the newspapers that fall. That was a real eye-opener, for Orv and me both. The worst of it was, the tragedy could easily have been avoided if Stef hadn't been so irresponsible. It was entirely as a result of his negligence that four men perished in a misguided attempt to claim that godforsaken island for Great Britain. By the time the rescue ship finally cut through the ice, only the crew's Eskimo seamstress and her cat were left to tell the tale. Although Stef didn't actually accompany the expedition, he came in for a stiff dose of criticism—every ounce of it thoroughly deserved, in my opinion! Little Brother thought his behavior was unforgivable. One half of me did too—the other half couldn't help sympathizing with Stef and wishing I could be something to him in his predicament.

Orv and I had just gotten home from the bay that September when a telegram arrived from Harry telling of Isabel's death. Naturally, we set out for Kansas City at once. Without giving it a second thought, I tucked into my bag a special copy of *The Friendly Arctic* that Stef had given me to use as a guest book. Owing to a typesetter's error, only the first few pages were printed; the rest were blank. Stef had written a personal message on the flyleaf: "I hope many good friends will write their names in this book, and that you will always value mine as somewhere near the top." Dear Stef—so many vain wishes I had about him! Some way that blank book is a perfect picture of our friendship, with all its promise and all its disappointment.

I finally got around to asking Harry to sign his name when he came to Dayton on his way to Europe, a week or two after Isabel's funeral. My heart fairly skipped a beat as he leafed through the book, page by page, looking for a space to write in. I was on tenterhooks for fear that his eyes would fall on Stef's inscription and he would suspect something. Doesn't that beat all? There was nothing to suspect, nothing whatsoever. Stef and I were never more than good friends—were we?

Harry

Isabel slipped away so quietly that we hardly knew she had left us. Shortly before she drew her final breath, I leaned over her pillow and she whispered in my ear, "Father"—we always called each other Mother and Father—"Father, you've been the dearest husband in the world. It's been wonderful, all of it." That was all. Her courage and cheerfulness put me to shame.

After her years of suffering, Isabel's peaceful death came as a blessed release. But the idea of staying on in the house that we had planned and saved for and built together was almost unbearable to me. It had been hard enough when Henry went away to college and I could scarcely bring myself to look into his old room. Without Isabel's warmth and gaiety, the whole house felt empty and barren. I had a good mind to lock the door behind me, move into an apartment hotel, and start a new life.

The Wrights saw me at my worst when they came to Kansas City for the funeral. And when I passed through Dayton a couple of weeks later, I must have looked as low as I felt, judging from Katharine's solicitude on that occasion. The *Star*'s owners had generously insisted on my taking a sabbatical at their expense. Reluctant as I was to travel alone, I did look forward to exploring Europe at my own pace, with no fixed itinerary and no obligations beyond filing an occasional piece for the paper. I was glad to find that Orville's spirits were on the mend as well. He was weighing a proposal to loan the original Wright flyer to the Science Museum in London. Griff Brewer, the Wrights' longtime patent agent in England, had come up with the plan. It appealed to us all as a way out of the standoff with the Smithsonian.

First thing upon arriving in London, I arranged to meet Griff and tour the museum in South Kensington. I had a notion that I could make myself useful by giving Orville a firsthand report on the aeronautical section. My impressions were mixed, and I told him so. Apart from a handful of life-size exhibits—the Rolls Royce plane that crossed the Atlantic, the Chanute glider, and another glider similar to the one Otto Lilienthal had been using when he was killed—all the planes on display, including the Wright flyer, were small-scale replicas. Moreover, the museum catalog mentioned the Wright plane merely as one in a succession, which was right enough but gave no idea of its real significance. Evidently, the Smithsonian wasn't alone in undervaluing the Wright brothers' magnificent achievement.

Katharine and Orville hadn't been abroad since before the war, but they still had many friends in Europe. Practically every city I visited, from London to Berlin, seemed to have an association with the Wrights. The Germans had given them a royal welcome a decade earlier. Reports of Orville's demonstration flights for Kaiser Wilhelm and Katharine's forthright Yankee charm had filled the newspapers for weeks on end. That world, I quickly discovered, had vanished beyond recall. The once-mighty Reich was on its knees in 1923, its economy in shambles. In Düsseldorf I bought a single sheet of letter paper to write to Katharine. My jaw dropped when the clerk told me the price: one hundred billion marks! I shut my eyes and counted out the bills until he told me to stop. Runaway inflation made it impossible to predict how much anything would cost from one day to the next. The entire country felt like an insane asylum.

I breathed a sigh of relief when my train from Munich crossed over the Austrian Alps into Italy. Mussolini's Fascists had restored at least a semblance of order after the war. An old friend of Katharine's and mine, Louis Lord, was spending a year at the American Academy in Rome. Louis teaches classics at Oberlin and knows the Eternal City as well as any man alive. He must have shown me every sight there is to see, down to the last temple, triumphal arch, and aqueduct. But we spent as much time discussing Katharine as Roman antiquities. Louis had heard through the grapevine that President King intended to appoint her to Oberlin's board of trustees. We agreed that a strong, independent-minded woman was precisely what that hidebound fraternity needed. Whether Mr. King knew what he was getting himself in for by appointing Katharine Wright was a different matter.

On the way to catch my boat in Cherbourg at the end of January, my eye was caught by an etching on display in a shopwindow in Paris. It showed a narrow street in old Rouen, with the great Cathedral of Notre Dame rising up through the haze in the background. I had been hoping to find something to bring home to Katharine, something that would remind her of the happy times she had had with her brothers in France in the old days. That print just fit the bill. In fact, I was so taken with it that I went back the following day and purchased another copy for myself. It was the next-best thing to being in France together.

All too soon my busman's holiday came to an end, and by the time we made port in Boston, my state of mind was considerably improved. Henry had a break between semesters at Harvard and joined me for a short vacation in New York and Washington. It was then that I first told him about my special interest in Katharine. She claims she always knew he was in on our little secret, but from what I observed he kept it pretty close to his chest. He didn't even give the game away when Katharine surprised us both by sending him a graduation present that spring. At that point, of course, she had no grounds for suspicion that my feelings toward her had changed. On the contrary, she was worried that Henry might suspect *her* of having an ulterior motive!

Katharine was in her bedroom when I reached Hawthorn Hill, and she fairly flew down the stairs to greet me, as if I had been gone a year instead of only three or four months. A few minutes later Stef joined us. Katharine had alerted me in advance that our visits would overlap, but she assured me that she and I would have plenty of time to talk one-on-one. Normally, Stef and the Wrights constituted a kind of mutual admiration society. On this occasion, however, the tension in the air was almost palpable. From something Katharine let drop, I gathered it had to do with the Wrangel Island tragedy I had read about in the London papers. Whatever the reason, she was visibly unsettled by Stef's presence. The very thought of his visit was a nightmare, she had written me, and my being there would help immensely.

Toward me Stef was his usual hale-fellow-well-met self. But his relations with Orville were unmistakably strained. Katharine explained that her brother had been somewhat touchy on the subject of Stef ever since the news about Wrangel Island came out in the fall. And she herself had clearly run out of patience with our intrepid explorer friend. Katharine was determined to give Stef a piece of her mind and impress on him how reckless and unprincipled his behavior appeared to others. Her stern tone and the steely glint in her eye made me almost pity the poor fellow. The perils of an Arctic voyage are as nothing compared to the fury of a woman whose trust has been betrayed.

My memories of that visit are crystal clear, not only because Katharine seemed especially pleased to see me but also because it was the first time she had taken me into her confidence about Stef. Always before when we had spoken of him it had been in connection with his or Orville's scientific work, the Smithsonian controversy, or some equally impersonal topic. Now Katharine seemed positively eager to open up to me and share her sense of disillusionment. That she liked and admired Stef as a friend came as no surprise, but up to then I hadn't realized how deeply she had become involved with him on an emotional level. Nor was I accustomed to hearing her voice her most intimate feelings so freely and forcefully.

Little by little, as Katharine let down her guard, my own defenses began to crumble as well. One afternoon, she and I were setting off for a stroll in the woods above the house. A few pieces of firewood had fallen off the veranda, and we both knelt down instinctively to toss them out of our way. As my hand brushed against the sleeve of Katharine's coat, I was seized by a sudden impulse to throw my arms around her. The force of my emotions caught me by surprise, and only in the nick of time did I manage to control myself. Katharine stood up and started to walk, apparently none the wiser, while I fell into step behind her, quaking like an aspen leaf.

Katharine

The winter sun was lowering when I happened to glance out of my bedroom window and saw Harry striding up the drive in that brisk, boyish way of his. "Four months in Europe have worked wonders for my dear friend," I thought. Harry had given a talk at the Oberlin Faculty Club the day before and looked mighty pleased with himself. Apparently, his observation that the Germans in the Ruhr Valley were not so oppressed by the French occupiers as had been reported in the American press made some impression on the Oberlin outfit. It was absolutely the first time that anything pro-French had been so much as *mentioned* in that setting!

I can understand why people like to hear Harry talk on European problems and such. He has so much judgment, and he sees the fun in pretenses and schemes and so on. When I get clear to the depths and decide that there isn't a bit of sense in the world, it does me good to see what influence a little real character does have, after all. More than anything, though, I was relieved to see Harry looking so much less on a strain. When he came through Dayton on his way to England, he had a look on his face that stayed with me long after he was gone. At first I thought I had said something that hurt him—brought up some painful memory—and I could hardly go on talking. Later I saw that it couldn't be the things I said, but the expression would come and go. That nearly finished me, seeing him go off that way.

With all the physical and emotional stress he had been under for the past few years, I was worried sick about him traveling in Europe without a companion. And when he wrote from Paris about suffering from nervous chills and being unable to sleep, all my maternal feelings came rushing out in full flood. I know only too well how draining such an affliction can be. My nerves have always been prone to acting up at the least sign of trouble, ever since I was a little girl. When Harry marched up to our front door, I saw immediately that the rest and change had done him a world of good—although a little voice told me that it would not be strange if it took more than five months after Isabel's death to get back to himself again.

As a matter of fact, I was in such a tight box myself that I could hardly concentrate on Harry's problems for two minutes straight. Was it fate or sheer serendipity that brought him and Stef—the two men I cared for most in the whole world, apart from Orv—to Hawthorn Hill at the very same time that winter? The situation was the least bit *difficile*—for me more than for either of them, I daresay! Stef and I were determined to have a good long talk and get past all the misunderstanding that had come between us in December, when he and his friend Mr. Akeley had come to Dayton for the big celebration. What with Stef's lame excuses for the Wrangel Island fiasco and the politicians' high-flying speeches, the truth was murdered enough that day to make one weep. Orv and I were both glad that the twentieth anniversary of the first flight came only once in a lifetime!

One morning Stef and I had to ourselves, and he insisted on telling me the whole Wrangel Island story from start to finish. We were interrupted a good deal, and the whole thing made me so sick anyway that I didn't care. But I think I made some impression on him about his recklessness in spending the money of people who couldn't afford to contribute to his schemes. I told him I was afraid of his ambition; that he had done enough remarkable things for one man; that, with his fine abilities and personality, he had a lot ahead of him if he would be content to devote himself to quiet, solid work. Ha ha! Stef took my grandmotherly advice very well—and went on doing just as before, I suppose.

I have no illusions as to my influence with Stef, but on that occasion I actually believe I made him uneasy—a thing he had never been before—about owing money to everyone and his uncle. I put it on the ground of his own interest. I tried to make him see that he couldn't afford to have a reputation for unreliability, no matter what the excuses were. It was a miserable business. I couldn't go back on Stef even if he was wrong. But I wouldn't pretend I thought he was right. All in all, it has been the most puzzling experience in friendship I have ever had. Stef and I are really attached to each other. Yet everything has conspired to make us as different as day from night. Sometimes I want to sit down in the middle of the floor and cry. What unreasoning and unreasonable creatures we women are when our feelings are involved!

Those few days with Stef in the house were a strenuous time for sure. After it was all over, I begged him to destroy all my letters to him, as a Christmas present to me—but I fully expect he didn't honor *that* request either. For crying out loud, what could Griff Brewer have been thinking of—to let Stef have $1,250 of our money for the relief expedition to Wrangel Island, without so much as a by-your-leave! At the end of the day, Griff was out nearly six thousand dollars and we forty-five hundred. Orv and I did not offer to share Griff's loss with him. It was high time he learned that Stef was an expensive luxury as a friend. I often get out of patience with Orv because he is so overscrupulous in money matters, but how thankful I am that he is, as I see what grasping for a few pennies does to people.

As I think back over my whole early experience with Stef, it was not a natural friendship for me. I can't see now how he could have had any reason for being a special friend of mine. I'm sure he must have found me insufferably stupid, and we hadn't other things in common to make up for that. It was a very great loss to me, for, as he expressed it once himself, I had given him an "idealized friendship." Stef wasn't the only one with stars in his eyes. I thought he was something altogether different from what he was. Never in my life have I so misread anyone. I didn't have it in for Stef—I just saw that there was no substance to one of my dreams.

I am not especially unsophisticated about people, and yet I am so inclined to idealize and idolize the few that I am really attached to. I should know better—but living with nothing but hard realities is a bitter business. Harry understood all about such things—that is why I could speak to him about my feelings for Stef. I've never felt any need to idealize Harry. He has none of Stef's shortcomings— his ambition, his recklessness, his fear of "entangling alliances." He has made his way all right without a brass band. Harry prides himself on being a rationalist when it comes to religion, but he isn't vehement or vulgar about it. And he doesn't scoff at tradition the way Stef does. I do think Stef would be an entirely different kind of person if he had grown up in the wholesome surroundings Harry had as a young man.

I often think about what it is that makes some people really superior, and I have come to believe it is capacity rather than anything else. I suppose character and originality enter into that—I am not sure—but at any rate it is something more than ability.

I have great admiration for the kind of people who always hold something in reserve, with whom you never strike bottom. Harry is one of those special people—I never fear I'll get to the bottom of *his* love—and Orv, of course. Time was I would have said Stef was special in that way too, but not anymore—I got to the bottom of *him* long ago! This great capacity impresses me to the point of awe. I am so lacking in that very thing, and the special friends I have had the luck to make have so much of it, that I have grown self-conscious and timid—*sometimes*, not always!

It wasn't until Harry went abroad that I came to appreciate what a truly superior person he is. His letters brought back my own experiences in Europe, and I could see that it struck him much as it did me. I loved the strangeness of hearing people speak our language when they were so obviously foreign. And the place names delighted me—Stoke Poges, for instance. Isn't that quaint? I went out there on a lovely day with an English wine merchant named Frank Hedges Butler. We walked across the fields to the church, and afterward we "butted in" at the old Penn Manor House, where the painter Landseer lived. We wound up by making the rounds of Mr. Butler's various clubs—such as a mere *woman* could be admitted to—and finally saw the skating at the Princess's Skating Club, where Mr. Butler fished out celebrities of all sorts for me to meet. Oh yes, that was a day to remember!

When Harry wrote about exploring Rome with Louis Lord, I "flashed back" to my first visit there with Will and Orv. It was the spring of 1909 and the city was packed for the beatification of Joan of Arc at St. Peter's Basilica. We had to go around to eighteen hotels before we found one that would take us in. A miserable, uncomfortable place it was too. The waiters in the restaurant were so dirty that I could hardly eat a mouthful of food. One day the boys and I went to see the Pantheon. Then we took a long walk and stood on the hill overlooking the Roman Forum and looked up in the guidebook all the things we could see. We walked around past the palaces of the Caesars to where the Circus Maximus used to be, over through the Arch of Constantine, and back to the Colosseum again. All the fine old ruins, straight out of my history books—another dream come true!

And France—how I do adore that country! I've always thought I would feel at home in Le Mans, among Will's friends. The boys and I didn't have nearly enough time to sit back and be tourists. We never got to Nîmes or Avignon or Carcassonne, or any of the other important cathedral towns. How does the poem go? *Tout le monde a son Carcassonne*—"Every man has his Carcassonne." Each of us has some goal, sometimes near at hand, that he simply can't reach. When Harry and I get to Europe, we are going to see all the places I missed, starting with Rouen. I've been longing to go there ever since he brought us that lovely etching of the cathedral. I hung it in a place of honor in the "cold storage room" at Hawthorn Hill, facing the *Muse of Aviation* sculpture that the Aero Club of Sarthe presented to the boys. Harry and I have the selfsame picture in our dining room—and it makes me homesick every time I pass by!

Harry's letters from abroad were a joy forever. They were the first love letters anyone ever wrote to me—if only I had had the wit to see it! A regular storybook lover he was. He cared a good deal for my letters too, he told me. How queer it is to remember that I used to feel uneasy about corresponding with him—as if I were some sort of temptress, a white-haired, bespectacled Circe. Isn't that the limit? After Isabel died, the very act of writing made me feel closer to Harry. It was all I could do for him at a time when I wanted very much to do *something*. I had come to realize that Harry needed me in a way that Stef was incapable of. I told Stef that one reason why Harry and I were such devoted friends was that we *sometimes* needed each other, whereas he could *never* need me for anything. In fact, I don't believe Stef could ever need anyone—not in the way I mean.

Harry seemed needier than ever after he got back from Europe—which is no wonder considering all the troubles that had been heaped upon him. It was on that visit to Hawthorn Hill that he came within a whisker of sweeping me up passionately in his arms. Fancy that! He confessed it to me later, after we had officially become lovers. And to think I used to believe that Harry was all head and no heart! I hated like the dickens to see him go off with Orv to catch the train *that* time—but Stef and I had things to thrash out between us, and we could hardly talk freely with Harry under the same roof. Orv's presence was trying enough! I survived the ordeal as fine as silk, barring a mild thumping in the back of my head and a few other disabilities. But I wouldn't want the combination of Orv and Stef in the same house very often.

One perk of becoming an Oberlin trustee was that it gave Harry and me a readymade excuse to be by ourselves from time to time, without giving Orv reason to worry. Of course, that was long before Little Brother knew there was anything to be worried *about*. I was still in the dark about Harry's intentions myself—not that he was trying awfully hard to keep them secret. At the trustees' meeting that November, for instance, I was talking on the telephone at the Park Hotel one morning when he and Professor Stetson unexpectedly came into the lobby. I can't think why I hadn't told Harry about the meeting—maybe I had—but anyway I was surprised to see him. I was even more surprised when he admitted that he had planned to come to Oberlin to visit his mother at precisely the time when he knew I would be there. That was just the last straw!

Then there was the time when Orv sat next to Harry's sister at lunch. We were all Mr. Stetson's guests at the Faculty Club, and Mary Haskell told my brother that I reminded her of Harry's favorite cousin—the one who unwittingly did me a favor years ago by insisting that Harry must on no account become a missionary— more than any lady she knew. I took that as a high compliment coming from Mary, who is a missionary herself. What I didn't realize was that Harry and Mr. Stetson were in cahoots—or that I was the innocent prey they were pursuing! Harry says he owes more to the Prof than to any other person for starting him to thinking while he was at college. I guess I owe the Prof a debt of my own— for helping steer Harry through the labyrinth of the female heart!

Mr. Stetson calls me the "lady trustee" and likes to pretend I intimidate him—ha! We know each other too well to have any illusions on that score. I may look fierce sometimes, but I'm meek enough at heart. In point of fact, the Prof is one of the most perceptive people I know. He told me some lovely things about Harry's work in Kansas City in the years when I didn't have any contact with him. I suppose it was inevitable that my casual friendship with the Prof would set tongues wagging in a small town like Oberlin. From what I hear, Mary was responsible for spreading the rumor that Harry and Mr. Stetson were "after the same girl." Can you beat that? "So you see," I said to my future husband, "your little sister isn't so innocent and unsuspecting as you thought!"

Orville

I confess I had my suspicions about Stef even before the Wrangel Island business blew up in our faces in the fall of '23. Up to then I had done my best to be agreeable, knowing how attached he and Kate were to each other. But the news reports of the incident left me no alternative. Kate showed me a letter that Harry had sent her from London, and I was glad to see that he sized Stef up in just about the same way I had come to think of him—as someone who sincerely believed that he was a special pet of the gods. Even Kate had to admit that his conduct toward me in that matter showed that he was not to be trusted.

Things had looked very different two years earlier, when Stef launched his first expedition to the island. In those days he could do no wrong in our eyes. He impressed both Kate and me as a romantic adventurer straight out of the pages of *Robinson Crusoe*. And Wrangel was his very own Island of Despair. Nobody could have been more taken aback than I was when Stef announced his intention to colonize it in the name of King George. The ship's crew was ludicrously small—three American sailors and one Canadian, plus an Eskimo cook—and they were woefully unprepared for the harsh conditions they encountered above the Arctic Circle. A year later, when it proved necessary to send fresh supplies, I loaned Stef three thousand dollars to outfit a relief ship. But ice prevented the *Teddy Bear* from getting through to the island, and no further attempt was possible until 1923.

That summer, while Kate and I were at the bay, Griff Brewer decided to raise money for a second expedition through a public subscription in England. Imagine my surprise when I learned that the biggest contributor to the Wrangel Island Relief Fund was the British Wright Company. The board of directors had blithely voted to give my money away and notified me after the deed was done. Both Griff and Stef betrayed my trust in the most inexcusable fashion. But their underhanded scheming came to naught. By the time the second relief ship reached the island, the white men were all dead. Only the Eskimo cook and her cat had survived. A few months later, a Russian crew arrived and planted the Soviet flag on the island. In the end, those men's lives had been sacrificed for no nobler cause than to feed Stef's insatiable ambition.

It goes without saying that I wanted nothing more to do with the man after that. But Stef was still Kate's friend, and I couldn't very well *not* invite him to Dayton for the twentieth anniversary of the first flight. He and Mr. Akeley came from New York for the ceremony at the National Cash Register Hall. Stef was one of the featured speakers, following Governor Cox. The poor governor was so anxious to do well that he did his very worst. He didn't get any of his facts straight but soared and soared into the stratosphere until at last he ran out of steam and sat down. After that sorry performance, it was a relief to listen to a scientist who actually knew what he was talking about. The gist of Stef's remarks was that Will and I had made the world round a second time because the aeroplane can go east or west right over the poles. He said people had grown accustomed to thinking of the world as a cylinder and not as a sphere.

Stef is a splendid talker, but actions speak louder than words. When he returned to Dayton after Christmas, I read him the riot act. He actually had the good cheek to tell Katharine he was glad in a way that the *Teddy Bear* had not gotten through the ice in 1922, because the Canadian government had not yet taken responsibility for occupying Wrangel Island. Kate reminded him that in his letter asking me for money, he had emphasized that lives might be at stake. That embarrassed him for once! Yet even then Stef continued to defend everything he had done. From his point of view, his schemes were so important for the advancement of science that he was justified in carrying them out at all costs. I was more than ever convinced that Kate was unwise to trust Stef a bit. Either he lacked conscience or he simply had different ideas of right and wrong from ours.

I was still reeling from Stef's behavior when I discovered that Griff—of all people—had gone back on me in an unbelievable way in connection with the sale of British Wright. As he well knew, I was anxious to wind up the company's affairs and prevent anybody from peddling our patents in Belgium and Italy. British Wright had already lost thirty-five thousand dollars over the past five years. Griff actually expected to use up all the remaining funds—between twenty-five and thirty thousand, half of which was rightfully mine—on his own salary and expenses. He was planning to travel to Alaska to make sure that the one surviving white man and the ten or twelve Eskimos still stranded on Wrangel Island in the wake of the various relief expeditions could return to the mainland, if they wanted to. As Kate observed, between enjoying grandstand plays and liking to travel, Griff's "duty" would have been very clear to him and very expensive to us.

By a stroke of sheer luck, the deal for British Wright fell through at the eleventh hour, so Griff was beaten at his own little trick. Swes and I even wound up getting more than seventeen thousand dollars out of the company. We had been prepared for years to have that all used up by Griff, and it would have gone that way without protest on my part if he hadn't gone a little too far in contributing my money to Stef's plans without my knowledge. The whole business left me sick to the stomach. I arranged to have the sale of my stock in the company taken care of through the bank. I knew it would hurt Griff's feelings, but I was in no mood to let him handle any more of my affairs.

Still, I never can stay mad at Griff for long, not after everything he has done for us—not least making the arrangements for sending the flyer to London. I had about reached the end of my rope with the Smithsonian when he came up with his proposal, and I jumped at it. In fact, I was all ready to start reassembling the machine for shipment when, as luck would have it, my back gave out again. Something seemed to snap while I was bending over the washbowl in the bathroom, and I realized too late that I had neglected to put on my supporting belt. The ensuing attack of sciatica put me out of commission for weeks. It was more than a year before I had the strength to get back to work on the flyer—and another four years before it finally went on display at the Science Museum. Five years! Why, it didn't take Will and me that long to invent the confounded machine in the first place.

Katharine

Between Orv's busted back, Harry's loneliness, and getting my feet on the ground as an Oberlin trustee, I had my work cut out for me in the early months of 1924. At least I could make Bubbo's life easier by doing things around the house, even if I was a miserable failure at making progress on the book. But Harry was so far

away—and so very, very vulnerable. I knew all about the things he
found so dark and forbidding when he returned to Kansas City as
a widower. I loved him for that—for all the loyalty and devotion,
and for all the heartaches too. Will's death had affected me the
same way. A kind of numbness came over me, and I was unable
to sleep for weeks on end, until at last I got so worn down that the
doctor had to be called in. And later turning my back on Orv and
all my Dayton friends—oh yes, I know what it's like to feel alone
and bereft!

It comforted me to know that young Henry would be spending the summer at home with his father. They have always been
the best of friends. But Henry was planning to go abroad in the
fall for a year of postgraduate study, and I dreaded it so for Harry.
He would need companionship more than ever when his only
child was gone. I bucked myself up with the thought that writing
an account of his travels in Europe on his sabbatical would keep
him from brooding on his troubles. I told him that we sorely need
a book or two, now and then, that has some sensible, unaffected
ideas. That cheap bunch of New York "intellectuals" that I fear
Harry admires somewhat are so far beneath what he has always
been that there is no comparison to be made.

I understood Harry's saying that he wouldn't have cared so
much, for himself, to go on living after Isabel died. When Will
was taken from us, I had the same feeling of emptiness—the world
seemed to have lost its meaning. Yet life does go on, willy-nilly,
and I did my best to convince Harry that the future was far from
bleak, for both him *and* me. I told him that we had a good many
years before us, years that were sure to be filled with satisfaction
and happiness. I was right about *that*, at least, however cloudy

my crystal ball may have been about other things. We have made each other very happy indeed. I'm not altogether pessimistic, if I do growl and fuss a good deal. When all is said and done, I have found a few people who make living well worth my while!

Was Stef one of those people? I used to think so, but now—now I'm not so sure. My mind is in an uproar. Some of the best memories of my life are bound up in my friendship with Stef. There was a time when I wanted to write to him every single day. I longed to know where he was and what he was doing when we were apart. Then, practically overnight, our friendship simply fizzled out. After that agonizing visit when Orv and I let him know how we felt about his disgraceful conduct in the Wrangel Island affair, his letters pretty much stopped coming. About every three months I would receive a line or two saying that he was very busy—that was all. I didn't blame Stef. Liking goes by favor. But it felt funny to be discussing solemnly whether he and I were friends any longer. If not friends, just what were we, I'd like to know?

Try as I might, I couldn't drum Stef out of my head. I kept hoping I'd find a letter in the mail when I got home from a trip. I wondered if he ever missed me, just the least little bit. Then I'd pinch myself and say, "It's all right if he doesn't. I don't know why he should miss me nor why I should wish he would. Everything is all right just as it is." Stef was a dear comfort to me when Reuch died and Orv was having such a bad time with sciatica. I never can forget the lovely things that existed between us. I wished with all my heart that I could do something worthwhile for him—not to make demands or be "forward," as he put it, but just to let him know that I thought of him with sympathy and affection, and that I would lighten his sad times and increase his happiness if I could.

But the case was hopeless—I see that now. The longer I thought about Stef and how little I could actually do for him, the clearer it became that he wasn't to blame for my restlessness. The real reason I was so unsettled was that I had *nothing to do*. I couldn't comfort Harry or Stef. I couldn't force the Smithsonian to do the right thing. I couldn't even get Orv to write that blasted book! No one ought to be without some useful occupation, yet women and girls nearly always are. There is no incentive for us to go out and find something meaningful to do. On the contrary, we are actually *blamed* if we take up any regular, honest-to-goodness work outside the home—as if it meant taking a job away from someone who needed it more. No wonder so many women don't do anything but give orders to servants and dress and fill up their time with nothing!

It isn't that I am bored—far from it. I have never been bored in all my life, except for a few hours at a stretch. Why, then, do I find myself with the same old weariness every afternoon? It has always been my besetting weakness, this getting so tired, ever since college. It often comes over me that I could hardly earn my own living anymore—if it should ever be necessary, I mean. I have so little endurance, so little strength, so little sustained energy. I don't know what makes me so mortally exhausted all the time. Maybe it's just pure laziness. My honest opinion is that I would be less tired if I had some good, hard work to do!

Harry

In the first few months after Isabel died, it was only my writing that kept me going from one day to the next. Never have I been so grateful for deadlines; without them, even the best of us might wake up one morning and find that he has nothing left to say. The articles I mailed to the *Star* from Europe were a lifeline for me. My colleagues reported that they went over well with readers, and Katharine even encouraged me to put them between hard covers. After reading the first draft of my manuscript, however, she changed her tune. Her Criticalness declared that my "Notes from a Kansas City Traveler" were all very well for a newspaper audience, but when it came to writing a book, she was sure I could "do better." Well, what did I expect? I asked for her opinion, and she has never been shy about speaking her mind.

In any case, I had other things on my plate after my sabbatical. Henry had decided to see the world for himself and spend a year at the University of Toulouse. Shortly after he set sail, in the fall of 1924, my mother's health fell into decline. I held off going to Oberlin as long as I dared, for fear of alarming her, and by the time I arrived she was so weak that she could talk only with considerable effort. One day, to break the routine of reading aloud to her, I told her about one of the widows back home who had been pursuing me. Her son, it seemed, had suddenly become one of the most eligible bachelors in Kansas City. As my sister was putting her to bed that evening, Mother burst out indignantly, "To think of those widows going after Harry. They deserve to have their necks wrung, every one of them. I guess they will learn my son is capable of selecting a wife for himself when he wants one!"

Later Mary told me that when she broached the idea of my marrying Katharine, Mother dismissed it out of hand. "She will never leave her brother," she declared. For a long time I too took it for granted that no matter how much Katharine cared for me, in the end she would be unable to tear herself away from Orville. It was the combination of Mother's death and Henry's absence that brought home how much Katharine's companionship had come to mean to me. I resolved to unburden myself to her on the subject the first chance I got. But before a suitable opportunity presented itself, another springtime was upon us, Henry was coming home from France to take a job on the *Wichita Beacon*, and the Smithsonian controversy was bursting back into bloom like a hardy perennial.

In April 1925 the *New York Times* belatedly caught wind of Orville's plans to send the flyer to London. He promptly put out a statement confirming the report, without volunteering further details. Off the record, he told me that the loan would probably be permanent, but he preferred to say nothing to the press. Then, to my surprise, Orville went on the offensive. He publicly challenged the accuracy of the Smithsonian's label describing the Langley aerodrome as the first machine in history "capable of sustained free flight." This salvo produced the desired effect of ruffling the feathers of officials in Washington. The Smithsonian's secretary, Dr. Walcott, duly issued a statement of his own in which he reviewed the Hammondsport trials of 1914 and concluded that the label was fundamentally correct.

Katharine accused me of "taking to the woods" just as the story was breaking, since I had gone to Quebec to meet Henry's ship. On my return I instructed the *Star*'s Sunday department to get up a general piece on the controversy. Meanwhile, I turned out another in a long series of editorials taking the Smithsonian to task. Not that I was under the illusion that it would do any good. I had told Katharine more than once, at the risk of making myself a terrible nuisance, that the only way to settle the matter once and for all was for Orville to publish his monograph. She protested that her brother was so worn out nervously and so lacking in vitality that she didn't think he could do it, and that it distressed her to have it urged. Much as I hated to be disagreeable, I insisted that it was a vital matter and really must be done.

Orville's resistance was nothing short of heroic. No force on earth could shake him loose. Each time after issuing a statement to the press, he would duck down out of sight, grumbling that the row about the machine going out of the country had so interfered with his work that there was no telling when it would be ready for shipment. I was just about ready to throw in the towel when, one day at the beginning of June, a large, flat package arrived in the mail from Dayton. Inside was a copy of the famous photo of the first flight at Kitty Hawk, inscribed to me by Orville. I knew what that meant. It was his way of saying that I was no longer just a friend of Katharine's but a trusted ally, almost one of the family. Nothing could have pleased me more.

Orville's magnanimous gesture demanded a response. But what did I, a humble denizen of Grub Street, have to offer a man of his stature? The problem occupied me for some time. At length I realized that the solution was literally staring me in the face. I recalled the portraits of Stef and other friends that I had seen on the Wrights' bookshelves in Dayton. I would send them a photo-graph of myself to add to their collection. Katharine wouldn't consider it immodest of me, I felt sure, and if Orville happened to notice, he wouldn't give the gift a second thought. To tell the truth, I was warming to the idea of being something more than a bird of passage at Hawthorn Hill.

Katharine

I was awfully glad to have Harry's picture, and it pleased me that he wanted to send it. A real "speaking likeness" it was too. I half expected he would open his mouth and start talking to me when I looked at it! He pretended to be surprised when I wrote to thank him, but he knew perfectly well how much I liked to have it. I told him I intended to keep it out in plain sight somewhere, either in the library or in my bedroom. That way, I told myself, Little Brother wouldn't get any silly ideas into his head. Not that there was anything for him to have ideas about—not just yet!

I tried to get up the nerve to send Harry a portrait of me, but my activities in that line had not met with a very enthusiastic response. The most recent photograph was the one that had been published in the *Oberlin Alumni Magazine* when I went on the board of trustees. Orv and Lorin and the children all made more or less insulting remarks about it, saying that it made me look like a "delicate old lady." I hinted as broadly as I knew how that my feelings wouldn't be hurt if Harry didn't want the photograph—but he went ahead and asked for it anyway. Serves me right for making the offer! So there I sit on the bookcase in his study, perched between Isabel and his dear, sweet mother.

Poor Harry—to lose both the women in his life one after the other. I had hoped he was through with his troubles for a while. I only saw his mother twice before she died. How I wish I could have been something to her, for his sake. Some way, Harry brings out all my mothering instincts in spades. And why shouldn't I mother him, I'd like to know? A mother's is the most lasting and genuine of all kinds of love. Harry's love for his mother was as fine as his devotion to Isabel. It was because he and Isabel had been so much to each other that he was lost without her. They grew up together and while they were still young learned to adapt themselves to one another, just as Orv and I did. Everything, on both sides, in their life together was a revelation to me of the lovely possibilities of marriage.

Katharine Wright Haskell. I still can't quite believe it's real—my new name, my new husband, my new home. Everything has changed so quickly! Four years ago I was a confirmed old maid with no thought or hope of marrying. All my plans, all my interests had gathered around the kind of life I had been living up to then, with Orv my central interest and Harry, Stef, and a few others a very dear and necessary part of my existence. Then, seeing that living was such an anxious and almost overwhelming thing to Harry, I began to transfer more and more of my interest to him, until at last I was drawn into his orbit and away from Orv's, like a stray asteroid captured by a passing planet.

I had a funny whim about wanting Harry to show me little attentions. I often wished that Orv would do some of the nice little things that other men do when they don't think half so much of any woman as he thought of me. Harry understood that without a word on my part. One Christmas, before his mother died, he sent me the most exquisite scarf to go with a blue velvet dinner gown I was having made. The scarf was a different shade of blue, and much prettier. It caught the same tones in the changeable velvet at times and was sometimes much deeper. For the fun of it, I cut a swatch of the dressmaker's fabric and slipped it inside a letter I sent to Harry. How deliciously daring it felt to have our own little secret!

Orv never pays the slightest attention to my clothes, whereas Harry is forever paying me dear little compliments. A shameless flatterer he is—and one more-than-loyal supporter too. He proved it when the Smithsonian flap reared its ugly head again. Orv and I were awfully sorry that Harry wasn't around when the storm broke in the spring of 1925. He had always done more than anyone else, and we did want him that time. It was nice of him to offer me his shoulder to cry on afterward, but I need a good open space when I really let loose. Bubbo had half a notion that Harry was the source of the leak to the *New York Times*. All I've got to say about that is—bully for him if he was! We thought he could probably start something, and Orv was so glad to have his help.

The tide was beginning to turn in our favor—for one thing, the aeronautical journals were all coming out on our side. But there was no doubt that Walcott would fight to protect himself. We never underestimated his prestige and power as the head of the Smithsonian. He was one of the best politicians in Washington and knew all the influential people in Congress. Orv always wanted an investigation by scientific people, but he had to be very careful not to let it fall into Walcott's hands. I have my suspicions about his successor, Dr. Abbot, too. Anyone can see how the so-called scientists have to curry favor with these men. So much money and so many opportunities for advancement lie in their power to distribute.

My opinion is, if people don't want the machine to stay in England, they will have to stir Congress up to take hold of the Smithsonian and do something about it. If they are not interested enough to do anything, I don't see how they can reasonably blame Orv for trying to get the machine settled in a permanent home while he is still here to see about it himself. Little Brother is very bitter and disgusted beyond words with the howl that has gone up. The nervous shocks have reduced his vitality and energy beyond belief. No one but myself can understand that.

I know what they all think—that if he had published more stuff and so on that it would be different. What people don't understand is that Orv looks on the writing as only a minor obligation. He truly despises the idea that telling about what you have done is the chief thing, that the actual doing is liable to be thought nothing at all unless you keep calling people's attention to it. It isn't because Orv hasn't written a book that the Smithsonian has been able to get away with murder. It is because talking and writing impress "scientists" much more than any "scientific" doing ever could. The scientists have been cowards, every one of them. No one who should have taken an interest and could have done much has done anything to help us. I despise the whole superficial spirit of the scientific world. Scientific fiddlesticks!

I knew, and Orv knew even better, that it would be more work to do the thing well through another person than for Orv to do it himself. Yet year after year it was the same old story. Each fall I would be looking forward hopefully to getting to work on the book, but Bubbo always had some plausible excuse. When I got too insistent, he would report that he was "looking up things" and getting all the material ready to use—"indexing" and so on. It was almost comical. He looked and acted exactly like a small boy trying to dodge a disagreeable chore.

Orville

Toward the end of 1924, I finally felt fit enough to set up the 1903 machine on the floor of my shop. Before it went to England, I needed to check that everything was exactly as it had been originally. A few pieces had been replaced when the flyer was sent to New York for exhibition some years earlier, and they were not quite right. I had hoped to get the flyer safely out of the country before news of its going got out, but unfortunately there was a leak at New York. I suspect Harry told someone out there confidentially and, like most confidences, it didn't keep. But we could hardly fault him for having no stomach for a fight. When I sent him the photograph of the first flight as a token of our appreciation, he wrote back, "Yours for knocking Walcott into a cocked hat!"

As a consequence of the leak, a mighty hue and cry had broken out over letting the flyer go abroad. One congressman even threatened to introduce a bill to prevent the exportation of such historic relics—as if that would have solved the problem. Kate said she wanted to pass a law against people expressing opinions on things they wouldn't take the trouble to read up on. Hardly any of the people who were creating such an unholy uproar understood the first thing about my dispute with the Smithsonian. A reporter from the *New York World* spent two days here, and I was frantic with the job of trying to explain anything to him when he didn't even know what an aileron was. That took all the life out of me.

I have tried and tried to get these elementary points across, but it's no use. Aeronautical engineering is simply too complicated a subject for general discussion. Everyone says it is a great pity that I dislike writing so much and am so unwilling to hand it over to anyone else. If they only knew how hard it is to get anyone to understand and to do anything but ball things up when it comes to the technical stuff, they would have more sympathy. Even Kate never seemed to get things quite right. If she tried to write anything, she missed the point just enough to exasperate me. In the end I always have to word the statement myself or it will make me look ridiculous before aeronautical men.

The most important thing, as far as creating an impression goes, is for other people to talk in a general way about Will's and my work as *scientists*. It isn't because anyone has read Langley's book that he is established as having contributed the scientific foundation for the aeroplane. Not at all. It is because the Smithsonian bunch and their supporters have continually talked and written, in vague generalities, about Langley's "scientific" work. They are the ones who deliberately began the references to Will and me as "mechanics." That didn't just happen. It was methodically planned and persistently done.

It is ridiculous, when you come to think of it, how the Smithsonian has succeeded in twisting all this. Langley didn't contribute nearly as much as Lilienthal did. Lilienthal was a much better engineer than Langley, yet he is never mentioned. Langley got his idea of using curved surfaces from Lilienthal. He used them after visiting Lilienthal but never mentioned Lilienthal in speaking of it. Of course, I know exactly what Lilienthal did and what the rest did. Walcott and Abbot don't know. None of them has ever studied the subject as Will and I did. I don't think I ought to have to call attention to the points in which Will and I excelled the rest. Our work is all on record.

Nothing will be gained by belaboring the issue further, especially now that the machine is safely out of sight in England. When the news of its going first became public, though, Kate and I were of two minds whether it would be better to give out the exact wording of my agreement with the Science Museum or let the matter drift along. After all, what difference did it make that I reserved the right to bring the machine back to this country after five years if a proper home could be found for it? At bottom, I expected that it would have to stay in England permanently, and I did not like to open a possibility of a lot more explanations. Even now I don't expect that the Smithsonian will ever make the wrong right—and I refuse to let them have the machine until they do.

As a last resort, I let it be known that I was open to keeping the machine in the United States provided the Smithsonian truthfully labeled the Langley plane, published both sides of the controversy in its annual report, and identified the Wright flyer as the first man-carrying aircraft in the world. But the Smithsonian didn't rise to the bait, even after the president of the National Aeronautic Association called attention to the fact that the Langley machine on display in the museum had no way of being launched. He said you might as well hang up the body of a legless man and label it capable of winning a footrace in the Madison Square Garden races!

Two distinguished scientists did suggest a revised label that the Smithsonian finally deigned to accept. They dropped out all reference to Curtiss's Hammondsport trials of 1914 in favor of a bland statement that "in the opinion of many competent to judge," the Langley machine of 1903 was capable of flight, et cetera, et cetera. Practically the only thing left to criticize now is the expression "competent to judge." So that is where things stand today.

The Smithsonian has come down from the claim that the Langley machine *did* fly in 1914 to the opinion of some that it *could have* flown if it could have been launched. Eventually, that claim will go too—but I don't expect I will be around to see it happen.

Katharine

By the spring of 1925, Little Brother was looking more tired and frustrated than ever. His strength and spirit had been pretty severely tried by the Smithsonian's scheming. I suppose none of us quite realized what a tremendous strain he had been under the last twenty years. Will and he had had to win the patent suits for themselves. No lawyer could handle them all. Sometimes it was maddening to have to let the lawyers talk for them when the lawyers themselves didn't half understand the fine points in the case. After Will died, I tried to convince Orv that he shouldn't put so much of himself into the fight. Curtiss didn't, after all. But Orv would always shoot back, "Yes, and Curtiss loses all the suits too, and I can't afford to do that."

Just as I was coming to my wits' end, Harry reawakened my slumbering genius for worrying. Something he said about the widows in Kansas City, when he came to Dayton that Easter, made me uneasy. A woman's eye is awfully sharp when she gets the least inkling of schemes afoot. I can jump at conclusions fifty feet away! I was ashamed of my sect that some of those "vidders" should have such dreadful taste as to be out hunting already. Try as I might to put the idea out of my head, when I heard of Mrs. Kirkwood having him over to meet her friends, and of his going out to a lecture with Isabel's former nurse, and later his letters in which he spoke of his loneliness and his not enjoying going around alone—well, the whole combination was too much for me. I felt like screaming, "Tell all the matchmakers to go to thunder and please, *please* don't let anyone make your future life for you!"

With Harry's fine ideas of honor, you see, I was afraid he might slip into something that didn't really satisfy him just because it was expected of him—or, worse still, that he had decided to drift along and see what happened. I had wanted to say something ever since Isabel died, but I'd always held back. At last I decided that I must tell him how I felt. I wouldn't for the world have interfered with any of Harry's private affairs. I only knew that I would have been glad to have a friend suggest a similar thing to my brother if he were to be left alone. How I used to laugh at the thought of Orv marrying. Harry must have laughed too at my grandmothering care of him!

I won't deny that my concern for Harry wasn't entirely disinterested. It came over me that maybe one reason I had thought what I thought and felt what I felt was that I saw a probable end of any—what shall I call it?—active friendship with him. I knew that I would never feel any differently toward *him*, and I wanted so much that he would never feel differently toward *me*. For so many years we had helped each other the best we could to weather the storms. But I knew how easily we could lose the chance to express the old friendship. Even so, I told myself that I could get along with that if it meant seeing him have what he deserved—comfort and peace of mind and real companionship.

Mind you, Harry was caught in a situation that wouldn't be easy for anyone. Many calamities have befallen very fine people under similar circumstances. As one grows old, one's powers of adaptation diminish. When we were both young and had nothing and were too inexperienced anyway to look for our own advantage, we could be freer and surer of ourselves when it came to falling in love. But Harry and I were long past that stage in life. I wanted him to have real companionship and thought he might possibly find it someday, but there was no chance of it just then. What he needed, more than anything, was understanding and sympathy and comfort. How I longed to be his fairy godmother and give it all to him!

My biggest fear was that Harry would end up disliking me if I kept on talking about these intimate things. Or that he would avoid telling me anything for fear I would read all kinds of things into nothing. It would have broken my heart to bring him uneasiness and uncomfortableness, when I wanted to do just the opposite. It was because in all my long friendship with him I had seen absolutely nothing I could not admire that I had this deep feeling about his future. He was so generous with me—to allow me so many privileges and to put the best possible meaning into what I did and said. Our long, long friendship meant so much to me. I would have been the unhappiest of unhappy mortals if we had lost what was really a prize to us both. There was never any real danger of that happening, of course, but sometimes perverse Fate does try to get the best of such a friendship. Here's for snapping our fingers under her nose!

Early that summer I went to Geneva, Ohio, to see my friend Mella's daughter, Katharine Wright King, graduate from high school. Mella and I have been friends since college. Katharine took special honors—she and one boy, a regular Harry Haskell from the look of him. The boy had a higher average, but Katharine had been in high school only three years and was the youngest in her class.

It was sweet to see her so happy and altogether lovely in her simple graduating dress, looking forward to everything with eagerness and a certainty that her dreams would come true. Katharine deserved nothing but the best, for she had a good mind, a fine start in character, and an attractive, winning personality. She wasn't pretty, exactly, but she was charming—at least to her "Aunt" Katharine.

All through the ceremony I couldn't stop thinking of Harry and me at Oberlin and how bright and eager *we* had been. The Order of the Empty Heart indeed! My girlfriends and I weren't exactly starved for attention from the opposite sect. When I think how naive I was about accepting Arthur Cunningham's engagement ring, it makes my heart go down to my boots. Well, the very first thing Mella told me when I got to her house was that Harry had sent a book to Katharine for her graduation. And when she said how pleased she was that he wanted to send her daughter a remembrance, there did flash through my mind the least suspicion that *he* was pleased to be sending it to *my* namesake!

Mella, in some way, gave me a little feeling that she had her own thoughts about my frankly confessed interest in and concern about Harry. It was a peculiar look she had when I said I had been writing to him a good deal since he had been alone. She said she had often thought of writing to him, to say she felt sorry for his loss, but lacked the confidence to actually do it. Well, I didn't know quite how to respond, so I just said, "Harry is safe with me"— thinking that maybe he wasn't quite safe among all those "vidders" in Kansas City. Ha ha! If I had known what lay in store for me when I went up to Oberlin for commencement that year, I would have turned tail and scampered straight home to Dayton!

Interlude

The Explorer,
Vilhjalmur Stefansson

Which of us can say when devotion turns into love, tenderness into passion? With Katharine one could never be sure where to draw the line. One minute she was all sweet reason, calmly discussing her "interest" in me, and the next minute she was practically begging me to make love to her. What puzzling creatures women are. I have devoted my life to unlocking the mysteries of the Arctic, but when it comes to the wilds of the female psyche, I'm in uncharted territory. Katharine once said the difference between us was that I had a "thinking heart," whereas hers was a "singing heart." Was it really as simple as that? Or was there some deeper mystery in our natures that made our misunderstanding inevitable?

Katharine has always been something of a mystery to me. Doubtless I am a mystery to her, though I can't imagine why. The life of a public figure is an open book. Anything I didn't tell Katharine wasn't worth telling in the first place. That wasn't enough for her, however. She accused me of holding things back, of being incapable of intimacy. But I never bargained on intimacy. What I wanted from her was something far more precious: an idealized friendship, a meeting of minds—and, yes, of hearts—but without emotional entanglements and the forwardness they engender. Unfortunately, Katharine's way of idealizing me was to idolize me. Her insatiable demands finally made it clear that she had mistaken my honest friendship for love, and I had no choice but to pull back. Since then, her letters have been sporadic and measurably less personal. I understand, of course, that she is simply paying me back in my own coin.

When I first got to know the Wrights, they desperately needed allies in their battle royal with the Smithsonian Institution. Admiring Orville as I did, I was only too happy to take up the cudgels on their behalf. Orville reminded me of the wounded elephant in the little sculpture that Akeley made before the war: he was exhausted and needed the support that Katharine and I were eager to provide. As a close family friend, I stood in for Wilbur in a manner of speaking. Katharine used to hold forth on how her two brothers had differed, always with what seemed to me balanced and impartial praise. I eventually came to feel, however, that she was a bit fonder of Orville. She said she was even "sillier" about him than about me. So although no one could take Wilbur's place with her, she took comfort in lavishing on me the interest and affectionate sympathy that he had always inspired in her.

Katharine is one of the warmest and most genuinely sympathetic women it has ever been my privilege to know. But it does her no injustice, in my opinion, to observe that she does not possess what one would call a fundamentally passionate nature. Enthusiastic and excitable, yes, but not passionate. She is far too sensible and levelheaded to abandon herself to her emotions. In fact, for all her "singing" heart, she clearly distrusts passionate love and greatly prefers the gentler kind—call it sisterly love or what you will. Her devotion to Orville is the purest expression of that love. Indeed, there is a question in my mind whether there is room in her life for any other kind of love—or any other man.

Passion

Harry

The explosion, as Katharine so indelicately calls it, had been building a head of steam for months. Sooner or later it was bound to burst. I don't wonder she was "dumbsquizzled" by my blowup; it took me by surprise as much as her. She's right: I was acting more like a callow youth than a hard-boiled newspaperman. Never in my life had I felt so worked up and out of control. In my experience, "overmastering passion" was the stuff of romantic poetry and novels. Once I began to tell Katharine how many years I had loved her, ever since our time at Oberlin, and how eager I was to share my life with her, the words came gushing out like molten lava from a volcano.

It was what she said about the scheming widows in Kansas City and the likelihood of our paths leading in different directions that lit the fuse. Despite her protestations of innocence, I have a notion that she deliberately brought the situation to a head just to see what I was made of. Not that I'm entirely innocent myself.

All that bellyaching about how lonely I was after Isabel died was sure to stir up her mothering instincts. I see that now. And I may have been ringing her bell just a bit when I went on and on about chaperoning Miss Farmer to those country-house parties—as if for one moment I would have seriously considered leading Isabel's sickroom nurse to the altar.

Then again, my escape may have been narrower than I care to think. Katharine hit the mark when she said I needed to be rescued. Miss Farmer had me in her sights. She planned to let me drift along like the heartsick widower that I was, plying me with tea and sympathy until I was too weak to resist. Then, if I tried to extricate myself, she would create a scene and make me feel that I had put her in an embarrassing position. Katharine and Dick Sutton saw what was afoot sooner than I did. When he told Katharine with tears in his eyes that it was all settled between Miss Farmer and me, and that he didn't understand why on earth I didn't "camp on the trail," Katharine knew full well that she was the game he wanted me to bag.

One way or another, I was pretty much a wreck by the time Oberlin commencement rolled around in 1925. I had shed thirteen pounds and was so overwrought that I could hardly concentrate on my work. I wrote to my old professor Raymond Stetson and asked what he thought I should do. With his profound knowledge of psychology, the Prof would surely have some insight into my feelings for Katharine. I should have known better than to turn to a lifelong bachelor for advice in an affair of the heart. As I recollect, he suggested that I dream up some sort of conversational pitch and send it to Katharine in a letter. That was about the craziest idea I had ever heard. It sounded to me a good deal as if, not knowing about such things himself, the Prof had copied it from a novel.

I had tried the literary approach before, as an underclassman at Oberlin, and it didn't get me far. I was a bashful youth with little experience of girls outside of my parents' small missionary circle. One year I got up the courage to invite a nice young woman to the Thanksgiving class party. Immediately, I began to worry whether I would be able to think of anything to say to her. To be on the safe side, I made an outline of what I might talk about and decided on a general discussion of Dickens's novels as offering possibilities. The evening passed pleasantly enough, but I never got another date with the young lady in question. I was in no hurry to repeat my mistake.

After I rejected his first proposal, the Prof counseled me to make a beeline for Dayton and get things settled face-to-face before I suffered another "attack." That struck me as a more promising strategy. Knowing that Katharine had gone to Oberlin for a trustees' meeting, I sent her a long letter by regular mail and two more by special delivery, suggesting a discreet rendezvous at a big hotel in downtown Chicago. We were both getting a little old for such lovers' trysts. On the other hand, as the Prof put it, I owed it to Katharine to let her "deal with the impossibilities" as she saw fit, in full possession of the facts. He dismissed my qualms about trifling with her happiness. "The only way to live is to risk being unhappy," he said, "and I'd rather be unhappy with the person I loved than as contented as a cat by the fire."

The idea of meeting me in Chicago without telling Orv offended Katharine's sense of propriety. She proposed instead that I come to Dayton a week later, while her brother was out of town, on the pretext that I was passing through on newspaper business en route to Washington. Apparently my campaign of love letters and telegrams was having an effect. It was not quite the one I intended, however. Almost at once Katharine was assailed by doubts. She had been unwise to be so affectionate and intimate with me, she wrote. Couldn't we remain just friends? I don't know how I had expected her to react, but I was definitely taken aback by her claim that she was in a state of shock and hadn't understood in the least what I was "hinting" at.

Hinting? I had all but professed my love for her on any number of occasions. Is it conceivable that she had no inkling of how I really felt—that to me she was worth more than all the rich old "vidders" in Kansas City lumped together? And couldn't she see how she had been blithely leading me down the garden path with her motherly concern and pledges of undying friendship? Whether her own moves were as calculated as mine had been is another matter. It may be that she is genuinely unaware of the effect she has on the opposite sex. The Prof says she is one of the few women of whom he would be willing to admit the possibility of such artlessness, so I suppose I must consider it too. After all, how else to explain her behavior toward me—and toward Orville?

Katharine

The wild, heart-stopping ride I took that never-to-be-forgotten weekend started out tamely enough. I arrived in Oberlin on Thursday for the trustees' meeting and checked in as usual at the Park Hotel. No sooner had I begun unpacking my bags when the telephone rang. The operator had Harry on the line from Kansas City.

He was all at sixes and sevens—some hopelessly twisted story about a letter he had written but had had second thoughts about sending. It wasn't like him to be so addled. I thought at first that I had touched something deeper than I had intended on the "vidders" situation and that was what had set him off. But then I saw that it was something else altogether—something much, *much* deeper— and all of a sudden I didn't know how to talk to him.

What, I asked myself, could have happened to make Harry feel so differently toward me? I dimly remember saying that I wished we could go on just as we had always been. Then I got the telegram saying that he had mailed an "important letter" and two more by special delivery. And—this was the kicker—he proposed that we spend Sunday morning alone together at the Blackstone Hotel in Chicago talking things over! I was with my friend Kate Leonard, having a nice, quiet chat—and just like that my whole world was turned topsy-turvy. There I sat, rooted to the spot, with Kate sitting in my room while I opened and read the telegram about coming to Chicago. With my heart standing still, I tossed it over onto the dresser and said, in answer to Kate's kindly anxiety, that I might have to leave before I had planned, but that it was nothing serious. I was getting to be a gifted fibber already!

Telling a little white lie for Kate's benefit was one thing, but the thought of not being completely straight with Little Brother was more than I could bear. I couldn't bring myself to go to Chicago to meet Harry when I would have had to do it in an absolutely secret way. Mind you, there was nothing *wrong* with a pair of old friends meeting like that—but if it had ever come out, Orv simply wouldn't have understood. He never interfered with what I did, but I always liked to tell him, just as he told me all such things. I knew I couldn't live with a secret of that kind preying on my mind. Orv didn't know anything about what Harry and I had been writing to each other, and he would have thought I had been very unwise to do what I had done. Only I didn't *know* I was doing what I had done!

On Friday afternoon, after the trustees' meeting, Frannie Lord and I popped into Tobin's drugstore for an ice cream. We had been making small talk for five or ten minutes when suddenly she blurted out, "Katharine, I have been thinking—you *will* forgive me, won't you dear—but I have been wondering why *you* can't do something about Harry. You and he and Orville belong together some way or other!" Well, I never batted an eye, even though I had already had Harry's letter telling about the unsent letter—the contents of which I had partly guessed, though it didn't come till the next morning, but I had had the telegram saying it was coming, and so on. What could I possibly say that wouldn't give the game away? So I just kissed Frannie to assure her that she hadn't offended me by speaking so freely.

Sure enough, all three of Harry's letters arrived as promised on Saturday morning. I collected them at the front desk of the hotel just as I was about to sit down with Mr. Stetson to have a long talk about Orv's "situation" with the Smithsonian. Then who should show up but Harry's missionary sister! Quick as a wink, I stuffed his letters into my pocketbook, where nobody could spot the tell-tale handwriting, and tried to compose myself. Whereupon Mary proceeded to take a letter out of *her* handbag—a letter from Harry's son, who had spent the past year studying abroad. And there we sat, the Prof and I, two most interested people—one of whom was struggling valiantly to keep her thoughts from wandering—listening to an account of young Henry's adventures in Europe!

After her reading was over, Mary got up and excused herself, and Mr. Stetson and I were finally free to broach the subject that was on both our minds. Because I wasn't sure how much Harry had already told him about our friendship, I made a guarded comment about how strange it was that Harry still didn't seem to be getting settled down, nearly two years after his wife's death. The Prof replied that *he* didn't think it strange in the least—from which I naturally deduced that he knew a good deal more than he was letting on. I was slightly self-conscious to begin with because I knew the letters buried in my handbag were sure to tell *why* Harry hadn't settled down. I consider my sitting there calmly with his sister and Mr. Stetson as positively heroic. And all the time there was poor Harry in Kansas City waiting anxiously for a telegram that wasn't being sent!

Before I got a chance to call the Western Union, I had another cable from Harry suggesting that he spend part of the following week with me in Dayton. This was a new fly in the ointment. Quick thinking was clearly in order. Orv, I knew, was due to receive an honorary degree that week from the University of Pennsylvania. He planned to leave for Philadelphia on Tuesday for Wednesday, the day of the award ceremony. From there he would go on to Washington for a meeting and return home Friday morning. That gave us our window of opportunity. To be absolutely safe, I told Harry to come to Dayton Tuesday evening and stay only through Wednesday. It wasn't like me to keep things from Orv, but I had no choice. I wouldn't for anything have worried him so just then. I was a bit unsettled myself, I fear!

The worst was Sunday morning, when I came in from commencement exercises and found that heartbreaking telegram from

Harry—"It's all right. Please don't worry," and so on. Of course it *wasn't* all right, and of course I *would* worry. So I sent an answer and again asked him to come—but I didn't know myself to *what* I had asked him to come. I felt I had done something horribly wrong in letting the situation get out of hand. I had given Harry so much advice about not getting involved in entanglements that I, in my superior wisdom, thought he wasn't quite ready to go through with. Why hadn't somebody given *me* a little advice? Everything I had tried to be and do my whole life seemed to be tumbling down around me. I felt doubly to blame because I couldn't change my feeling for Harry—but it would have been even worse if I could!

It was all so unreal, like a waking nightmare. I scarcely recognized the person who was walking around Oberlin in my shoes. Harry seemed almost like a stranger to me as well. All of a sudden he had become a different person, with this overwhelming feeling for me that I hadn't suspected. That curious sense of unreality about him was one of the most paralyzing things about the whole experience. Not until I got back home Monday night and had a chance to take a good long look at his photograph in the privacy of my own room did he become his old familiar self again. I could have shouted for joy! There he was, gazing calmly at me out of the picture frame, the same as he had always been. Out of my wild desperation, out of all the fog and commotion of the past few days, I suddenly found a certain measure of clearness and peace. I was myself again too—for a brief spell, at least.

Orville

Kate generally was dog tired when she got back from one of her trustees' meetings. This time, though, she seemed uncommonly listless and fidgety. I couldn't put my finger on the problem—she just couldn't settle down. Naturally, I assumed it was the Smithsonian's latest piece of chicanery that had upset her. They had offered another half-baked proposal for changing the label on the Langley machine without coming straight out and admitting that it was physically incapable of ever getting off the ground. That so-called compromise was unacceptable to me, of course, and I needed Katharine's advice on a statement to give out to the newspapers. Then there was the article the editor of *Liberty* magazine had written about me, which I had asked him to submit for her approval. What with one thing and another, it was close to midnight by the time we went up to bed.

First thing the next morning, while we were sitting at breakfast, Carrie came into the kitchen and said the Western Union was on the line with a telegram for Katharine. She got up and went into the telephone closet to take the call. When she got back, she announced casually that Harry would be coming the next night.

"He is?" I said. "How does that happen?"

"Going east," she said.

"Going to Washington?" I asked, thinking I might arrange to meet him there.

"No," Katharine answered, a little too eagerly, I thought. "New York."

My curiosity was piqued. Still, Harry did do a good deal of traveling in connection with his newspaper work, and he had gotten into the habit every so often of dropping in to see us on short notice. Despite Kate's peculiar behavior, there was nothing out of the ordinary about his visit as far as I could tell. I was about to leave for Philadelphia and wouldn't be home until the end of the week. So I said I was sorry I couldn't stay to greet our guest and went back to reading the morning paper.

It seems I wasn't quite myself that day either. Upon boarding the afternoon train, I was chagrined to discover that I had come away from home without my tickets or my wallet. I didn't even know who was supposed to meet me in Philadelphia. There was nothing to be done but get off at Xenia and turn back with my tail between my legs. I caught the next train back to Dayton and walked over to my office on North Broadway to finish up some work. From there I rang up our neighbors, the McCormicks, and they came to pick me up in their motorcar.

Carrie had gone home for the day, and the refrigerator was empty. So Frank and Anne roused Katharine, who was upstairs napping, and the four of us headed out for a bite to eat. When we returned, the telephone was ringing off the hook, and Kate dashed down the hall to answer it. It was the Western Union again—two telegrams in one day!—this time with the message that Harry had postponed his trip and wouldn't be coming the next day after all. To my surprise, Swes seemed more relieved than disappointed by the news. The thought crossed my mind that she had been playing me for a fool all day long. But it was such a preposterous idea that I put it out of my head.

In any case, I had more pressing matters to deal with, what with the Smithsonian situation and the latest flap over the flying machine being sent out of the country. Harry would have been the least of my worries, even if I had realized what he and Kate were up to. A week or so later I was called to Washington for a meeting, and this time Swes took care to remind me to check my pockets. When I got back to Dayton, who should I find waiting for me but her future husband!

Katharine

Orv and I were at breakfast when the Western Union rang with Harry's first telegram. It said if I still thought it "wise"—or some such foolish thing—he could come to Dayton the next night at six. As soon as Orv was safely out of the house, I wired back that I did want him to come. I dropped Little Brother off at the train station at three o'clock and came home to lie down—only to be awakened around five-thirty by a phone call from Anne McCormick. She told me Orv *hadn't* gone to Philadelphia after all and was *at his office waiting to be picked up.* I was so scared I couldn't say anything but "Hasn't gone? Hasn't *gone?*" I nearly had a fit—as soon as I was sure Orv was all right—for then I began to think how my one chance to talk to Harry was all knocked up.

My first thought was to tell him that Orv hadn't gone so he wouldn't come all the way to Dayton for only the short talks we could get in between times. Before Orv and Frank came, the telephone rang again and Anne answered. "Western Union for you," she called out. That was the message that said something—I was too excited to hear straight—about some *other* message being reported undelivered and saying Harry would come the next night. As soon as I could, I got to the telephone and called the Western Union. No answer. Called again. No answer. Called again. No answer. Then I tried the Postal. I got hold of a blockhead—*man,* of course!—who couldn't understand anything. Finally I got the message through that Orv had missed his train—but I told Harry to come anyway if he would and that we could manage somehow. Talk about getting our wires crossed! It's a marvel that Harry made any sense of those messages. I was so worn down I couldn't say anything sensible to save my soul. To cap it off, later that night, after we got home from dinner with the McCormicks, there was another call from the Western Union saying that Harry *wouldn't* be stopping in Dayton. So as casually as I could I told Orv he wasn't coming after all. I felt as if Little Brother could see right through me in my new role of creative artist. Harry dear, the lies I told for you that day ought to be on your conscience. I regret to say they are *not* on mine!

Now that the terrible strain of the last few hours had been lifted, I wanted to laugh out loud. And yet I couldn't help feeling it was God's judgment on us that Orv had missed that train. Truly, I never spent such a disturbed day in my life, except when someone was dangerously ill. Altogether, my world was in a state of great disquiet and uneasiness. It wasn't just that I had begun to feel differently; I realized that I couldn't keep from letting Harry know it any longer. I couldn't tell him anything of what was inside me, but I had to try because it was so awful to let him think anything different from what I really felt—always s'posing I knew what I felt myself!

Isn't it funny trying to *feel* your feelings? What slippery, ill-mannered things they are! Just as I get them well settled, in a Punch and Judy box, so to speak, something touches a spring and up they jump. For years I had wanted to give Harry all the affection and sympathy I could muster, but I worried over the effect of having his feelings stirred up so. Where was that peaceful and splendid future I was trying to hold out to him? All I could tell him truthfully was that I had found something in my heart that *might* be love. I wasn't even sure what love was. How could I tell where affection left off and love began? The thought of his loving me or my loving him was overwhelming. "Please, Harry," I wanted to cry out, "don't care so much—and please *do*!"

I wasn't jealous of Harry's friendships with other women—or if it *was* jealousy at the bottom of my concern, I didn't know it. I think he more nearly diagnosed my feelings when he told Mr. Stetson that he appealed to my "mothering instincts." I have a mighty big lot of those, to be sure! Back of everything was the feeling that I couldn't fail Harry when he needed me most, any more than I could fail Orv. I was in such a tight box and saw no way out. I couldn't even promise Harry that I would dare the great adventure anyway, if it came to that. When I was young the girls always laughed at me because I was so enthusiastic about *other* people getting married but was so thankful in each individual case that I was not the one involved. Now things looked very different—and it scared me so!

As a rule I despise playing safe—nothing risked, nothing worth having won, I always say. My experience has not been such that I take much stock in the Freudian theory of suppressed desires. I believe William James is nearer the truth in saying that feeling grows with expression. I am sure it has been so in my life. I don't mean that I have been able to control my feeling always, but I have found that unexpressed feeling usually gets weaker, especially if I don't act on the impulse. If it hadn't been for Orv, it wouldn't have taken me one second to know what to do! I'd have run the risk of finding that I had affection instead of love for Harry. There is always a possibility of unhappiness in every friendship, of course, but not enough to justify one in avoiding every possible chance. Each one knows his own heart, which no one else *can* know.

I believe one could live on the kind of feeling I had—and have—for Harry. I was proud of his love because it was a beautiful love, kept in his heart so many years but not allowed to prevent him from doing and being what he ought to do and be. It would have been a horrid, ugly thing if he had not treated it as he did. While I teased him by telling him he was good when he wanted me to tell him I loved him, still that was a fundamental part of all my feeling for him. It was because I saw him doing everything he ought to do always that I wanted to get in and help him. Of course, I didn't know I was getting in quite so deep—but never mind!

Truly, Harry gave me a great shock by telling me he had loved me from those far-off days in Oberlin. He had always been a special person to me, but only as an especially interesting friend. I had no idea that he had any "thoughts" about me. If I had for one moment suspected his feeling for me, I wouldn't have felt free to write to him as I did after Isabel died. I wouldn't have dared to do it even if I could have gotten rid of my pesky conscience. I would have thought I was just making everything more difficult for him. There are half a dozen reasons why I wouldn't have added fuel to the fire if I had known there was even a spark there. I couldn't bear to think I had worked my way into his heart when he was in trouble and needed support and sympathy. I despise that. It is one of the commonest tricks of my sect.

I always thought I was not an upsetting person. That was one reason why I allowed myself to be rather queer and unconventional.

I fancied I could be as good friends as I wanted to be with men like Harry and Stef without involving a thing but common interests. Ha! I've learned my lesson! Harry was so dear and I had such a tender feeling about him, and still I had to be careful not to say anything I couldn't stand by later. I wasn't at all sure I really loved him, and yet I wanted desperately to *tell* him I loved him—*if I did!* Only one thing was absolutely clear to me: it was too late to go on a strictly "pre-explosion" program anymore. We were out of danger of the hazards of friendship and now had to consider the hazards of love.

How tortured I was! I was sure almost everyone would think it right for me to leave Orv, when I knew it wasn't. Harry kept insisting that I had the same rights to satisfy my own heart that Orv would have had, and that everybody would have thought it all right if he had married without considering me. But I knew I couldn't live with myself if I left Orv in the lurch. We had been more to each other than many married couples. After Will died, he built Hawthorn Hill with the idea of my being there with him just as much as any husband builds a home for his wife. Everything was planned for the future with the idea that we would be together always. The very suggestion that I could ever leave him drove me nearly wild.

In short, there was Orv on one side, to whom I owed a great obligation, and there was Harry on the other side, to whom I would owe a greater one if I said or did anything to make him care more for me. I was trying so hard to love him *and* be a friend at the same time. It nearly broke my heart to have him thank me for my "goodness through it all." Oh, what an idea!

Harry spoke about our not being young and romantic any-more, but if I were expressing my honest opinion, I'd say we were acting like a pair of headstrong children instead of mature middle-aged folk. To be precise, *he* was acting like an impetuous twenty-year-old—and *I* was acting like a hopeless old maid! I hadn't wanted to marry anyone since I broke up with my college beau. As I got older, I realized that the chance of making even a reasonable success of marriage grew more and more unlikely. But I couldn't get along with a merely reasonable success—*my* marriage had to be a very beautiful thing. One minute I was all my years and knew that no ideal can ever be realized; the next minute I had the feelings of a girl and believed that an ideal *can* be realized—but all the time experience came in to temper my dreams with reasonableness!

Of course, I can never be a girl again—and I'm glad of it. I've often thought how nice it is to be past youth and most—not all!—of the perplexities that go with it. It was interesting to be young and now it is interesting to be middle-aged, but really there is no comparison. For one thing, I couldn't have had a friend—let alone a *lover*—like Harry when I was young. And I couldn't have cared so much for him at Oberlin. I didn't have it in me to love him back then as I love him now. I might have married him thirty-odd years ago if he had wanted me to, though. It would have been so much easier to think of marriage when we were young. Yet even then I was worried nearly sick over the thought of leaving the family without a woman to take care of the things that only a woman can look after very well.

I seemed to be on the verge of an explosion myself—and I had nobody to share it with, nobody to turn to or confide in. None of the family would have understood how I felt—Little Brother least of all. I *couldn't* add to Harry's disquiet, and yet I wanted to tell him so much more than I did. I couldn't see which was worse—refusing to let him know how very, very dear his love was to me and letting him get over that as soon as possible; or admitting that his love did awaken something way back in my heart, which might come to be something neither of us could manage. I couldn't see how I could go ahead with that—with the possibility of unendurable pain for us both.

I was just beside myself when Carrie brought in the special-delivery letter saying that Harry had postponed his trip. Such a time as I put in at the breakfast table that morning! Unless Orv is a good deal stupider than I think, he saw that something was wrong. Lies are always a mess. I believe you have to begin younger than we were to arrange for these secret meetings. I was just possessed to talk to Harry, but I didn't want him to come in any but an open and aboveboard way. It happened that Orv had another trip planned the following week, so I wired Harry to come on Wednesday evening. Then he could stay until Friday and see Little Brother after he got back from Washington. We could never have lived through an evening and a day together with no chance to be by ourselves. Harry was so sweet about it. He said he would feel paid for coming if he could just be alone with me for three minutes so he could hold me close to him and kiss me.

A funny, smothery feeling comes over me when I think back to the night he arrived. It just *poured* while I was at the station waiting for him. The train was late, and Harry looked so strained when I picked him out in the crowd on the platform. And then I didn't know what to do with him—any more than he knew what to do with me, I 'spect. But I couldn't endure his having any more heartache. I was so afraid that anything I did would make the situation worse than it already was. My blessed, blessed boy! He had been so good and so brave and so unselfish and so hurt, and had found out he could have rest and comfort and peace if only I loved him. I was so anxious about him, and I didn't want to mix up sympathy and love—and all the time I felt as if I couldn't love anyone because of what it would mean to Orv.

One day, one short day, was all we had to ourselves. Harry was so dear, and I should have been happy—but for some curious reason it nearly broke my heart. My feelings were all jumbled up like a pile of pickup sticks. The last time I saw him, I hadn't thought of anything more than our dear friendship. I couldn't talk much about marrying him and living with him, even though I knew that was uppermost in his mind. I felt I would be to blame if I let him think of marriage unless I was sure I could satisfy that longing eventually. Finally, since I had no idea what to say, I just put my arms around him and let him see what he could in my face. I wanted to shut out all the perplexities and love him and have him love me. I couldn't bear not to go all the way now that I knew he wanted it so much.

Orv got home Friday morning, and by lunchtime poor Harry was so wrung out that he had to lie down for a rest. It was just *too* bad to waste all that time before his train went. Why, oh why didn't we talk more? So many things I wanted to tell him and have him tell me. All the dear things he said to me—and all I didn't say to him—kept coming back to haunt me. I could see how hard it was for him too to go off in that way. He wanted, just as I did, to have one more chance to hold each other very, very close and forget everything else. How safe I felt in the circle of Harry's arms! Some way his being there and the things that happened, the memories left with me and so on, had rather cut off the past and even the future. I'd be a pretty stupid companion if I were like that for very long!

After Harry left, I sank into another one of my black times. Everything worried me—Harry and all *his* problems, Orv and all *his* problems, myself and all *my* problems. I couldn't sleep for days on end. It seemed to me the Smithsonian business was hopeless, that anything I could do would be wrong and would make someone unhappy, that I was nothing but a troublemaker and should have foreseen what my dear friendship with Harry was leading up to. It was plain enough that he had given the subject a great deal of thought! If Orv's eyes had been sharp, he would have seen in the expression on Harry's face when he said good-bye to me something different from anything he'd seen before.

Harry

My furtive visit to Dayton, while Katharine's "little brother" was away on business, was meant to clear the air between us. Instead, the fog settled in thicker than ever. As much as I wanted to help Katharine find out what was in her heart, I couldn't possibly ask her to do what she thought she shouldn't do. The one thing I was burning to discuss—marriage—was the very subject she seemed determined to avoid at all costs. I tried reasoning with her. I argued that she had her own life to lead and that Orville wouldn't have hesitated to leave her if he had taken it into his head to marry. But Katharine reasoned right back at me. She pointed out that Orville didn't want to leave her and had planned their lives with a view to sharing everything with her. I departed in a deep funk, convinced that we had reached an impasse.

I did take away one small shred of consolation, however: Katharine and I would see each other again in a month's time. She and Orville had invited me up to their summer "camp" on Georgian Bay in Canada. I had heard about Lambert Island for years and was curious to see the place that meant so much to them both. Katharine insisted on taking precautions to avoid arousing her brother's suspicion. She urged me not to write too frequently in advance of my visit. It would be awkward, she said, if there were five letters waiting for her every time they called at the village post office. I was to avoid sending telegrams and address all my letters on the typewriter. And from time to time I was to write a chatty "business" letter that Katharine could share with Orville, to show him we had no secrets. To keep tongues back home from wagging, I was to put it out that I just happened to be coming near the bay on my way east. With luck, nobody would check the timetable and find out that there was only one train to and from Toronto each day.

At the appointed hour, Katharine and Orville met me at the little station in Penetang and took me out to the island on their motor launch, a distance of some ten or twelve miles across open water. I recognized the compound immediately from the snapshots Katharine had sent me. We pulled up at the dock alongside the boathouse. The main dwelling with its inviting screened porch sat on top of the hill, with two smaller cottages and various outbuildings scattered among the rock outcroppings. All the buildings were painted the same light green and were unfinished inside. Orville had jury-rigged a pull cart, using old airplane tires, to haul luggage and other cargo up from the jetty. I had one cabin to myself, Orville slept in another, and Katharine had her bedroom just off the enclosed porch in the main house.

I'll say one thing for the bay: it hasn't been overadvertised. It is about the loveliest place I have ever seen. The Wrights made me feel at home straight away. They even had the daily *Star* delivered by mail. Orville had had the happy inspiration of decorating the cabins with works of art reproduced on the covers of our Sunday magazine. Twice a week we rode into Penetang to pick up supplies and letters. And each day we took the launch to a nearby island and brought back three quarts of fresh milk, which we bought off an Indian family. Orville wasn't a milk drinker, so Katharine used his share to make cottage cheese. She insisted on serving my favorite breakfast of shredded wheat biscuit laced with fresh cream. Now that's my idea of roughing it!

The Wrights led a quiet, simple life on the island. No "fancy togs" or other luxuries were permitted to spoil the rustic atmosphere. They both needed to put the workaday world behind them for a few weeks. Katharine asked me to bring the manuscript of a book I was working on, but we never got around to discussing it. In fact, we didn't do much of anything that required mental or physical effort. Day after day we rocked on the porch, read our books and newspapers, foraged for wild blueberries, and bathed in the pure, ice-cold water of the bay. A few nights, after dinner, Orville brought out a deck of cards. The Bishop would have turned over in his grave to see his two well-brought-up children playing a spirited round of poker at the kitchen table. We placed bets with matchsticks and used regular poker language. None of the niceties of the polite bridge game for us.

Orville got special pleasure out of taking his guests on long boat rides to view the sunsets over the bay. I must have been a satisfactory audience, because Katharine said she never knew him to be so anxious to show anyone Go-Home River, Honey Harbor, and all the other places they liked. Orville's launch had an aviation motor so powerful that the boat occasionally seemed to leave the water and take to the air, skimming over the tops of the islands. Every now and then the motor seemed to fall to pieces, but Orville would patiently dive in with some heavy wire and a pair of pliers, collect the pieces, put them together, crank up, and on we went. I never had had the opportunity before to watch a distinguished inventor at his relaxations. It was a fascinating experience.

It was just as Katharine had described: Orville is a completely different person up at the bay. I can still hear him singing in the distance as he tinkered away at one of his pet projects. He is constantly designing, building, or repairing one thing or another—Katharine says the natives think he is a little "touched" to work so hard when he doesn't have to—and he prides himself on doing it all without special tools. His reconstruction of the water system at the compound to give a direct pressure line connected with the hose—to fight fire, as he said, or maybe just to amuse himself sprinkling water—was especially impressive. Ah, them were the days!

With so many agreeable distractions, it was easy to forget that no progress was being made in resolving Orville's dispute with the Smithsonian. The label on the Langley machine still made the patently false claim that it was capable of flight. I was of the opinion that a congressional investigation would be a good deal of a farce. The influence of the Smithsonian was too pervasive. What was needed then, as it is now, was a detailed account by Orville of the state of aviation at the time he and Wilbur took it up, of their own laboratory work, and of the way they applied it in actual flight. Such a book would settle the matter once and for all. But he never will write it unless he has somebody cooperating with him to spur him on. I know it, Katharine knows it, and deep down Orville knows it too.

Orville

Once word got around of my decision to ship the flyer to England, my days of peace and quiet were numbered. You would have thought I was public enemy number one. What really got my goat was the way certain individuals who had not lifted a finger to defend me from the Smithsonian's scurrilous attacks now had the cheek to accuse me of being selfish, shortsighted—even un-American, for pity's sake. Senator Norris, for one, was furious at the prospect of the machine going out of the country. Earl Findley of the *New York Times* told him why I was doing as I was, and how all my dealings with Secretary Walcott had led nowhere, but even then he refused to back down. "That old man won't always be there. He isn't the Smithsonian Institution." That's easy for Norris to say—he isn't in the Smithsonian's line of fire.

Katharine and I had always planned to get up a good, fair, clear statement of the situation when the machine was ready to be sent. It would have recalled Will's and my early experience with the government, the years of trouble because of government patronage of patent infringers, the years of endurance with the unfair treatment of the Smithsonian. We would have told how, in spite of early snubbing by the Ordnance Department and the chance to sell the machine abroad, *always* the US government was excepted, in every exclusive contract proposed; how we kept still about all the rest and hoped the matter would be cleared up when there was a chance to know the facts; and how, even now, the offer to the Science Museum in London is restricted so that if there is a change, the machine can come back where it belongs.

Now that Kate has taken herself out of the picture, I hardly see how that job will ever get done. There is no one else I can trust to do it right, no one else who knows the full story of what Will and I put up with all those years. Just think: it's been a quarter of a century since we took the machine up at Kitty Hawk. The 1903 flyer is a piece of history now. I saved it from the flood and preserved it and patched it back together again—and all for what? So it could be put on display in a *British* museum! Two or three years ago, before Swes ran off and got married, I still had a sliver of hope. But I was worn to a frazzle after the long, hard fight. It seemed every time I turned around I bumped into a reporter asking for a comment or a politician lecturing me on my patriotic duty to keep the machine in the United States.

The twenty-fifth anniversary of the first flight is over and done with—and good riddance. I've had my fill of speeches and awards and parades and brass bands. All I crave now is to get away from it all. If it wasn't the middle of winter, I'd shut up the house and head up to the bay tomorrow. A day on the island never fails to set the world to rights. Kate and I fell for the place the moment we laid eyes on it. Course, I saw right away that it would take a lot of work to make it as comfortable as it is now. Back then it was just a bunch of shacks sitting atop a barren rock out in the middle of nowhere. A Canadian gent had built the main cottage for his bride, but she took one look at their new home and hightailed it back to civilization. Kate, I'm glad to say, was made of sturdier stuff.

Scipio, our dear departed Saint Bernard, loved to splash around in the water and sun himself on the rocks. After Father and he died, Kate and I would stay up north for weeks at a spell with just ourselves for company. Visitors were welcome, so long as they were tolerably self-sufficient and not overly particular about the accommodations. Harry fit in nicely, I'll say that for him. He was always good company—able and conscientious, with not a bit of conceit. I remember meeting him at the train in Penetang. He had come straight from Toronto and still had that nervous, jumpy look about him that people get when they're in the big city. It took him a few days to fall into the rhythm of island life. Every day he looked a little more rested, and by the time he left he was fully restored. The bay has that effect on people.

Visitors or no visitors, Kate and I observed our daily routines. I had my chores and hobbies to keep me occupied, while she read, wrote letters, tidied the house, and fixed meals. In the long summer evenings, when the dusk lingers long past bedtime, we would sit on the porch with Harry and talk for hours, the way we used to do at Hawthorn Hill. I took him around in the motorboat to see our favorite spots—past Franceville, through the Freddy Channel, past Whalen's store, the McKenzies and Williams places, and so on. We saw some beautiful sunsets out on the bay. Sunsets on the island remind me of the ones we used to have at Kitty Hawk. The clouds light up in all colors in the background, with deep blue clouds of various shapes fringed with gold.

Harry stayed with us two weeks, and not once during that time was the Smithsonian's name so much as mentioned. We could hardly avoid reading reports of the controversy in the newspaper, but there was an unspoken agreement that no serpent would be allowed in to poison our island paradise. So we cheerfully put the unpleasantness out of our minds and got about our business. Kate and I generally went our separate ways at the bay, just as we did back home. Some days we hardly set eyes on each other from dawn to dusk, save for mealtimes. And Harry couldn't have been easier to have around. For once, I was genuinely sorry to see one of our guests depart. He had begun to feel almost like a member of the family.

Katharine

It nearly made my heart stop beating to think of being with Harry at the bay. I wasn't at all sure we could carry it through without letting Orv see any difference from the past. I had a dreadful time acting unconcerned and casual about his coming. At the last minute I had a crazy idea about not being able to invite him to the bay after all, but it was just the result of my supersensitiveness and guilty conscience. What can have been the matter with me that I blew around so like a weathercock? I was deathly afraid I was doing the wrong thing to let Harry come and to assume that I loved him. And I don't know how I would have survived if he had repeated one of the off-color stories he picked up in Sinclair Lewis's so-called Sunday school class in Kansas City. Little Brother never could appreciate that vulgar brand of humor!

Even the letters Harry wrote before his visit made me self-conscious. I had my own room where I could be alone, just off the porch, but it wasn't easy to read with Orv sitting on the other side of the door waiting for me to come and talk. I felt guilty to be doing something I couldn't tell him about—but Harry's love letters were worth having some perturbation of spirit over! It took some doing to hold up my end of the correspondence. The big table in the living-and-dining room was the only place where I could write with any comfort, and I could write to Harry in peace only when Orv was busy somewhere else. Once I managed to do it with Orv playing solitaire right at the same table. Can you beat that?

I had worried that Harry would find our life on the island dull and primitive compared to the life he was used to, but he came to love it as much as Orv and I did. The bay grows on people that way. We had spent all our summers there since the end of the war and looked forward to it more and more every year. The two of us always had lots of fun in the simplest sort of ways. We went around in our old clothes and enjoyed not having to get dressed up for anything. The days were never long enough for all the idling we had to do. I warned Harry that he was in for a few surprises when he saw me in action—or *in*action. About the most energetic thing I ever did was picking wild blueberries. They were ripe by the time Harry came in July, and we had delicious blueberry pies, if I do say so myself.

I'll never forget how comfortable Harry was at the bay. I could never get him to admit he was uncomfortable, despite the primitive accommodations. The two weeks he was with us passed like an enchanted dream. All the things I had wanted to discuss sort of faded into nothing when we had a chance to talk by ourselves.

I was as tongue-tied as a schoolgirl. So many thoughts I had—so much I wanted to say, and so much I *couldn't* say a word about! Nothing of all Harry said to me seems dearer now than that he was "home" at last: "Home is the sailor, home from the sea, and the hunter home from the hill." I dived down and hid my head on his shoulder when I couldn't say how I loved him but was just overwhelmed with it. I knew then that we were both home and safe with each other.

It was a blessed, perfect time. I knew Harry was special, of course, but I had no idea he was so nice to have around—let alone some of the other things we got up to as we poked around the island foraging for berries and lounged in the big chair on the porch! He seemed to be a kind of tempter. I grew to love the characteristically crisp way he has of saying words, and his movements—and everything about him. One rainy, blowy night, Orv went to bed early and left us to our own devices. It was so lovely to be with Harry all alone. That was the only evening we had—and then only an hour, and that only five minutes long! I was getting to be a regular lotus eater—no cares or responsibilities. And the less my conscience troubled me, the more I liked to think about all the dear things that made up the bond between us.

You see, I looked upon Harry's visit to the island as a kind of test, for him as well as me. I had a notion that I could tell whether I loved him or not by having him very near me—that if I felt the least repulsion I could be sure I must stop short, even if I hurt him mortally. It was such a serious thing to me—more than that, a life-and-death matter—for I had two people to think of, and I couldn't see how to live either way. If I didn't love Harry, it would be a tragedy for him. If I did love him, I had an unmanageable situation for myself and Orv. It made me almost stop breathing to think of it!

Well, I hardly know what happened, but I realized right away that Harry was dearer to me than I had thought. I didn't feel any repulsion at all. I loved to have him hold me as close as could be. He was so gentle and tender, and it was natural enough for me to be tender with him. I had felt that way ever since he had been so troubled, and especially after he went off to Europe alone. I loved him sitting on our porch at the bay and not seeing how to "get started." We just sat silently together and loved each other. When I couldn't get a word out, I'd scrunch up my shoulders and snuggle as close to him as I could. And he would just shake his head at me when words failed him. He frightened me when he showed so much feeling. That is the side of him that I didn't know existed at all, and it almost hurt me.

Funny—with Stef it had been exactly the other way around. At first I thought he was much more responsive than he actually was. It took me a long time to realize that it was just a superficial closeness, or rather a closeness that existed mostly in my mind and not in reality. Stef has an outer layer of extraordinary friendliness and interest in people, but inside of that is a place where no one is admitted in a really intimate way. There is nothing wrong with Stef—he is just being himself. But having once started on the wrong track, I had to have a lot of collisions and smashups before I got it into my head what was the matter between us. I was ridiculously sensitive and full of absurd ideas and awfully hard to get along with. I just wobbled around, ashamed of thinking so much of him one minute, and ashamed of being ashamed the next minute.

The two experiences were so similar, and yet so completely different. With Stef I never dared to trust my feelings for fear that he would find them a burden and shut down without reciprocating. With Harry—well, let's just say I was afraid I had got hold of something that was too much for me. Even now I sometimes wonder if I am not still living a dream. I am so old to have such a beautiful thing come to me. Harry loves me as if I were a girl. No one could ask for anything more! Because he loves me as if I were a woman too, and that makes it perfect. These thoughts and feelings come to me over and over and are lovelier all the time. I have such absolutely perfect confidence in his character. I love him so surely—and so irrevocably.

One thing followed another, and by the time we saw him off on the train in Penetang, Harry and I were engaged to be married—at least, *I* considered us engaged. If it comes to that, Harry didn't make a formal proposal until several weeks later—and then only after I had written demanding to know if I was ever going to get one! Of course, I knew that we were a good deal better than engaged, but Harry had made some frivolous remark about suing me for breach of promise if I didn't agree to marry him, and I couldn't resist pointing out that he had never actually *asked* me to marry him. What's more, I said, if he could find anything actionable in my foolish talk, it wouldn't impress any court of law very much!

If it makes Harry feel like a regular caveman the way he rushed in and grabbed the woman of his choice, all right. My impression is that he had to have a good deal of help. Either way, the die was cast. We had gotten past the explosion stage and "plighted our troths." The only thing now standing between us and the altar was Orv.

Harry

That first trip to the bay convinced me once and for all that Katharine and I were made for each other. Being together on the island seemed to light a special spark, like two pieces of kindling that blaze up together. Everything Katharine said and did—and everything she *didn't* say—told me in no uncertain terms that she felt the same way toward me as I did toward her. By the end of my stay I thought we had come to a mutual understanding about getting married. But she was still playing hard to get. It wasn't until I joked about suing her for breach of promise that she finally consented to an engagement. Even then, she insisted that I make her a proposal in writing!

Popping the question to my college sweetheart was a snap compared to the hoops Katharine made me jump through. Isabel and I were so young and innocent. My brother Ed had offered his fraternal advice about the rituals of courting and marriage, but to me the prospect of "going with" any girl seemed far off. Sometimes I actually dreaded it, for fear that the girl I fell in love with wouldn't care a jot for me. And what should I expect, I asked myself, when there were so many other boys who took class parties in stride, always knew the right way to act, and could talk with girls by the hour and never stop to take a breath? Upon surveying the field, I made an inventory of myself and concluded that I was lacking in most of those desirable qualities.

So I could hardly believe my luck when Isabel told me she loved me. We were both such kids when we got engaged at the beginning of my senior year—Ferdinand and Isabella, my sister used to call us. Mind you, Katharine has a point: we were all children in those days. And yet one is only as old as one feels. To hear Katharine tell it, anyone would think she had at least four or five years on me. In fact, we are closer in age than Isabel and I were—less than six months apart. In some ways we have more in common than Isabel and I did too. Our backgrounds, experiences, and interests are remarkably compatible. If only I had had the wit to propose to her when we were at Oberlin. But I didn't, and it's no use crying over spilled milk.

Isabel and I were engaged four years before we got married. Katharine and I were in a hurry to make up for lost time and waited only one. But no year ever passed so agonizingly slowly. Katharine insisted on keeping our plans under wraps until she worked up the courage to talk to Orville. That was completely unrealistic, of course. It wasn't long before a number of our mutual friends saw through our charade. One day in the fall of 1925, after I got back from the island, Katharine had Anne McCormick to lunch at Hawthorn Hill. Anne surprised her by asking if she thought I would ever remarry. Before Katharine could think of a suitably diplomatic reply, Anne said, "I suppose you would really be sorry if he did." To which all Katharine could think to say was "Um"!

In short, the cat had one paw out of the bag already, and the longer Katharine dillydallied about bringing Orville into the picture, the shorter the odds were that he would learn about our engagement from somebody else. Either way there was no telling how he would react. Katharine swore up and down that she would find an opportunity to talk to him in her own way and her own time. All I could do was to be patient.

Orville

After Harry departed that summer, the Deeds had us up to their camp near Hudson's Bay. Kate wasn't especially keen on the idea. She joked that the Deeds were so formal that they had to outfit on Fifth Avenue just to go up into the woods. But there was no way of wiggling out of the invitation gracefully. Besides, the Canbys were going to be at the camp too, and we always enjoyed Frank and Bertha's company. In the end, it turned out to be less of an ordeal than Kate feared. One morning she and I escaped, just the two of us, and paddled around Marshallito Island and up the creek to Muskrat Lake. There was nary a sound but the note of a bird, rarely, and the dip of the paddles. It was a beautiful day, clear and crisp and warm in the sun. That excursion alone made the trip worthwhile.

The Deeds were such gracious hosts that we felt almost ashamed to be so eager to get back to our humble abode on Lambert Island. From their camp to the nearest railroad depot was a journey of two days by canoe. The first part passed without incident, but as we were leaving the last portage, I hurt my back while trying to pull up a small fir tree to bring home with us. The pain was so intense that the Canbys had to practically carry me back to the cabin. All night I lay flat on my back, unable to move, and next morning I could hardly dress myself without help. Fortunately, Frank had brought a small pneumatic mattress that made the train ride bearable. By the time we got to Toronto, I was able to walk the couple of blocks to the Queen's Hotel for breakfast, using Kate as a crutch.

It was thanks to her we had another little adventure on the way home from the bay in September. George France had ferried us to Penetang in his dory. We arrived ten minutes before the train was due to depart, but for reasons best known to herself, Swes insisted on collecting the mail. She appealed to the stationmaster, who promised not to let the train leave without us. He hailed the express man with a horse and wagon, Kate hopped in, and they went galloping up the street to the PO. I watched in amazement as she jumped out over the wheel, rushed in to get her armful of mail, jumped in over the wheel, and back down the street they came dashing again—in the nick of time to catch the train. It was a most ridiculous performance, a sort of wild John Gilpin ride, but everyone had a good deal of fun out of it, Kate most of all.

The house felt mighty good to come home to that time, with a nice, warm bed to sleep in, a needle shower to soothe my aching back, and my special reading chair to relax in. The first night Kate and I sat up in the library, catching up on the news and talking over some items that had come in my mail. Kate had a thick pile of her own correspondence to deal with. As a rule she preferred to type her letters on the Hammond machine I gave her for Christmas a few years back. But lately she had taken to staying up after I switched off the light, writing letters in longhand at the desk in her room. One evening that fall I found her studying some drawings of Harry's house that the postman had brought. A few days after that an album of photographs came from Kansas City.

She and Harry were as thick as thieves, and I—I was as thick as a plank!

Katharine

Our wedding day may have been put off indefinitely, but that didn't keep me from fantasizing about living in Harry's house and imagining how it would be when I was its mistress. After Orv and I got back from the bay that summer, I asked Harry to draw me a rough sketch of the layout of the two main floors, so I could start to plan a little. Later he sent some snapshots of the inside that young Henry had taken. I needed to refresh my memory because it had been some time since Orv and I had seen the house when we went out to Kansas City for Isabel's funeral. I had forgotten about the dry stone wall that encircles the property, like a pretty New England homestead. In my mind's eye I was already laying out a little flower garden in the backyard, beneath the library window. Cut flowers for the table are one of my extravagances!

Some way flowers always put me in mind of Mother. Pop and I used to plant flowers at her grave in Woodland Cemetery, and I made a pressed-flower album in her memory. Come to think of it, I must have been working on that very album the first time I visited Kansas City, when I went out to help Reuch and Lulu make ready for their first baby. I was still a child myself. Ever since I can remember I have been playing nursemaid to *somebody*. If it wasn't Lou, it was one of the children, or Mother and Father, or Will and Orv. It seems to be my calling in life! Everyone expected me to drop everything and rush home from Oberlin when Little Brother had his typhoid attack, same as they expected me to quit my teaching job and run off to Europe with the boys. And what thanks have I ever gotten for my pains? The more you do for a family, the more they take as a matter of course.

If only Orv didn't hate so to be read aloud to—it would have made it ever so much easier for me to work up a proper bedside manner. That's one thing Harry and I never tire of, reading to each other. Luckily, our tastes in literature run pretty much along the same lines—always excepting that insufferable smarty-pants Mr. H. L. Mencken. I can't fathom why Harry considers him such hot stuff. If you want my honest opinion, he's the worst go-getter imaginable. It's a queer thing—Orv and I see eye to eye on practically everything under the sun, but when it comes to books and reading and such, we might as well live on different planets. Sometimes I think Little Brother's idea of romance comes straight out of the pages of Booth Tarkington's *Seventeen*—and mine, I daresay, comes from *Middle Aged Love Stories* by Miss Josephine Bacon!

Dear, sweet Orv—he was utterly oblivious to my feelings for Harry. How blind he was, so unsuspicious of us both. Surely it must have been obvious. Are all men so unobservant? Perhaps they are. After all, it was easy enough to keep my college romance with Arthur Cunningham a secret from the family. And no one was the wiser the time Pop's friend, the elderly temperance preacher, made a pass at me in our parlor on Hawthorn Street. I was so innocent about being friendly, and he was terribly bright and interesting. The first thing I knew he was altogether *too* interested in me. I ought to have kept him from coming out, but I let things drift on until I finally came to my senses and sent him back to his hotel. I swore that was the last time I would ever let myself get wound up with a married man!

Will always said how glad he was that I was on hand to keep an eye on the young ladies who fluttered around Orv like butterflies wherever he went. Bubbo would have been quite a catch in his salad days. Now that I'm safely out of the way, I can easily imagine that some older woman has had ideas about him. But I guess he can look after himself well enough if it comes to that. Little Brother has a positive phobia where most members of my sect are concerned. He can be perfectly charming and talk a mile a minute in mixed company—but put him alone in a room with a woman and he clams up as tight as Silent Cal!

Orville

Barring Kate's sudden addiction to secretiveness, our lives that fall went on much as before. In October I was called to Washington to testify before the president's Aircraft Board, and Mr. and Mrs. Coolidge invited us to luncheon at the White House. At the appointed hour, we and four other guests were ushered into their private dining room. True to form, the president said very little at lunch, though he was sociable enough. He asked me a few questions, Kate made two or three innocuous remarks, and that was that. After the meal we retired upstairs, the men to the library and the women to the drawing room. Almost as soon as we sat down, Mr. Coolidge jumped up, announced that he was going to the baseball game, and excused himself. The rest of us took the hint and called for our coats.

To my disappointment, if not my surprise, Mr. Coolidge showed no more inclination than Chief Justice Taft to take on the powers that be at the Smithsonian. Nor did he rise to the bait at the Gridiron Club dinner that fall, when the newspapermen put on their little skit about the flyer being snatched up by a foreign museum. The leaders in the House, both Republican and

Democrat, came up to me afterward and offered to help, but I asked them not to do anything in Congress without letting me know. If there was going to be a showdown with the Smithsonian, I would have to furnish the ammunition, and I didn't want the thing stirred up in some half-prepared way. I already had my hands full setting up the 1903 machine so it would look the way it did originally when it finally went to England.

It was the *Star*'s Washington reporter, Roy Roberts, who brought me to the Gridiron shindig. I suspect he wangled the invitation to the White House as well. As Harry was unable attend the correspondents' dinner, I was obliged to listen to my host sing his praises all evening long—how he was the best friend Mr. Roberts had, how everyone liked him around the office, how he was able get the essential points out of any subject, and so forth and so on. Mr. Roberts regretted that Harry could not be "down east" more, mixing with the people who were "running things." I refrained from observing that one reason Kate and I liked and trusted Harry was that he *didn't* put himself forward and get mixed up with the politicians and opinion makers, the way most reporters do.

We had become so accustomed by that time to seeing Harry pop up every few months that I didn't bat an eye when he showed up in Dayton at the end of the year. Swes made out that he was "just passing through" on his way home after spending the Christmas holiday with his sister in Cleveland. We had a pleasant visit and saw him off to Kansas City a few days later. I still find it hard to believe that he and Katharine were plotting and scheming behind my back the whole time—after all the three of us had been through together. If you ask me, that sister of mine has a lot to answer for. I honestly believe that Harry and I would still be close friends if she hadn't come between us—and if he hadn't come between me and Swes.

Harry

I told the men at the office that I would be spending Christmas with Mary that year. For once it was unnecessary to invent a cover story. I suppose there was some risk involved in showing up in Cleveland on Christmas Eve without giving my sister more than a few days' notice. But I counted on Mary being so happy to see me that she wouldn't ask too many awkward questions. In any case, my interest in Katharine was no secret to her. What I didn't realize at the time was that Mary had actually discussed the prospect of our getting married with Mother before she died. It seems she divined my intentions more than a year before they revealed themselves to me.

I arrived at Hawthorn Hill the afternoon of Christmas Day. I had sent Katharine her package in advance so that it wouldn't look as if I had planned all along to present it in person. She took some leftover turkey out of the oven and the three of us sat down to a late supper in the kitchen. Afterward we moved into the library to open our gifts. It was the first time in more than thirty years that Katharine and I had exchanged Christmas presents, and I had my work cut out not to show my state of mind to Orville. Katharine created a smokescreen by reminiscing about the copy of Thomas à Kempis's *Imitation of Christ* that she had given me at Oberlin. She said she chose it because my missionary people were all so far away and she thought I might be lonely. And all the while I was thinking that with any luck I wouldn't be lonely much longer.

The Wrights put me in my usual room at the end of the hallway, across from the "blue room" where Katharine and I liked to hold what the young people call petting parties. That first night, after Orville was safely in bed, we tiptoed back downstairs and sat up for a long while talking—and doing "other things," as Katharine says. She plied me with questions and ideas about redecorating the house in Kansas City. She even asked for an inventory of the furnishings in every room so we could get the wallpapering done and new rugs ordered before she moved in. There was just one hitch: she still couldn't, or wouldn't, say when she would be ready to move.

When I came to Dayton that Christmas, I expected we would announce our engagement to Orville together. It had been several months since I proposed, and it didn't feel right to keep her brother in the dark about our plans much longer. But Katharine had her own ideas. She said she wanted to feel happy about my visit and preferred to wait to break the news after I was gone. If I had known that months later I would still be waiting for her to make up her mind to leave Orville, I might have taken a firmer line. But it went against the grain with me to push her. I cared for her too much to let her go ahead with the wedding against her better judgment and just because she had said she would. There wouldn't have been happiness for either of us in that.

So I assured Katharine that there was plenty of time to think it over. If she finally decided she couldn't leave her brother, even for the part of each year we had talked about, I would do my best to live with it. After all, I could hardly ask less of myself than I was asking of Orville. All the same, I believe Mr. Stetson got it about right when he said that Katharine's making herself indispensable to her brother was partly a game, a way of making herself feel useful. Deep down, he told me, she knows that Orville could dispense with all that indispensability. She could dispense with it too—or perhaps not. Sometimes I wonder if Katharine doesn't need Orville even more than he needs her, to give her a sense of doing vital work.

What a tangled web we had woven for ourselves. Orville could have brushed it away in an instant if he had chosen to. He could have taken the high road and said, "I don't want to be the occasion of one of these fine martyring devotions," and wished his sister well in her new life. Unfortunately for all of us, he had come to depend on Katharine's unstinting devotion, and she seemed bound and determined to play the martyr.

Katharine

The moon shone all the time Harry was here—a bright, Christmassy moon, like the Star of Bethlehem, streaming through the windows in the "blue room" while we spooned like a pair of young lovers. I hardly slept a wink those three nights. How sweet it was to have Harry so close to me and to give something of myself to him. We snuggled together in the big chair and he slipped his hand down where I love to have it and held it against me. It was so good to feel it there. It seemed to stop a sort of aching. Harry was so dear—*so* dear! I wasn't afraid of anything with him. I knew he would never be anything but delicate and that we would never get common with each other, no matter how completely we let the bars down.

That Christmas would have been perfect bliss if only I hadn't been so uneasy in my mind about Orv. Try as I might, I couldn't force myself to tell him about Harry and me—and I will never, ever let him know how long ago I decided to move to Kansas City. That's one secret I will guard to my dying day. I started several times to talk to him about being married, but I couldn't get anywhere when I saw the look on his face. It's what I call his "little boy look"— the pathetic, appealing look he always gives me when anything hurts him. It nearly breaks my heart. I couldn't bear to make trouble for him, for I knew that he would be so absolutely alone without me.

Harry tries hard to sympathize, but he simply can't imagine how inseparable the relation has been between Orv and me. Up to now, our interests and our friends have been together always—just exactly as much as a husband's and wife's are. It felt like the most natural thing in the world to be wearing the solitaire ring that he gave to me when I graduated from Oberlin—as if I was "his girl." Orv is like a boy in some ways—like all men, I think. He has worked so hard, risked so much, accomplished so much. Just at the time Harry asked me to marry him, Little Brother had a wearing, hard fight on his hands and needed me more than ever. It was wonderful to be needed, in a way, but at the same time I felt as if I were in chains—and I wasn't sure I had the strength to break loose.

How can I ever explain all this to Harry? His feelings about his sister can't be compared with Orv's feelings about me. They haven't lived together all their lives, shared everything all their lives, enjoyed everything together, endured everything together. It wasn't just Orv who depended on me—I didn't know how *I* would ever be satisfied away from *him*. He never went anywhere without me, except for some affairs for the men. He never considered anything without asking what I thought about it, just as any good husband would do. Always everything that interested Will and Orv interested me, and they took up all my interests in just the same way.

But what if I'm wrong? I might be mistaken, and that's a fact. What if Orv doesn't need me as much as I think he does? I can only judge his feelings by my own. I hardly know what I would have done if he had told me that he planned to marry someone and was going somewhere else to live. I can just imagine what Orv must have thought of my proposing to go off—at *this* stage of the game. On the other hand, I sometimes wonder if he didn't suspect something and wasn't much disturbed by it. It seems unlikely that he had plans of his own, but maybe he hadn't thought of marrying because we had each other, and if I left him, he would find someone else.

It's a queer thing about love. Everybody knows the more you love, the more you *can* love. I loved Harry more because I loved Bubbo so much, and I guess I loved Bubbo more now that I loved Harry so much. Sort of a polygamist attitude—the more, the merrier! Sometimes I had a wild hope that we could all be together—that maybe, some day, Orv could come and live with Harry and me in Kansas City, and then I'd not have a trouble in the world. I could do everything they *both* wanted. I could be with Harry alone a lot and still not make Orv feel left out. Little Brother is so companionable, so quiet and gentle—surely, I told myself, Harry wouldn't mind.

Living as a threesome never would have worked, of course. It was just another one of my fairy-tale schemes. On top of everything else, the *Star* was put up for sale in early 1926, and it seemed probable that Harry would not want to stay on in Kansas City after the paper changed hands. We had spoken once or twice of the possibility of his moving east to do his writing. If he did want to try his luck in Washington or New York, I was in favor of making the change sooner rather than later, while he was still in his prime. I had always thought the *Star* might be bought by someone with such an entirely different idea of a newspaper that Harry wouldn't be interested in staying with it. But that didn't matter. We weren't dependent upon any place or anyone for our real happiness, as long as we had each other.

Harry

It was beginning to feel as if we were all characters in a drawing-room comedy—or perhaps a Shakespearean tragedy would be closer to the mark. There Katharine and I were, two star-crossed lovers, young at heart but growing longer in the tooth with each passing day. We couldn't even call ourselves masters of our own fates: my happiness lay in Katharine's hands, and our happiness lay in Orville's. Then, just as we were all hunkering down for a long, hard slog, the future of the *Star* was suddenly cast to the winds as well. I can still picture the scene at the office when we got the news of Laura Kirkwood's death that February. Everyone knew what that meant: her father's great creation, the "Daily William Rockhill Nelson," would be consigned to the auction block and all of us on the staff would be sold down the river, like chattel.

Against the odds, the paper won a new lease on life. Mrs. Kirkwood was less fortunate. She had everything to live for, but threw it all away on drinking, horse racing, and high living. So much for the privileges of the leisure class. Toward the end, Mrs. Kirkwood seemed to have lost all interest in life. Somehow she had persuaded herself that her husband had stopped loving her. It wouldn't surprise me to learn that she deliberately drank herself to death in that hotel room in Baltimore. And to think that only a few months earlier she had been trying to throw me together with one of her widowed lady friends. I expect I should be grateful to her. After all, it was her well-intentioned matchmaking that finally pushed me into Katharine's arms.

Katharine was all for cutting my ties to Kansas City and moving east, or even living abroad for a time. But I had invested too much of my life in the *Star* to walk away without a fight. A few men on the paper reckoned we had a shot at buying it from the Nelson estate. The other bidders had deep pockets, but we pooled our resources, secured a bank loan, and pulled it off. Katharine practically begged me to let her put in some of her own money. She had a sizable nest egg that her brother Will had left her, as well as some property and other investments, all more or less safe and sound. But I wouldn't hear of her taking such a gamble with her life savings. As she often reminds me, money is important in its place, but its place isn't above everything else.

Katharine seems content to be cutting our pattern according to our cloth. But it's no use denying that in the eyes of the world she took a step down when she came to live with me in Kansas City. I almost hated to disabuse her of the illusion that Colonel Nelson had left me a small fortune in his will. I was making less than ten thousand a year when we were married and had nothing in the bank to speak of. Katharine once told me that Orville was worth some five or six hundred thousand dollars. They both lived comfortably on his savings, had a large house and servants, entertained lavishly, and traveled as much as they cared to. Who was I to ask her to give all that up and leave one of the most distinguished men in the world to become the wife of an obscure midwestern newspaper editor?

Orville

No sooner had Harry left that Christmas than Kate started acting on edge again. Once or twice I feared she was close to breaking down. She even paid a department store bill with the wrong check—that wasn't like Swes at all. When I questioned her, she dismissed it as "just some trouble in my upper story." Ha! The constant stream of letters from Kansas City—two or three a day sometimes—should have opened my eyes sooner. But the bits that Kate read out loud to me sounded innocent enough. One day she had her nose buried in Harry's essay on the founder of the *Star*. The next thing I knew, the paper was for sale and the staff was moving heaven and earth to raise the money to buy it. Swes even talked about chipping in some of her own savings. She said it would be a safe investment—in the newspaper and her sweetheart both, no doubt!

Harry has been a friend to us through thick and thin, but he never was as hard-boiled as Kate made him out to be. No, he needs a woman's companionship and support as much as any fellow does. The signs were staring me in the face all along: the stacks of letters and telegrams; the flowers he sent every year on Kate's birthday and Valentine's Day; the surprise visits when he just "happened" to be passing through town. It's not as if it was the first time my sister had turned a man's head. Young Lieutenant Lahm was mighty chummy with her when I was laid up in the hospital after my accident. Gentlemen admirers were forever giving her boxes of candy or bouquets or fancy tea sets. That ornithologist fellow, Frank Chapman, inscribed several of his books to her. And then there was Stef, always showering her with presents—books, pictures, even sculptures.

Swes is a handsome and intelligent woman, beyond a doubt. I don't wonder that men like Harry and Stef are attracted to her. No man could ask for a better friend, a better helpmate, a better, more loyal sister. Love is a different proposition, however. Willie Baxter learned that lesson soon enough when he lost his heart to Lola Pratt at the tender age of seventeen. You have to hand it to Booth Tarkington—he understands a thing or two about relations between the sexes. Follow your head, not your heart, and you won't go far wrong, that's always been my motto. If Will and I had frittered away our time chasing skirts, I reckon I would still be selling bicycles down on South William Street.

Katharine

I was sure crazy after Harry went away that Christmas. I can't imagine now how I got into such a state. My thoughts were like the monkey's tail, going around and around. I was in such a peck of trouble and such a peck of happiness, all mixed up together, afraid to enjoy the happiness that Harry offered because of the specter of Orv in the background all the time. The harder my darling boy pressed me to make up my mind, the more confused and frantic I got. I was in the vicious circle—not free to love him as I might, not free *not* to love him. I almost despaired of finding a way out.

Harry will never know how my conscience fought with my feelings. I had finally begun to realize what our loving each other meant for Orv. The thought of what was coming stabbed me day after day when I thought what the house would be to Little Brother without me there. I dreaded what I had to go through—and what he had to look forward to. The tears were very near the surface all the time. Even if I had known what to do about Orv, I would have had bad moments over making the plunge into marriage, because I knew there would be no going back. Whichever way I looked, a door seemed to slam shut in my face.

To make matters worse, the fate of the *Star* was hanging in the balance, and Harry's future along with it. I had long felt that the life of the paper, under the old management, was very uncertain. And I was as full as Harry was of utter amazement at the selfishness of the Nelson family. Most people who do big things, as Mr. Nelson did, are very selfish. But not to leave so much as a penny to any of the people who had worked with him and for him—for him, in the sense of devoting themselves wholeheartedly to his plans and profit and pleasure—that was cruelly selfish. Imagine deserting the men who had been with the paper so long and made it what it was, especially after not letting them have any credit before the public.

Thinking only of one's family is a very common weakness. It was disgraceful for the name of Mr. Nelson's son-in-law to appear at the top of Harry's editorial page—as if he had the least thing to do with what went into it. As close as our family has always been, I have less and less admiration for "family spirit." No doubt Mr. Nelson thought his daughter would outlive all of his old associates—at least the years of their activity in any work. Laura Kirkwood was naturally a fine woman, but someone with her lack of self-control should not have been in the position of running a newspaper. She had grown too used to the loyalty and ability of the staff to get its true value. Harry was devoted to the Kirkwoods, but if you ask me, they owed a good deal more to him than he did to them.

My blessed boy deserves everything that's coming to him. How good it is to see Harry reaching independence while he is still young enough to enjoy it. I believe I have sort of an obsession about that. I want him to be free from worries of all sorts—not just financial ones. He's had so much anxiety in his life. It will be lots of fun to watch our pile getting bigger and bigger, until finally we can snap our fingers at everybody! I grow more determined every day to do as I please. What I want most of all, for both of us, is peace of mind. I don't have to compete with other women in clothes and such like, but I do have to have some feeling of security. I don't want to be dependent on *anyone* when I'm old, any more than I want Harry to be.

My dearest! I want to be so much to you to make up for all the time that is gone—for all you have suffered that I couldn't help, for everything that has troubled you since you were a child. We'll finish up life with as near a perfect love as we can make it, won't we, dear? And we'll be so gentle with each other and so tender and loving. We have nothing behind us to be sorry for and such a chance for the future—all so full of promise because we understand so much more than most people can when they are married and we both realize the possibilities and want to do so much for each other. Oh, my boy—I do want to satisfy you—be everything you want me to be that I can be—a sweetheart, friend, companion, helper—everything that you can wish!

All that long winter and spring, Harry was a pillar of strength—which is a sight more than I can say for myself. Little Brother was bound to catch wind of our plans in time, whether I told him or not. All our friends in Oberlin seemed to know about the letter Harry sent me at the Faculty Club in November—I must say Frannie Lord didn't act so very surprised when I finally divulged our secret. We figured out that it must have been someone in President King's office who gossiped to Mrs. Hemingway in Kansas City—who naturally broadcast it to the world. And then there was that corker of a letter from Doctor Dick: "If only you lived in Kansas City and could adopt the best white man on earth—his initials are H.J.H.—then my happiness would be complete." Talk about dropping heavy hints—*that* one landed like a ton of bricks!

Fancy—I still hadn't told anyone the most important news I ever had to tell. I hadn't even told Lorin yet, partly because I dreaded it so and was on the verge of tears all the time, and partly because it wasn't easy to get a chance to talk to him alone. To think that he and Orv actually spoke about the wedding that spring and neither of them said a word to me. I didn't know anything at all about that until months later. They were both waiting for me to say something first!

Carrie was good as gold—carrying my letters to Harry to the post office, taking confidential phone messages, and generally running interference with Orv. But I could see that it was pointless trying to keep our plans from him much longer. I was more and more afraid that I would slip up and call Harry "dear" in front of Orv or one of our friends. That would have been a mess! And I was positively paralyzed with fear that Little Brother would hear the news from someone else, which would have been even worse.

Finally, I couldn't stand the strain any longer. I broke down and told Harry that *he* would have to talk to Orv—all by himself.

Harry

In May of '26, as soon as we wrapped up the purchase of the *Star*, I made another excuse to stop in Dayton on my way east. This time it wasn't a pleasure trip, however. Katharine had finally thrown in the towel and decided she couldn't face telling Orv about us after all. She entrusted the thankless mission to me instead. I was to speak to her brother alone, man to man, for all the world as if I were asking a father for his daughter's hand. Katharine declined even to be present during the interview. She was afraid she would cry if she was in the room, which was the last thing either of us wanted.

She met me at the station on the morning train, and we drove straight out to the house. The hillside was a mass of pinks and reds, with the hawthorn trees and redbuds in full glory. Orville greeted me as affably as ever, but I could see he was under a cloud. The tension in the air must have been contagious. When Katharine started in once more about deserting her poor little brother who needed her so much and so on, I'm sorry to say that my patience wore thin. I pointed out that it was pretty late in the game for her to speak of being uneasy about what we were doing. Moreover, she was being unfair to Orville. Katharine had made up her mind to be married months earlier. Her own brother had a right to be told.

When I broke the news to Orville the next day, he listened politely to my little speech. If he had already guessed what Katharine and I were planning, he gave no sign. On the contrary, it was all too clear to me that he had never seriously entertained the possibility that his sister might actually leave him. He had gotten it into his head that she had prevented him from marrying when he was a young man, and that an implied agreement resulted that she should never marry. The truth is that Orville was so absorbed in his work he had no inclination to marry. Through Katharine's companionship and her part in making a home, he felt no need of taking a wife. If he, with his determination and will, had met somebody he had wanted to marry, I believe he would have gone ahead. And it would have been Katharine's duty to accept the situation, just as it was his duty to make the best of her decision.

Orville is not a man who can be argued with, however. He made his great success in aviation through his independence of character and his refusal to listen to others. The same qualities now got in the way of his taking a just view of Katharine's needs and desires. She has been a devoted sister to him all her life. She gave up her career as a teacher—work that she enjoyed more than anything else she has ever done—to devote herself to looking after him and Wilbur. He waves all that aside as negligible. He has convinced himself that she is indispensable to his happiness, and I fear his attitude will never change.

Orville put on a brave front when the three of us talked things over together that evening. I almost began to hope that we had brought him round to our view of the situation. Not until after I left the next day did he let his true feelings come out. According to Katharine, he refused to speak to her. He wouldn't even stay in the same house with her. Naturally, she was devastated. Her worst fears had come to pass. It felt like someone in the family had died, she told me. For my part, I wasn't convinced that Orville had taken it all in. Katharine insists he didn't suspect anything at all until I talked to him. Is it possible that he failed to see what was in his own sister's heart? Or did he see it and shut it out by the sheer force of his stubborn, indomitable will?

Orville

To give credit where credit is due, when push came to shove, Harry didn't beat around the bush. He came straight out with the bad news, even knowing as he did that it would cut me to the quick. Would I could say the same for my sister. She let me coast along month after month in blissful ignorance, without so much as a hint that anything was going on between her and Harry. When the three of us sat around calmly discussing the situation after dinner that night, I was at a loss for words. What did they expect me to do—congratulate them on their happiness and wish them well? All I could think of was that they had been carrying on behind my back for months, not only here but on the island too.

Evidently, Harry isn't as unselfish and high-minded as I took him to be. I guess that shouldn't surprise me, in light of what I've seen of human nature. But I fault Katharine more than I do him. She lied to me—or at least failed to tell me the whole truth, which comes to the same thing. And she sided with Harry against me—*me*, her own flesh and blood. Getting held up by professional bandits like Glenn Curtiss is one thing. Distasteful as it may be, it's just business and nothing personal. But for Kate to go back on me like this is unforgivable. After all I've done to make her comfortable and secure, to build her a proper home and give her a place in the world, this is how she repays me.

We always agreed, Kate, Will, and I, that we would never marry. Not in so many words, perhaps, but that's neither here nor there. Where family is concerned, it shouldn't be necessary to spell out such mutual obligations, as if we didn't trust each other implicitly. Did Will and I need a contract to set up the Wright Company? Did I need to sign a piece of paper saying that I would remain a bachelor for his and Kate's sakes? Did Pop need a legal document to ensure that we would look after him in his old age? Pshaw! The Wrights have always stuck together. It's how we were brought up. It's what is right.

There is such a thing as a code of honor, even among thieves. Whatever else people may say about us, we Wrights have always conducted ourselves in an open and aboveboard fashion. Kate never acted less than honestly and honorably toward me—until Harry came into her life. Blast you and shame on you, Katharine Wright! What can have possessed you to let an outsider break up our family?

Katharine

I ought to have foreseen how awful it would be. I didn't, quite, and I blame myself. Orv is so sensitive, and after Harry went away his face showed everything to me. He looked so pitiful, so dark under his eyes—just as he used to look when he was terribly worried and sick besides. Oh—my little brother! This is the first time there has been any trouble to amount to anything between us. Orv has always been so dear, and he has always been my special care. Harry can have no idea of how it hurt me to hurt him so.

Orv went into a kind of tailspin. Day after day he moped around, sulking like a little boy. He used never to come home without hunting me up right away—I loved to feel wanted that way—but now he wouldn't stay in the house a minute. He started leaving for his laboratory early in the morning, even before Carrie came. He didn't sleep a wink for two nights and was so sick that he had to take aspirin. I was walking around like an automaton myself. I couldn't think or feel or do anything but force myself to go through motions. I was sick with anxiety and doubt—so discouraged, so guilty of having done something awfully wrong. Harry used to say he hadn't quite realized how much we live in the future until Isabel died and he came up against having no future to look forward to. So it was—so it *is*—for me with every thought of Orv.

I was foolish, of course, not to have seen it coming. Little Brother hadn't been acting quite right, quite normal, for weeks. For one thing, he was a lot more clingy than he usually was, and even the least bit boastful—*that* wasn't like him at all. One day— this was before he and Harry had their man-to-man talk—he came home from his office looking like the cat that swallowed the canary. It seemed the chief engineer of the Missouri Pacific Railroad had put his private car at Orv's disposal for the ride from St. Louis to Little Rock, to attend a meeting of the local Engineers Club. Bubbo waved the telegram in front of me and said now I could see that he was "some punkins." If that doesn't beat all! I told him I wasn't bluffed a bit by his blow—I knew him a lot better than those people did!

After my engagement was out in the open, Orv became so desperately unhappy that I had to do something to console him. I told him not to worry so, that I never intended to go off and leave him, and that Harry didn't want me to do that either. Once more I held out the possibility of the three of us making a home together in Kansas City, or my coming out regularly to stay with him in Dayton, as Harry had proposed. I don't know whether it was quite right—quite *straight*—for me to give Little Brother that relief. But I couldn't leave him without comfort when he was so heartbroken. I told myself over and over that Orv would come to feel differently in time, especially if he saw that we were being considerate of him.

I should have saved some of that comforting for myself! Harry kept urging me to follow my heart, but how could I be sure where it was leading? The one thing I was absolutely sure of was that I loved Orv and he loved me. We had been true to each other for over fifty years—longer than most marriages last. My love for Harry was strong and enduring too, of course, but it didn't have such deep roots. I always thought that the possibility of his ever coming to care for me the way he cared for Isabel had passed in Oberlin. At bottom, I still couldn't quite believe that he wasn't so hard-boiled emotionally as we all thought in those days. How long would this new passion of his last? Could I trust it? For that matter, could I trust my *own* feelings, which seemed to be whipping me this way and that like a flibbertigibbet?

If only I had had Harry's sublime belief that it was so right for us to be together that everything else must get out of the way. He had become such a stormy person—the very last thing any of us would have thought of him in college. For him love is like a bolt of lightning, while for me it is more like a burst of anger or joy— something that has to be examined rationally and dispassionately, without being purely selfish about it. If I'm being quite frank, I don't feel so sure that the passionate love is absolutely necessary to our natures. It can be lovely—as it is with Harry—but it is not really a large part of our lives. The gentle love, the kind I have for Orv, is a much bigger part and has much more claim on us. That is the kind of love that lasts, I think.

What Harry said about it being pretty late to feel uneasy about what we were doing went in deep with me. It was so true, so unanswerably true. I had made my choice and there was no possible way out that I could see. Nothing could undo what had been done. I felt as if, after years and years of doing my best to be as much as I could be to Father and the boys, then to Father and Orv, and finally to Little Brother all alone, I had come to the end of it all.

Harry

Having done my duty and bearded the lion in his den, I was strong for moving full speed ahead with our wedding plans. Katharine, however, insisted on applying the brakes and letting Orville get used to the idea before we pressed it again. That approach might have worked but for one fatal flaw: her brother obviously had no intention of getting used to the idea—not then, not ever. He simply chose to walk away from it. He refused even to talk to Katharine about her forthcoming marriage. In a way, you have to admire Orville's ability to wall himself off from disagreeable thoughts and experiences. His whole character has been built on resisting outside influences. The relentlessness that makes him so absolutely honest and reliable is a wonderful asset to a scientist. But it won't do where human nature is concerned.

I had come to expect this kind of unreasonableness from Orville, but to run up against it in Katharine was disconcerting, to say the least. When she digs in her heels, she can be just as stubborn and hard to reason with as her brother. I felt trapped between a rock and a hard place—and there was no telling which of them was more immovable. Needless to say, Katharine took a different view of the situation. She still had visions of patching things up and bringing Orville out to live with us in Kansas City. As much as I would have liked to look through the rose-colored glasses she talks about, I judged the chance of that happening to be about as remote as traveling to the moon in a flying machine.

Katharine

The prospect of making a home together with Harry made me feel all shivery inside. It's what sustained me during the long, cold months when neither Little Brother nor I could find the strength to face up to hard reality. I had such dear fancies about feathering our nest and making it cozy and bright. Most of Harry's furniture was in the colonial style, and I wanted to keep it that way. I pictured chintz wallpapers in some of the rooms upstairs and maybe plainer paper and the little figured stuff for hangings and bed draperies. I had my two mahogany pieces—the chiffonier and the dressing table that I bought with money I earned when I was teaching—and the cherry bureau and table that were my grandmother's. That plus a pair of twin beds was all we would need to furnish our room.

To take my mind off my troubles, I started to make an inventory of things I wanted to take with me to Kansas City. All the linen at home was marked K.W., so naturally that would be part of my trousseau. All the silver in the house was mine too. It wasn't anything especially fine, but Will and Orv had started the collection for me the Christmas after they made their first flight, and I loved it. I had picked out the perfect spot for the polar-bear rug that Griff Brewer bought for me in Norway, between the living room and the library. I imagined a pretty Oriental rug in Harry's study upstairs, with a lovely big chair to sit in when we wanted to be close together and talk—and other things!

Orv gave me an allowance of four hundred a month to run Hawthorn Hill. The house in Kansas City doesn't cost us anywhere near that much, I'm happy to say. I love the idea of budgeting our income—and I've never been in favor of "keeping up" with the neighbors or anyone else. Father and Mother set an example on that, which I shall never forget nor cease to admire. I love fine things when you can have them easily and comfortably, but I certainly don't need them to be happy. I told Harry we could make a lovely home for each other by taking the greater care in all the things that didn't cost a penny. Then we would be able to have enough nice, fine things to add a little "velvet" to what was already lovely and sweet.

I was out in Kansas City a good deal of the time in my thoughts that spring and summer. I pictured Harry coming home from the paper in the evening—how he would burst in the door, full of boyish energy and enthusiasm, how he would call out to me, the way Orv used to do, and how he would always come hurrying up to kiss me if I should happen to be upstairs. I wanted that so much! I would be all dressed up for dinner and we'd have a pretty table and he'd "help me sit down," as one of my friends calls it when men pull out the chairs and so on for the ladies. Maybe he would even bring me a little surprise now and then. I was determined to keep up all the dear, sweet ways we had with each other when we were courting.

On Saturday nights, when Harry worked late, I'd be waiting up for him. He would honk his horn, and I'd run down and open the garage door. Then he'd get off his coat—maybe he'd have to do such a prosaic thing as look after the furnace for the night before we could go upstairs. But anyway, I'd have everything nice and cozy in the study, and we'd sit in the big chair and talk and talk and *talk*. Then I'd cuddle up close to him and tell him I wanted him to tell me again that he loved me—and we'd be off! I would stroke his face and hair and kiss him, and I'd want him to hold me close to him and love me the way I like to be loved. And we'd not have to hurry to bed because tomorrow would be Sunday and he wouldn't have to rush off to the office. We'd be all by ourselves, and we'd feel as if almost our *whole world* was in that one room.

I loved to tell Harry some of my little secret longings. I didn't want him ever to be indifferent about coming home to me. I knew I wouldn't feel alone in Kansas City ever, if he wanted me lots. I wanted to be with him a lot—a mighty big lot! I looked forward to getting all our interests and all our belongings in one place and feeling that everything in our lives belonged to us *together*. I had moments of wanting nothing more than the privilege of doing things for Harry's personal comfort—some humble little thing like getting him a good breakfast and sending him off in the morning happy and contented. It must be a "reversion to type"! I felt like the pathetic, middle-aged German teacher in the Josephine Bacon story who suddenly decides to chuck it all up and follow her heart.

In my daydreams, I saw myself coming downtown at noon once in a while to have lunch with Harry. Sometimes I would need the car during the day, and I could take him to and from the office, the way I did with Orv. But he would have the use of the car mostly. I wasn't going to have him going into the office on the streetcar regularly—no siree! He has earned more comfort than that. I am so proud of Harry's work—as proud as ever I was of Orv's. I can't imagine ever being jealous of it, the way some women are of their husbands' work, or foolish enough to want him to give it up for me. And I don't mind his going into the office evenings or Sundays or anytime he wants. After all, that care and devotion to their work are the reason he and Orv got where they are today.

Orville

As I had no intention of interrogating Kate about her wedding plans, and she was clearly in no hurry to bring up the subject herself, we pulled back into our shells, each of us waiting for the other to make the first move. At length, I decided to have a word with Lorin—only to discover that my older brother already knew about Kate's move to Kansas City, but hadn't wanted to be the first to tell me. As far as I was able to determine, there was no one but me in the entire family who wasn't in on the secret.

I waited and waited for Kate to lay her cards on the table, but she refused to give me even that satisfaction. It was just like after Will died, when none of us could find anything to say to save our souls. There was no consolation to be had in talking. Words were even more painful than the reality of Will's death—talking about it only made it seem more real. Kate and I spoke about Harry's new position at the paper, our trip to Kansas City in 1919, when he took me downtown to meet his associates—practically everything *but* her secret engagement. Harry came up to the island again for our joint birthday that summer, but we couldn't talk there either, and I for one was in no mood to celebrate.

I knew that Swes was counting on being married at Hawthorn Hill. Neither of us could ever forget Ivonette and Scribze's wedding—how the house was filled to the rafters with flowers and the minister got the wrong name on the wedding certificate and we all rolled up our sleeves and served a buffet supper to the crowd when the extra help we had hired failed to show. And we often recalled the summer Leontine and John got married here—the summer it was so beastly hot that I had to put an electric fan blowing over a tub of ice to cool us off. I can still see the look on the newlyweds' faces when I presented them with a pirate's chest supposedly full of nails that magically turned into gold coins!

Yes, this house was made for weddings, all right—*other people's* weddings. As I recall, it was Kate herself who made the observation that we had better import a few weddings, since neither of us planned on having one of our own. I was of no mind to change my ways simply because she had gotten some fool idea of marrying into her head. I made my position crystal clear to Lorin, but I might as well have been speaking Chinese for all the difference it made. He actually tried to persuade me to make it up with Kate and allow the ceremony to take place here. That was the limit. Evidently, my brother had forgotten how broken up Swes was when he and Netta got married. She moaned and groaned about each of us boys deserting her one by one. Well, it was time she got a taste of her own medicine.

I have no regrets about sticking to my guns. It was the right thing to do—the honorable thing—the only thing I *could* do under the circumstances, no matter what anybody says. If I can stand up to the secretary of the almighty Smithsonian Institution, I guess I can stand up to my own family sure enough. Not that it was easy, mind you. Saying no to Sterchens was one of the hardest things I've ever had to do. Even sending the flyer overseas didn't give me so much trouble. We had never had a serious disagreement before in our entire lives. But Kate finally left me no choice. If I couldn't stop my sister from leaving me, I could still be master in my own house.

Katharine

Orv's spirits seemed to revive as the summer wore on. I expect he had convinced himself that I wouldn't leave him when it came right down to it. So long as we gave the topic of marriage a wide berth, life got back to pretty near normal. At the island we did the things we always loved to do—fishing, swimming, boating, napping, and generally lolling about like sloths. I ought to have taken more pleasure in Harry's visit than I did. If I had been easier in my mind about Orv, I would have enjoyed nothing better than doing some honest-to-goodness planning for the house. Isn't that what people about to get married are supposed to do? But the only way I could have enjoyed thinking about coming to be with Harry was to ignore everything else.

The upshot was that I did practically nothing all summer long. I couldn't go ahead with Harry as long as things were as they were between me and Orv. It was my fault mostly. I was never able to talk to him about being married. I used to say I could always bring the boys around to my way of thinking if I just had patience enough to rely on the sun instead of the wind to produce the desired state of mind—but not this time. Every look at Little Brother was a stab in the heart. I began to see what a relief from responsibilities death can be. No one could help me in my particular trouble. No one else knew all the little things that made up the background of our story. Sometimes I had a notion to leave without telling Orv, but I was afraid I wouldn't be much good to Harry if I came that way. I *wasn't* free and knew it, and yet I went ahead anyway—and now I'm paying the price.

By the time we got back home from the bay in September, I simply had to confide in someone, so I decided to have a word with Lorin. He was so dear to me when I was a little girl and Mother was ill and couldn't do things for me. He brushed and braided my hair and saw that I was all right to go off to school. If Lorin understood and encouraged me, I thought I could go ahead with the wedding. I was afraid I was in trouble with the whole family, but it turned out I needn't have worried. Everyone was sympathetic—Lorin, Lou and Netta, all the nieces and nephews. Carrie too, of course—she did everything to help me when I got near the breaking point. Whenever I looked washed out, she said very little but stayed late and put dinner on the table. That was her way of showing sympathy. "It's all I can do for Miss Katharine," she said.

What a blessed relief it was to have the family behind me! All the girls, in particular, were interested in seeing that I had the proper clothes for the wedding. I believe women just naturally love romances! Netta wanted me to be married in white, but I didn't want a wedding such as young people would have—a plain traveling suit was just fine for me, thank you! Netta was so sweet to me. She said I had helped her more than anyone else when her children were little, and she had not forgotten it. She and Lorin promised to do everything they could to help Orv and to give me a pretty wedding. I wanted Netta to sing and Lou to play the piano at the ceremony—nobody from outside, just the family.

I had almost begun to hope that Orv would come around—until Lorin spoke with him and slammed up against another brick wall. When the Lords came to visit and Louis went to see Little Brother, it was the same story. Orv flatly refused to attend the wedding, which meant that we couldn't have it at Hawthorn Hill. He wouldn't even allow us to use his name on the announcements. I could hardly believe my ears. All my dreams for a lovely, simple afternoon ceremony at home went up in a puff of smoke. So that was that—Harry and I couldn't have a proper wedding after all. We had to be "just married" on the quiet in a small ceremony somewhere away from Dayton. I was so ashamed of myself, so sorry to spoil Harry's little bit of happiness—his *and* mine.

Harry sent me a lovely wedding ring, and we fixed the date for November 20, 1926. The Lords were happy to let us be married at their home in Oberlin, but everything had to be kept hush-hush. We tried to arrange it so no one would know that Orv wasn't there. We put it on the grounds of wanting to have President King marry us and so have the wedding in Oberlin—a pretty lame excuse! But I knew our secret was safe with the Lords. If anyone else asked who was going to be there, "the family" would answer. Mr. Deeds put a notice of the wedding in the *New York Times* and papers in Washington, Cleveland, Dayton, and Kansas City. That way people would assume that we hadn't tried to send announcements.

It was just too bad to have to scheme around in such an undignified way, but it couldn't be helped. The whole situation would have been utterly ridiculous if it hadn't been so terribly sad. Fancy two grown-up men waging a tug-of-war over little Katie Wright! I had been pulled in both directions so hard and for so long that I scarcely knew which end was which anymore. I only knew I couldn't go on much longer. I had been pretty poor in the pinch, but I couldn't fail Harry now and endure myself. Wasn't that a queer way to get married?

Orville

The strain between Kate and me didn't let up as time wore on. On the contrary, it got worse. We slunk around the house taking care not to cross paths, like enemy ships keeping each other at bay. Toward the end, there was virtually no communication between us at all. Swes thought that by holding the wedding in Oberlin and putting it out that no one but the family would attend, she could avoid offending our friends and causing a scandal in Dayton. But I let it be known that I would boycott the ceremony no matter where it took place. My word was final: if Kate walked out of my house, I said, the door would be closed to her for good and always.

The rest of the family took her side, of course. That was to be expected. Love makes fools of us all, it seems, especially women of a certain age. Kate always was impulsive and unconventional in her friendships with men. I almost think she took pride in being what she calls "queer." I could understand about Netta and Lou getting behind her—women can always be counted on to stick together in a pinch—but Lorin's attitude stumped me. Who would have believed that my own brother would fail to understand my position? Will and I helped Lorin out more than once when he was in a tight spot. I had a right to expect his support.

Kate was adamant about not letting me stay on here alone—a sure sign of a guilty conscience, if you ask me. She and Carrie fixed it up that Edwards, the colored man who used to work for us, would come back and live with me. He had run off to France to be a magician's assistant or some such tomfoolery, but apparently he let slip to Carrie that he would welcome the chance to come home. To tell the truth, I'm happy to have him back. Edwards is a man of good character, pleasant, trustworthy, and easy to have around the place. Between him, Carrie, and Miss Beck, I consider myself well taken care of. But none of them can ever replace my Sterchens.

Harry

Katharine's plans for the wedding seemed to change with the weather. One day the sun was shining and she was burbling on about gowns and invitations. The next day the sky clouded over and she was shrouded in gloom. But she remained a loyal sister to the bitter end. The one thing she insisted on absolutely was that we do nothing to cast Orville in an unfavorable light. We agreed to have a small, private wedding in Oberlin at the home of our old friend Louis Lord. Katharine had the happy idea of asking President King to conduct the ceremony. If she couldn't have a family wedding, she said, she wanted to be married by someone from Oberlin and from the old days.

I didn't mind so much for myself, but Katharine deserved more fuss to be made over her. It was her fondest wish to be married at home, surrounded by her family and a few close friends, and to be given away by Orville. She used to tell me about the big family weddings they held at Hawthorn Hill, complete with bridesmaids, fancy floral displays, and sit-down suppers. Our wedding, by contrast, was a simple affair, cloaked in darkest secrecy. I practically had to sneak into Dayton to get the marriage license. There was little danger of anyone recognizing me, but Katharine was a different matter. Pretty much all of Dayton knows the Wrights by sight, I should imagine, including the clerk at the Montgomery County probate court.

In spite of our elaborate precautions, the newspapers caught wind of our plans, which isn't surprising, really, seeing that the Wrights are the closest thing to royalty in Dayton. The next day's *Journal* carried a front-page story revealing that I had come to town, obtained the license, and proceeded to Oberlin for the wedding. The reporter telephoned President King for details but got no satisfaction. By the time he managed to track me down at my hotel, I had my speech all worked out. I told him that I wasn't married yet, but I declined to say I wouldn't be married within the next twenty-four hours. Katharine couldn't have done better herself—and she's a dab hand at telling little white lies.

After such a suspenseful buildup, the wedding itself was almost an anticlimax. My son and sister were there representing my family. Lorin and Netta finally decided they couldn't attend the ceremony without precipitating a breach with Orville. Consequently, no Wrights were on hand to see Katharine take the most important step in her life—none except Lorin's daughter, Leontine, who came down from Cleveland with her husband, John. As we predicted, the AP and most of the newspapers that covered the wedding automatically assumed that "members of the Wright family" included Orville. Katharine and I felt no obligation to set the record straight.

Apart from the Lords, the only other outside guest was our mutual friend Raymond Stetson. We wouldn't think of leaving him out. If it hadn't been for the Prof, I might never have asked Katharine to marry me in the first place. It must have given him particular satisfaction to hear us recite our vows. He had always urged Katharine to set Orville's feelings aside and do what was best for herself. She had been a "lay sister" a long time, he said, but had never actually "taken the veil." His words came back to me as I slipped the wedding band onto Katharine's finger. It hardly seemed possible that we were man and wife at last. And yet I couldn't help wondering whether the ring that Orville had given her years before didn't signify a stronger bond.

Katharine

In the end, I left Dayton without telling anyone outside the family but Mrs. Deeds and my old friend Agnes Beck. It was all so undignified, going away as I did, with little more than the clothes on my back. I shall never forget that. I hated it so! Orv wrote me a check for a hundred and fifty dollars—his way of squaring accounts, I expect. But I had to leave behind almost everything I owned—my silver, my china, my linens, my books, my typewriter, Mr. Akeley's bronze elephants—everything. I did manage to pack the pretty new dress I had just had made—black silk with a green trimming—along with a couple of old evening gowns. I was determined not to look shabby in Kansas City, or Harry's friends would be sorry for him!

The ceremony at the Lords' house was lovely, even if it was a far cry from what I had imagined my wedding would be. The family all wanted me to have a traditional white dress set off by a big, colorful bouquet. Instead, I wore a plain new suit and carried a nosegay of white carnations mixed with sprigs of holly. Simple elegance! Hawthorn Hill always looked so enchanting when it was gussied up for weddings, with flowers spilling out everywhere and food and music galore. Harry, bless his heart, wanted to make up for all that, so he ordered pretty arrangements of autumn flow- ers—including an assortment of my favorite roses, nestled among sprays of baby's breath—and the Lords laid on a small supper for the guests after the ceremony.

There was a big article in the Dayton paper, of course, accom- panied by that horrid picture of me—the one that makes me look as much too soft as the one with a hat makes me too hard. I shud- der to think how Orv must have reacted when he read about my contributing "money and an inexhaustible supply of enthusiasm" to the invention of the flying machine. Talk about a yarn that springs up out of nothing and travels a long distance! And then to have that mob of reporters descend on Hawthorn Hill after the wedding, pounding on doors and trampling on the flowers. Carrie says Orv was as mad as a hornet. Lucky for them I wasn't there— my sting is a whole lot worse than his!

Some way moving to my new home took it all out of me. If it had only been a matter of exchanging one house for another, my worries would have been nothing. But it is not so easy to say good-bye to things and people over and over at my time of life. I sometimes feel that I can't hope to see old friends in Kansas City. It is so far away from New York and everywhere that people naturally come. Only lately have my friends in Dayton been writing to me and sending me gifts and messages. As for new friends—close ones, I mean—I am afraid I won't make many here. In Dayton I grew up with everyone and never knew what it was to go out and make friends. Harry had to do that when he first went to Kansas City, but now he's been here more than half his life, so he has a big head start on me.

When it comes right down to it, I am pretty old to be starting afresh in a new place. What if I shouldn't make a success of it? I would never want Harry to be ashamed of me. All the women he knows are clever and energetic about their houses and know all the latest furnishings and gadgets. I don't know much about such things. And I've always had an inferiority complex about cooking. Our house is clean and neat as a pin, but not at all fancy. Harry is so considerate of all my "queerness"—but I try not to be so queer that people feel sorry for him! I'm just not built for stylishness and that's that. All those widows who seem to thrive in Kansas City—what must they think of me? "That little snip! No style—no nothing."

The debut of the second Mrs. Haskell left much to be desired, I fear. I felt as if I had been dipped into hot water, wrung out, and pulled through a keyhole. There was nothing left of me but some limp strings. I had sort of gone into a little heap, a pathetic little heap. I can never regret doing what I did—but Orv casts a great shadow over my happiness. If he would only let me come and stay with him all I can. I could be there often and stay for weeks, just as I intended. Will I ever wake up from this bad dream and find him as he always was? Oh, Harry, darling Harry—it is so hard to say the final word!

The Professor,
R. H. Stetson

So Katharine has taken the plunge at last. She led poor Harry on a merry chase, I must say—and it didn't take an expert in psychology to see where they were headed. It may be that Katharine didn't know just where her moves were to lead; they were definite enough and made the thing inevitable, just the same. I told them both at the beginning that there would be no peace till they had gotten through their emotional spree. Along the way, they were fated to do what all lovers do: speculate endlessly and invent, suppress, exacerbate, mitigate, and exaggerate at least seventeen different emotions. It's all there in that extraordinary series of silly letters that Harry wrote to me early on in their courtship. Ordinarily I destroy letters, but these I shall keep. I always need good material to illustrate emotional vagaries.

I did my part to assist Cupid by praising Harry to the skies every time an opportunity presented itself with Miss Wright. For instance, he may wonder why he got off so easy in my review of his little essay on Kansas City that came out a while back. It's *not* because one's to be gentle with old graduates and deal kindly with their efforts to write. Not at all. It's simply because I'm mortally afraid of the Lady Trustee. And I don't care how inconspicuous the review might be, or how quietly the thing might be done in the review itself, I should be found out by the woman in question and well scolded if I failed to do my duty. Consequently, for months on end I found it advisable to speak of Harry in terms of highest respect. I burned enough incense at his shrine to keep him in good fragrance for years.

Harry was just as crazy in his sane moments as he was in his insane, and I must say there was method in his madness. Katharine's too, I daresay. It was not all an impulse of the moment that led her to open things as she did. Nope, she wanted to have an understanding with Harry, whatever it might lead to. But then, having brought the marriage matter to a head, she dithered over leaving the inventor-bro till there was no hope of getting him to take a reasoned view of the situation. Still, what can't be cured must be endured. Orv's been her child for a long time. And of course she's been everything to him, though it's not the indispensability that she's assumed and that it's conventional to assume. If Orville had been attacked by general emotionality and wanted to bring a wife into his life, do you suppose he'd have hesitated? Not for a minute.

As difficult as it is for Orville to accept, there's no question that marriage is a great thing for Katharine. It will be a new and vital undertaking, far more rewarding, certainly, than staying home and keeping house for her bachelor brother. The question is, can she ever let him go?

Release

Orville

That day is etched in my memory for good and always. I drove home from the laboratory, parked the Franklin beside the garage, and called out to Kate as I opened the kitchen door. It was a habit of ours to let each other know we were home safe and sound. Ordinarily Swes would call back, but not this time. The house was as still as a tomb. Thinking she might be taking a nap, I climbed the stairs and found her room empty, with the door wide open. Kate was nowhere to be seen. She had cleaned out her drawers and closet, taken her travel bags, and laid the key on her writing desk, where I'd be sure to spot it. She had insisted on locking our bedroom doors at night ever since we had that rash of robberies a few years ago.

Surely, I said to myself, my sister has just gone off unexpectedly to Oberlin or Cleveland. She'll be home in a few days and everything will return to normal. I didn't want to admit that she had walked out on me. It was Carrie who finally broke the news. Swes hadn't said a word. She hadn't even left me a note. The typewriter was sitting empty on her desk. The photograph of Will and me that she hung on her wall, the engraving of the Greek dancers she brought from the old house on Hawthorn Street, the pocket-knife we sent her for her birthday one year from Kitty Hawk—all were in their familiar places. Everywhere I turned there was some memento of her—Mr. Ogilvie's coffee cups in the alcove, Mr. Akeley's bronze elephants in the living room, the big sculpture in the reception hall. To this day I can't pass by it without thinking of Sterchens—our very own Muse of Aviation, spreading her wings over us.

The day of the wedding, the house seemed to echo with the sound of her voice: "Orv! Is that you, Little Brother?" I plugged my ears, tried to distract myself by reading the paper and doing little chores—but nothing worked. My thoughts kept circling back to the ceremony in Oberlin. The *Dayton Journal* had announced that Kate was to be married "in the deepest secrecy." Pish-tush! She and Harry might as well have read the banns from the steps of city hall. Her face was splashed all over the papers from coast to coast. "Sister of Wright Brothers Weds College Mate—Her Sacrifices Helped to Conquer Air." *Her* sacrifices, for pity's sake! *I'm* the one who passed up the chance to get married for her. *I'm* the one who built this house for her and gave her every blessed thing she asked for. *I'm* the one who sacrificed—and this is how she thanks me, by running off with her college sweetheart like a lovesick schoolgirl.

Well, if my devoted sister is determined to make a spectacle of herself, there is nothing I can do to prevent her, not with the rest of the family ganged up against me. At least Lorin had the decency not to speak to the reporters who came nosing around here after the wedding. Isn't it enough that the whole world knows how Kate treated me, without adding insult to injury?

Katharine

Off with the old, on with the new—isn't that what they say? If only life were as simple as a change of clothes. My wedding didn't feel a bit like a fresh beginning—it was more like the end of the life I had always known and loved. Harry was so sweet and considerate. He insisted on taking me to New York for a few days, so I could see a few of my old friends before going to live in Kansas City. Some honeymoon that was! I love Harry dearly—I never dreamed that such a romance could come to me at this time of life—but we were never alone, really and truly *alone*, for a minute. Little Brother was right there beside us, inside my head and heart, day and night. I had quaked at the thought of leaving Dayton without saying good-bye; now I had actually gone and done the awful deed. It wasn't only Orv I had left behind, it was my family, my friends, the world of science and aviation—everything and everybody that had ever meant anything to me.

No one can ever realize how heartbroken I was to do what I did—but it came finally to the place where I thought it was the only right thing to do. After all, Harry needs me at least as much as Orv ever did—to say nothing of my own feelings in the matter. I don't expect other people to agree with me. In fact, I s'pose pretty much everybody was offended by what I did—everybody except dear, sweet Leontine. Bless her for coming to the wedding and braving Little Brother's disapproval. And young Henry—if he can welcome me into *his* family, not to take his mother's place but to be his friend, why can't Orv accept Harry into ours? Does he really hold Harry to account for stealing me away from him? Oh, if he only knew how little my darling boy is to blame! Or is it *me* he can't bear to lay eyes on—me, Sterchens, the loyal sister who abandoned him?

Listen! It will never do to dwell on hard realities when there is so much work to be done. Orv can sulk in his tent to his heart's content; I have a husband to provide for and a household to keep up, even if it's not as big a job as running Hawthorn Hill. From the get-go I made it my business to get on friendly terms with Ollie. She cooked all those years for Harry and Isabel and is as devoted to him as he is to her. Ollie has lots of nice dishes in her repertoire. I figured if she would let me give her some of my favorite recipes—my chicken-noodle-and-mushroom casserole, say, or my "famous" angel food cake—we could have a great collection. That's how it was back home with Carrie—share and share alike. Most cooks are touchy about taking tips from other people, but Carrie isn't a bit. She is always ready to pick up anything new and is grateful for suggestions from anybody.

Harry and I don't lack for creature comforts, and that's a fact. I don't suppose anyone could be so good to me as he has been. He is so concerned over having brought me away from all my family and friends—and life is very pleasant in Kansas City, in every way. There is always plenty of interest if one feels energetic, but I am not tied up in any real responsibility, as I was in Dayton. Our house is attractive and comfortable, and we have pretty much made it over inside. Our latest purchase was some lovely china—Spode-Copeland series plates, Minton's gold-band dinner plates, and Cauldon dessert plates, besides Minton's cream soup dishes. Harry has never had very nice dishes, and he is like a schoolboy about them. He was as pleased as Punch to have the carving set I sent him for his birthday before we got married. Mella King's husband picked it out for me. He never knew, good soul, where it was going!

I took the plunge into married life without making a big splash about it—apart from some niggling qualms about changing my name. I was proud enough to have Harry's name, only—well, Katharine Wright had meant *me* for as long as I could remember. It was a little pull for me to give that up, and I could probably have gotten some advertising on it if I had cared to try. But of course it would have been silly for me to keep my maiden name. It would have embarrassed Harry continually—to say nothing of irritating Orv—and people in Kansas City never would have understood. The first time I wrote a letter on my new stationery, with the initials K.W.H. woven into a neat little circle at the top, I thought they must belong to somebody else. If Little Brother is determined to disown me, I can get along just fine as Mrs. Henry J. Haskell. Nuff said!

Harry

The readjustment from a city where Katharine had lived all her life, and where her family and friends were, to a strange city where she knew almost no one would have been hard enough at best. But the circumstances have made it so unnecessarily and cruelly hard for her. There is not only the personal side, the intense personal affection and loyalty to Orville, there is the fact that aeronautics had become such an important part of her life. I am so dumb on all such subjects that I can be of little help to her in talking about aviation developments. Orville's unreasonableness has cut her off almost completely from one of her great permanent interests. His attitude is a calamity to Katharine, a calamity all around. But I see no way to change it. Orville is so kind and gentle and fine in his general relationships that his behavior toward Katharine is quite incomprehensible. The scientific mind is beyond me.

For as long as I've known her, Katharine's behavior—toward her brother and me both—has been above reproach. No one can accuse her of acting precipitately or without regard for the feelings of others. If anything, she has neglected her own feelings and needs. She gave Orville ample opportunity to come to terms with her engagement and get adjusted to the idea of living on his own. He refused. Finally, she felt she had a right to her own life and her own home. There never was any question of shutting Orville out. She made it clear to him that we both wanted her to spend as much time in Dayton as she could. That Orville was unwilling even to consider such an arrangement has been a bitter pill for her to swallow.

In spite of all the crosses she has to bear, Katharine has never complained about her life in Kansas City. No sooner had we returned from our excursion to New York than she was subjected to a grueling round of ladies' luncheons and teas, on top of which we had dinner invitations two or three times a week. Naturally, the fuss was all on Katharine's account. Now that I was no longer an eligible bachelor, the widows and matchmakers had lost interest in me. Katharine had been looking forward to fixing some of her favorite dishes for me on Ollie's nights off. As it turned out, she seldom set foot in the kitchen. We had talked about going out for a restaurant meal or eating at one of my clubs from time to time, but that didn't seem to be in the cards either.

My friends mean well, I have no doubt. They have been as generous and welcoming to Katharine as I could wish, every one of them. They are killing her with kindness, she says. But I have a notion that, in the beginning at least, there was more to their attentiveness than old-fashioned midwestern hospitality. People are naturally curious. I couldn't help feeling that my friends were looking Katharine over and sizing her up, almost as if she were some sort of exotic specimen in the laboratory—the one and only Wright sister, *Soror aviatrix*!

Katharine

We were invited out a good deal at first—that was to be expected. All Harry's friends felt that they must make me feel at home, especially his colleagues at the paper. Orv and I had been introduced to a number of them over the years, so I wasn't exactly a stranger. Mr. Longan, the managing editor, lives just up the street. Mrs. Longan gave a lovely tea party for me shortly after I moved here, with delicious cakes and fresh roses and everything. If you can credit what you read in the society newspaper, I made quite a respectable impression too—"a real acquisition not only to society but to the *intelligentsia* as well." Pretty hot stuff! The invitations have come so thick and fast that I've hardly had a moment to feel lonely, only a very few such social occasions go a very long way with me.

When you come right down to it, I am not accustomed to being the center of attention—and I am not at all sure I take to it naturally. I never had to think about such things back in Dayton. As a rule, people came to Hawthorn Hill to see Orv, not me—that goes for Harry and Stef too, when they were first getting to know us, anyway. Moving to Kansas City was a bit like traveling in Europe with the boys before the war—all those important people wining and dining us, treating us like royalty, and fussing over *me* as if I were a world celebrity instead of a middle-aged schoolteacher who had scarcely set foot outside of her hometown. Some way everything seems so much more complicated now. The older you get, the harder it is to keep what you *are* separate from what you *have*. As Orv's sister—and now as Harry's wife—it's much more difficult to tell who is liking me for my own sake than when I was just plain old Katie Wright, the Bishop's daughter.

Not that I had any worries about our first two visitors taking me just as I am. Griff and Stef both know me inside out. Was I ever glad to see Griff that first autumn in Kansas City—not least because he came straight from Dayton and brought us news of Little Brother. It felt almost like old times to be talking with someone who shared my interest in aviation, someone who worked with both Will and Orv and understood what we have been fighting for all these years. As for Stef, he was his usual incorrigible self. He waited until the very last minute to send a wire saying that he was coming to Kansas City to give a talk and that he would be staying downtown—at the Muehlebach Hotel, if you please! Of course, we insisted that he stay with us, but we were dining out that evening, so Harry had to make arrangements to leave the party and meet his train, at considerable inconvenience to both us and our hostess.

I hardly know what to think about Stef anymore. With that insatiable ambition of his, he seems to be dashing everlastingly from one speaking engagement to the next, writing book after book as if there were no tomorrow—always on the go, never settling down, never feeling truly satisfied with himself. And he *will* take after that vulgar crowd of "intellectuals" in Greenwich Village, no matter what Harry or I or anyone else has to say about it. Yes, my illusions about Stef have been well and truly shattered. Someday I mean to find out if the rumors we've heard about a special friendship between him and Miss Fannie Hurst are true. I 'spect they *are* true—but what of it? If there's one lesson the trials and tribulations of the past few years have drummed into me, it's that people like Stef and Griff have to be taken for good and bad. None of us is an angel—certainly not me!

Orville

The only surefire way I know to take my mind off a problem is to bury myself in my work, so that's what I did after Katharine left. The 1903 flyer was still sitting in my shop, waiting to be brought back to its original condition before I let it go to London. Once the hullabaloo over the wedding died away, Miss Beck and I got down to covering the wings with new cloth. Day after day, she worked the sewing machine while I marked places that needed stitching. Will and I had the same routine on Hawthorn Street. He would spin the sewing machine wheel around by the hour while I squatted at his feet, marking the places to sew. We made a frightful racket, but no one complained. In fact, Kate told Pop it was lonesome not having us around after we transported the flying machine down to Kitty Hawk. Life would be a darned sight simpler if feelings were as easy to patch up as a piece of sailcloth.

It was just before Christmas that year that Senator Bingham introduced a bill for the erection of a Wright brothers monument in Kill Devil Hills. Hallelujah, I thought, Secretary Abbot and the Smithsonian can go to thunder now. No matter what propaganda they put out about the Langley machine, the United States government has officially acknowledged that Will and I built the first man-carrying flying machine. Maybe there is some justice in the world after all. Griff Brewer was here when I got the news, and you can bet your bottom dollar I gave him an earful. There is no one but Kate with whom I would rather have shared the sweet taste of victory. I knew she would hear about it from Griff soon enough anyway, as he was going on to Kansas City directly from Dayton. I didn't begrudge Swes her right to celebrate. After all, it was always her fight as much as it was mine and Will's.

Katharine

Harry and I were just settling in after our honeymoon when a letter arrived from old Mr. Lahm. He too had just come away from Dayton and had been treated to a lengthy harangue about my running off with Harry and leaving poor Little Brother in the lurch. How I would love to have been a fly on the wall *that* time! Mr. Lahm's sympathy and understanding touched me very deeply. It was such a warm, friendly letter, recalling the old days when Father and Will were with us. Some way he manages to create an atmosphere that makes Will seem almost alive. Like father, like son! Young Frank—Lieutenant Lahm he was back then—was the soul of kindness when Orv was in the hospital at Fort Myer and I went out to nurse him. He found me an inexpensive hotel nearby, came every day to see how Little Brother was getting along, and even took me out to dinner. Fancy how many tongues *that* set wagging!

Hearing again from Mr. Lahm set loose a raft of memories—of Will and Pop, of our trips to Europe and my maiden flight that time in Pau, of Orv and his smashup and our happy family life in Dayton, of Hawthorn Hill and what it meant to each and every one of us. All that is water under the bridge now—and what's left behind is a sad little pool of heartache and regret. Sometimes, in my imagination, I walk through that house, looking for Little Brother and at all the dear familiar things that made my home. But I never find Little Brother, and I have lost my old home forever, I fear. When I married Harry, I forfeited the right to share in Orv's triumphs—or his troubles either. In all my happiness about my brothers there is a sadness nowadays and, in my pride, a realization that I have no part in it.

It's a full-time job to manage all my troubles—not that I've been such a notable success at it. Thankfully, my Oberlin work keeps me from brooding. Doing double duty as class secretary and trustee can put a terrific strain on the nerves, but I was glad for the distraction during those first few months in Kansas City. President King announced his retirement that fall, and all winter and spring were taken up with committee meetings to pick his successor. I had to make several trips to Oberlin and Cleveland, but never stayed longer than absolutely necessary. Even now I want to get out of Ohio as quickly as I can. Lorin has been pressing me to come to Dayton to see his family, and I have a tempting invitation from my dear friend Agnes Beck—but I couldn't go there yet. I don't see how I ever can—but I'll not worry about that now.

Agnes's letter made me good and homesick—almost the first time I have felt really homesick since moving to Kansas City. I want to go back to Dayton very much. As long as I'm here, though, I mean to make the best of it. I'll not give in to those old feelings of tiredness and good-for-nothingness. Just look at Agnes: she is a beautiful character and full of intellectual interest, but she stayed home to care for her grandmother instead of going to college. She became an excellent teacher and has two lovely daughters, but she has always tried to do too many things and hasn't managed her affairs well. The result is that she has always overworked and been in turmoil. Life has been rather hard for her, and she looks worn and a little restless. I so often think what she could have been, under different circumstances. I shouldn't wonder that people say the same of me when my back is turned!

What Agnes needs is someone to smooth over the practical things and give her leisure to pursue her own interests. Isn't that what I've done all my life—first for Pop, then for the boys, and now for Harry? They do say that behind every good man stands a good woman. Harry, I know, doesn't need me in the same way that Little Brother does, especially now that he's a big man at the *Star*. It does my heart good to see him getting the wider recognition he deserves. In the opinion of Louis Lord—hardly an impartial authority, I admit—I am married to "one of the most influential editors in the country." Listen! Not many women get to call themselves the wife of such a paragon. And what do I do all the time Harry is writing his "influential" editorials and hobnobbing with high-muck-a-mucks in Washington? I stay at home and pick out new china for the house!

I'm not complaining, mind you—Harry is everything people say he is, and more—but life in Kansas City isn't quite the dream-come-true that I imagined. For starters, I have entirely too much to fret about—and too little to do. Maybe that's why I felt so run-down when we got back from New York. I came down with the most terrific cold. My throat swelled up and I was nearly deaf in my right ear, until finally I thought I'd better have the whole works examined. Of course, the tonsils were ordered out—I saw *that* coming a mile away! Harry was with me most of the time I was at the hospital. He got his editorial pages made up in advance and so could be away from the office. I was uneasy about a general anesthetic, for no particular reason, and asked for a local anesthetic instead. I didn't dread it much, but I regret to say that I nearly fainted after it was all over!

Harry

I have been increasingly impressed with the terrible strain that Orville's attitude places on Katharine. She puts up a brave front, but the ordeal is clearly taking a toll on both her health and her spirits. When she was young, she had a bout with tonsillitis that prevented her from finishing high school. Afterward she suffered from frequent sore throats. By the time we got married, the discomfort had become so severe that she agreed to be examined by my old college roommate in Cleveland. He diagnosed the problem immediately, and she finally had her tonsils removed here in Kansas City. Why she didn't have the operation years ago is a mystery to me. When it comes to heeding the voice of reason, she can be as hard of hearing as her brother.

Katharine doesn't share my confidence in the skill and knowledge of doctors. That makes us even, because I don't share her faith in the consolation of religion. In my view, it's not a question of believing or disbelieving any particular dogma. The notion of a beneficent, all-knowing deity simply strikes me as inconsistent with everything we know about mankind's propensity for evil. Katharine long ago gave up attending church regularly, but she can't quite bring herself to reject the possibility of an afterlife, however slight it may be. She says speculation is more interesting and generally more satisfactory than a dead certainty of nothing ahead.

I expect she'll cling to that last vestige of irrational hope to her dying day, just as she refuses to face the fact that she and Orville will never be reconciled.

My "rationalist" religion is one of the few bones of contention between us. As the daughter of a God-fearing bishop, Katharine naturally considers Unitarianism no kind of religion at all. Before we were married, she said it would be a test of her love to see if she could get along with my Unitarian friends. I recall how indignant she was when I told her our minister had agreed to serve as Sinclair Lewis's religious adviser while he was in Kansas City writing *Elmer Gantry*. And she let me know in no uncertain terms what she thought about my hanging out with the fundamentalist preachers and freethinkers in Lewis's "Sunday school class." The only reason she read the novel when it came out was because Mr. Lewis had the publisher send me a complimentary copy. She insisted she would never have spent two dollars and fifty cents for such "trash."

Well, as Katharine says, religion will always be something to scrap about when other subjects fail us.

Katharine

I had lived in Kansas City only a few months when Harry took me to Oberlin for President King's retirement party and to see our friend William Allen White get his honorary degree. We had pushed hard for Mr. White's nomination and considered it quite a coup to win over several of the naysayers on the committee. Mr. White has many sterling qualities—for one thing, he hasn't a trace of smartiness, which is more than I can say for Sinclair Lewis and his ilk. If you ask me, though, his political biographies don't amount to so very much. The one of Calvin Coolidge is so sentimental—too racy and breezy. I often think he doesn't know much of what he's trying to talk about. As for his *Woodrow Wilson*, Mr. White admits that he had no special information on the subject—he even cautions readers not to treat it as a "source book." I should hope not! I can't imagine anyone taking such a potboiler seriously.

If Harry ever set his mind to write a book of that sort, it would be a very different kettle of fish. He is so much more solid and substantial and *sensible* than William Allen White—and his ideas are more interesting too. I can't help thinking his religious upbringing has a lot to do with it. In my humble opinion, Harry is far more deserving of recognition and awards than Mr. White or any number of other so-called celebrities I could name. He's not swelled-headed about it, either—that's what I admire most about him. When he got his honorary degree from Oberlin, back in 1917, he didn't puff out his chest and put on airs as most men would have done in his shoes. He didn't make any to-do about it at all, in fact. As I recollect, we celebrated the occasion by letting Lorin drive us out to the ball game after the award ceremony!

Still, Mr. White is unquestionably distinguished in his own way, and I painted him in glowing colors in my letter to President King recommending him for the degree. I pointed out that he was one of our leading contemporary writers, that *Woodrow Wilson* had been generally reviewed as one of the outstanding biographies of recent years (ha ha!), that his writings are constantly sought by the best magazines, and so on. Little white lies mostly, not out-and-out whoppers—but they seem to have done the trick. Mr. White got his degree and was thoroughly pleased about it, and all was well in the end. He is one of Harry's oldest and dearest friends, so I have to tread carefully whenever I have anything less than unalloyed praise for him.

When it comes to politics, though, I have to admit that few newspapermen hold a candle to the "Sage of Emporia." Harry invited him and Mrs. White out to the house that summer along with some colleagues from the paper. The men could scarcely wait to get up from the dinner table so they could rush off to the *Star* office and discuss the upcoming election. I 'spect they felt the subject would bore us womenfolk—as if I hadn't sat around with Orv and his scientist friends often enough not to be intimidated by "men's talk"! I know how deadly a bunch of American men can be when they can't, or won't, talk anything but business. My women friends try hard to discuss books and so on. They don't usually have any ideas of their own and they are kind of pathetic, but at least they *want* to talk about something. What do their husbands expect? When women are so occupied with taking care of houses and children that they *can't* think of anything else and never get out among other people, of course they are not interesting. I don't know what can be done, but I know that having the vote has already done a lot toward making men take us seriously.

Speaking of children, that summer we had a visit from the Bulgarian Haskells—Harry's missionary brother, his wife, and three of their ten children. They were touring the country on furlough, and Edward plied us with stories about the folk school they run in a village called Pordim, somewhere out in the foothills of the Balkans. It was a strenuous time for us, I can tell you, but we survived. If I had to judge from their activities on that occasion, I'd say the children of missionaries were no less inclined to Goopish behavior than the common garden variety. I gave the little boy a piece of my mind when he splattered water from the kitchen faucet all over the floor. That was just plain careless of him, and if there's one thing I can't abide, it's carelessness. I'm afraid I lost my temper and blurted out, "It's ridiculous—we have enough work without having any more." Maybe it's no bad thing after all that I have no children of my own!

Harry

It was a mortifying experience to attend commencement exercises as the husband of Oberlin's formidable "lady trustee." I never had any doubt that Katharine was a woman to be reckoned with, but to watch President King and his fellow worthies pay court and hang on her every word made me feel smaller than ever for having brought her into exile here in Kansas City. All I can say is, if the college trustees expect Mrs. Henry J. Haskell to roll over and rubber-stamp whatever they propose, they are in for a rude awakening. President King got a taste of Katharine's medicine the time he let one of her favorite professors go to Amherst without a fight and notified the trustees only after the fact. She made it known that the professor in question was the kind of teacher Oberlin could ill afford to lose, and that President King could put that in his pipe and smoke it—or words to that general effect.

To be sure, Katharine and I have the greatest respect and affection for President King. After his retirement was announced, I was moved to write him a letter saying how much his teaching and example had meant to me over the years. King was an advanced liberal of his day—advanced almost to the point of heresy, even at a progressive school like Oberlin. I recall a course in freshman psychology he taught in '92, when he openly espoused the theories of Darwin, and a course in evolution that he gave a year or two later. The interest in philosophy that he aroused in my senior year has remained with me. Since then hardly a year has passed that I have not read one or more books on philosophical subjects—mostly popular ones, to be sure, but books that have enlarged my experience considerably.

One time—it must have been in my junior year—I had a long talk with Professor King, as he was then, about religion. Suffice it to say that it was not a subject I was particularly eager to discuss with any member of my own family. I was in the throes of a spiritual crisis and had been having second thoughts about taking the missionary pledge. I confessed to Professor King that I felt out of place remaining in a church a large part of whose creed I didn't believe. I found it increasingly difficult to go along with my parents' belief that the Bible is to be interpreted literally; that if one part is rejected, the rest must go; and that God must of necessity have preserved men from error and left a word directly from himself. As I saw it then, and still see it now, the only ground of acceptance of any part of the scriptures is their reasonableness.

King is a kind, tolerant, and sympathetic man. He told me he was sure I believed the fundamental things, that my great aims were the same as those of the church, and that he saw no reason for my leaving it. To a young man beset by doubts, his words of wisdom were consoling, if not altogether persuasive. Eventually, I did come to a parting of the ways with the Congregational Church. Isabel and I felt more at home among the Unitarians, to the lasting chagrin of some of my family and friends. Bill White and Katharine take a dim view of my apostasy. On one occasion, when I must have drunk the cup of bile to the lees, I told Bill I thought the world was a good deal of a mistake and that perhaps God would be justified in wiping the slate clean and starting over again, though I wouldn't be particularly hopeful over the results.

Now, Bill happens to be blessed with the ability to see a silver lining in every cloud. That, I take it, is his religion in a nutshell. Every time he accuses me of harboring a "grouch on God," I come back with my standard reply: that we are simply calling the same thing by different names. My notion is that none of us lives to himself; that each of us has purposes and needs and loyalties extending far beyond our individual lives. Katharine and Bill call that enveloping whole God, and so can remain members of the Congregational Church in good standing. The real cleavage is between those who refuse to recognize obligations beyond their own interests and those who do recognize such obligations—not between those who use one terminology and those who use another.

Nor, in my experience, is this merely an abstract philosophical debate. Ever since I stood by helplessly and watched Isabel grow more and more frail from one day to the next, until I scarcely felt her weight when I carried her upstairs to bed, the problem of evil has seemed to me as a practical matter insoluble. Bible or no Bible, it is inconceivable to me that any all-powerful and allegedly beneficent deity would permit such tragedies to happen. The only consolation I found in Isabel's unfailing strength and good humor was the realization that joy and suffering are inextricably bound up together in the human condition. On this point, at least, Bill and I are in agreement. When young

Mary White had her fatal horse-riding accident, he didn't give way to grief as most fathers would have done. Instead, he sat down at his desk and turned out a column for his newspaper about Mary's immortal soul "flaming in eager joy upon some other dawn."

His words have the ring of eternal truth. Katharine too possesses a joyous soul, but she suffers deeply over Orville's attitude, and there is not a thing in the world that any of us can do about it.

Katharine

Carrie visited us later that summer, the summer of '27, and stayed for a fortnight. She told me all about home and the family and Colonel Lindbergh's recent visit to Dayton. I was particularly interested in her eyewitness report of that event. "Lindy" had just made his solo flight across the Atlantic and was hounded by well-wishers everywhere he went, the way the boys were in the old days. We read in the newspapers about Orv having him out to dinner with some other notables and taking him to the laboratory afterward to inspect the original flying machine. What the reporters *didn't* say, according to Carrie, was that a mob of celebrity seekers had surrounded the house while the guests were at the table and made a mess of Little Brother's precious plantings. What a disaster! In the end, Colonel Lindbergh made a brief appearance from the balcony off my old room and sent everyone home happy.

Carrie is taking good care of Orv—that is some comfort to me, at least. Heaven knows she's as devoted to him as I am. Such a hard worker too, ever since she came to us as a little spit of a girl. Even when she comes out to Kansas City on "vacation," it's as much as

I can manage to shoo her out of the kitchen. If I don't keep a close eye on her, she sneaks off to make a batch of her special orange marmalade or some other dish she knows I'll like. How she finds the time and energy to write so many letters I'll never know—but am I ever grateful that she does! If it weren't for her and a few other loyal friends, I would feel completely cut off from my old life. My own record as a correspondent is not what it ought to be, I fear. Writing, which used to be my delight, has become an almost forgotten art with me.

Carrie's visit sticks out in my memory because she happened to arrive just after I had my new will drawn up. Some way it seemed right and fitting to have a friend from home by my side as I made provision for disposing of my worldly goods—such as they are. Harry has always insisted on keeping our accounts separate—he wouldn't let me invest a penny of my savings to help buy the *Star*. A very safe and sensible investment it would have been too, as things turned out. But I got even with him: I left him my entire estate free and clear—apart from a few small bequests to Carrie, Lorin, and other special people. Orv will get a thousand dollars when I go to my reward. Of course, Little Brother has abundant means of his own—but I could never turn my back on him the way he has on me.

In some strange way, the work of toting up every one of my possessions, drafting my last will and testament, having it witnessed and notarized and everything—all of that made me feel *less* secure about facing the future instead of *more*. Dear, sweet, passionate Harry—sometimes I almost wish he didn't love me quite as much as he says he does. He has already lost one beloved partner; what if something should happen to *me*? That scares me to think about. Love conquers all—all except death, as I know from bitter experience! "Omnia vincit amor." How does the rest of the verse go? "Et nos cedamus amori"—"Let us give in to love." Aye, there's the rub! We have given in to love with our whole hearts, Harry and I—and we must both take our chances, it seems.

No sooner had we sent Carrie home than we packed up the car and set out for the Colorado mountains. Harry and Isabel used to vacation in Estes Park, until she became too ill to travel. When he proposed the trip, I jumped in with both feet. The altitude in the Rockies made me unable to climb or do much else, but we took some dandy automobile rides—and Long's Peak Inn is *nearly* as nice and comfortable as the camp on Georgian Bay. All the time we were there, I couldn't stop thinking about Orv summering on the island without me. To think that it had only been a year since we celebrated "our" birthday together with Harry at the bay. At least Orv had Griff Brewer to keep him company—and I was so glad that Griff was taking charge of the flying machine and seeing it set up at the Science Museum.

On the drive home from Colorado at the end of August, Harry and I had the surprise of our lives. He was called up at half past four in the morning, at North Platte, Nebraska, to hear that Mr. Kirkwood, the principal owner of the *Star*, had died unexpectedly at Saratoga, New York. By a quarter to six, we were on our way in a dense, ghastly fog, having had a good breakfast at the Union Pacific station. We drove five hundred miles that day and pulled up at the *Star* office at nine o'clock that night. We had a busy week, with out-of-town people coming for the funeral. We had nine to dinner one night and eleven the next—all in the hot weather too, but we survived.

Once the excitement died down, the staff had to consider the question of how to take up Mr. Kirkwood's stock in the company. Harry and his associates had begged, borrowed, and mortgaged themselves to the limit when they bought the paper the year before. The thought of taking on still more debt was more or less paralyzing. But it all turned out very happily. Harry even had a nice surprise when his next paycheck came in. He and two other men had a very substantial increase in salaries, on the ground that they had more responsibility. It has really been a fairy story for Harry, who has worked all his life for the *Star* on just a moderate salary. I tell him I brought him good luck! However, we're not spending any of the extra money. We are busy plunking it away for a rainy day.

Harry

Mr. Kirkwood's death, coming on the heels of his wife's, might have doomed the staff's dream of running the show ourselves. He had invested two and a half million dollars of his personal fortune in the *Star*, on top of the millions the bank had loaned us to purchase the paper. Fortunately, the directors had had the foresight to take out a substantial policy on Mr. Kirkwood's life. That enabled us to buy back his stock in the company without having to borrow to the hilt. Katharine and I received our share of the insurance money, but we never actually saw it: the bank took everything before we got our hands on it. Not that we have any reason to complain. Assuming all continues to go well, *Star* stock will be very valuable in a few years' time.

I admit I had my doubts about Mr. Kirkwood's fitness to run a great newspaper. Being the son-in-law of the founder was hardly sufficient qualification in itself. In the end, though, he did both the *Star* and Mr. Nelson proud. Not long before he died, he paid to have a Tiffany stained-glass window installed in the Nelsons' honor at Grace and Holy Trinity Cathedral. He may have lacked the Old Man's genius, but his heart was in the right place. When all is said and done, Mr. Kirkwood treated the staff more than fairly. How many other newspaper proprietors would have paid for my trip abroad after Isabel died? The employee stock-ownership plan was his creation, and he left the *Star* in a stronger financial position than it had been in for many years. It's thanks to him that Katharine and I are our own masters now—or will be as soon as we get the mortgage paid off.

Katharine and I are fortunate in so many ways. We have every reason to feel optimistic about the future. If only the past didn't weigh her down so heavily. Orville will never relent, I fear, and she can never let him go.

Orville

Kate wrote to me any number of times after she moved away. There was no mistaking the handwriting on the envelopes—the script neat and round and carefully formed, just like when she was learning her letters as a little girl. But the Kansas City postmark struck me like a slap in the face. I never could bring myself to open the letters, let alone answer them. Call me hard-hearted or what you will—as far as I'm concerned, Kate as good as died the day she walked out of this house. Carrie spent a couple of weeks in Kansas City that first summer. She keeps up a regular correspondence with Swes, as do Griff, Anne, and Stef. Between them, they tell me everything I want to know about her married life.

It's not as if I don't miss her, God knows. When Colonel Lindbergh was here and the house was overrun with gawkers and reporters, I'd have given my eyeteeth to have her back. Kate would have sent those hooligans packing in two minutes flat. Under the circumstances, I had no choice but to ask our honored guest to appeal to the trespassers to leave. He did it with good grace, I'll say that for Mr. Lindbergh. And he has always had the common courtesy to acknowledge that he is riding on the Wright brothers' coattails—which is evidently more than can be expected from the Smithsonian outfit. But I suppose the Wright brothers are ancient history now to most people. Watching Mr. Lindbergh fly over the city that day in the *Spirit of St. Louis*, I could hardly believe that twenty-three years had passed since Will and I made our first practice flights over Huffman Prairie.

Colonel Lindbergh was born and bred to take center stage. The public can't get its fill of him, and neither can the reporters. Well, he can have his "Lindbergh-mania," and much good may it do him. Will and I tired of "Wright-mania" fast enough, I reckon. Those interminable ticker-tape parades, luncheons, dinners, speeches, ceremonies—they were just a sideshow, an annoying distraction. Our work was the main thing. We never went in for self-advertising. We never sought fame or wealth. All we ever wanted was our just deserts. I ask you, is it right that the whole country was going gaga over Lindbergh at the very moment I was packing up the original Wright flyer to be shipped to England? Is it right that I should still be fighting for Will's and my work to be recognized, while those who profited from it are showered with accolades?

Katharine

Poor Orv! No matter how hard he tries, he can't seem to stay out of the headlines. Harry and I had to laugh when we read about the dedication of Wright Field a year or so ago. Bubbo looked fit to be tied in the newspaper photos, as if he were performing an unpleasant duty—which was undoubtedly true! The US Army has finally done the boys proud, and I for one am grateful for it. But goodness me, how Orv does hate making a spectacle of himself! It must have been like pulling teeth for him to watch President Coolidge present the Hubbard Medal to Colonel Lindbergh. I can just see him on that stage at the Washington Auditorium, sitting as quiet as a church mouse and hoping no one would notice him for all the other dignitaries.

Harry and I celebrated our first wedding anniversary in November of 1927—a milestone! I remember thinking that it had been a happy year on the whole, but all the time I'd had a cloud over me. Harry still doesn't know, I hope, how much I worry over Orv. It does no good, but I can't forget him and I don't *want* to forget him. Dear Little Brother! There is no use to write to him. He returned my last letter unopened. It was a long time before I could tell Harry about it, and I have told no one else but Griff. It is so incredible. To think that we used to shun reporters like the plague, and now I depend on them for news of my own brother!

Lulu is the only member of the family we see on a more or less regular basis out here. Poor Lou—she has been almost a vagabond since Reuch died and hardly calls Kansas City home any longer, I believe. She is unsettled and doesn't know just what to do with herself. We still get together for Christmas with her and her children and their families. There are several small children in the outfit, and we all enjoy their enthusiasm over the Christmas tree. When I was a girl, I resented Lou for taking Reuch away from home—but she was lovely to me when I told her about Harry's proposal of marriage. I know she would have been pleased to accompany Ivonette at the wedding, if I had asked her to. Lou is a real musician. I used to keep the Steinway piano in the living room tuned for her—she plays such fine music always and makes no virtue of it at all!

Kansas City would feel much more like home if only Reuch were still here to keep me company. Harry includes me in everything, of course, but the newspaper is a man's world, and I don't have much to contribute to it anyway—though he does try to share it with me and always asks my opinion on whatever topic he happens to be writing about. But I do so miss my family and friends—women friends especially. I like women awfully well, in spite of some of our shortcomings! If circumstances were different, I wouldn't think twice about taking part in an interesting, worthwhile organization like the Association of University Women—only I fear it would be like rubbing salt in the wound for Orv to see my name in print.

For all my disappointments, I find life here interesting, and all the *Star* connections are likewise. Harry is pure gold. I never saw such unselfishness and consideration for other people, and he is always cheerful and good-natured. I was afraid I would find it quiet and dull out here after all the excitement we have had in our family for years. Not a bit of it! What with our trying to own the *Star* on a shoestring and the owner of the rival newspaper suing to upset the sale, it hasn't been boring for a minute. After what I went through with Pop and the boys, it feels like second nature to be caught up in another lawsuit—and we are having a picnic seeing how much money we can save, to put into the *Star*. It is a wonderful thing for Harry. In just a year or two, he will be independent—unless the *Star* loses the lawsuit or business blows up entirely.

I always seem to be in the thick of something, and I don't really mind if life is unpredictable. I would find it awfully dull if everything ran along in a groove. Harry and pretty much everybody else think I am happy in Kansas City—and I am happy—I am—I *am*! And yet—part of me will always be back home in Dayton, wishing I never had left and searching in vain for Little Brother. That sadness casts a shadow over me every waking hour, whatever I do and wherever I go. It just goes to show that you can never step into another person's shoes. It's as Jessie Rittenhouse says in my favorite poem:

> I looked through others' windows
> On an enchanted earth,
> But out of my own window—
> Solitude and dearth.
>
> And yet there is a mystery
> I cannot understand—
> That others through my window
> See an enchanted land.

Orville

A year or so ago, Anne McCormick came marching into the house to have it out with me. She wanted to discuss Kate and thought she knew me well enough to talk me around to her point of view. Nothing doing. I told her the same thing I told Harry when he informed me of their engagement: it was on account of Kate that I refrained from getting married thirty years ago. If she had not made it as plain as day that she didn't want Ullam and me to run off and leave her, and insisted on staying home and looking after us, I would have gone out with the girls like any other fellow my age. Anne just laughed and said that was about as flimsy an excuse as she had ever heard. She said I was simply making myself unhappy and hurting Katharine without any real reason. Hurting Katharine, for pity's sake! As if I was the one who skipped out on her and not the other way around.

I am well aware of how the situation *looks* to other people, most particularly members of my own family. What not a single one of them seems to understand, or even care to understand, is how it *feels* to me—how Kate's betrayal gnaws away at me day after day, how it turns my heart to stone and makes me never want to trust a living soul again. Swes wasn't just my sister, she was my friend, my partner, my protector, my better half. Only Kate knew everything I had been through—the accident, Will's death, the patent suits, the sciatica, the battle with the Smithsonian, the relentless pressure to write the book and prove what never should have needed to be proved. Only Kate understood how much it has cost me all these years to stay the course and stand on principle. Now it seems principles are all I have left to stand on.

A few weeks after my set-to with Anne, Miss Beck and I finally got the flyer packed up and shipped it off to London. It took the two of us working together the greater part of a year to make it ready to be displayed in public. Griff sent newspaper clippings about the opening of the new exhibition galleries in South Kensington last spring, with King George and Queen Mary and the cream of the British aviation world in attendance. From all reports it was an impressive show, but I have no regrets about staying home. In fact, now that machine is finally off my hands, I feel like a man who has been released from prison after serving a long sentence at hard labor. I have even dismantled the laboratory so I can no longer put in time playing there. Who knows, I may yet get down to writing the history of the development of the aeroplane. If I have to do it without Katharine's help, so be it. The Wright flyer may be a museum piece, but Orville Wright is not ready to put himself on the shelf—oh no, not quite!

Katharine

Anne McCormick came straight to us from speaking with Orv. To hear her tell it, she did her level best to talk sense into him, but it was no use. His defenses flew up at the first sign of trouble ahead and she didn't get anywhere at all. Ordinarily, Little Brother is the most reasonable of men—except when he decides to be *unreasonable*. There isn't a blessed thing that anyone can do when he once makes up his mind on a course of action—or inaction either. I've battered my head against *that* particular wall so long that it's more or less permanently black and blue! I saw no point in pursuing the topic any further, so instead Anne and I got to work rearranging the furniture in our living room. Shifting tables and chairs around is a whole lot easier than getting Bubbo to budge.

Griff sent us photos of the flying machine hanging in its new home in the Science Museum, looking as good as new—*and* correctly labeled at long last! It almost hurts me to admit it, but maybe it's for the best the flyer left the country after all. The fight with the Smithsonian has been a wearing, wearying, heartbreaking thing to go through for all these years, and I am glad for Orv's sake that the ordeal is over. As a matter of fact, I have quit worrying about the Smithsonian. I don't imagine they will correct their past misconduct, but if their attitude changes and the machine *can* come back home, all right. The main reason I want it back is because I think it made Orv feel very depressed to send it away. Several friends who visited him about the time it was ready to go said that he was depressed—noticeably so.

I could have put the whole wretched business out of my mind long ago without batting an eye if it hadn't been for Mr. McMahon pestering me about the series of articles he's been writing on the boys for *Popular Science Monthly.* Orv won't like that one bit. He always complained that McMahon's approach was too personal and chatty—he said so in as many words, in fact, the first time we rejected his book many years ago. But Mr. McMahon seems incapable of taking no for an answer, and I was too much of a lady—or maybe too much of a coward—to turn him away. Anyhow, he spent a couple of weeks at our house in Kansas City gathering material for his new manuscript. He was evidently under the impression that I could—or ever would—persuade Little Brother to change his mind. Ha!

They do say that no man is a prophet in his own land—for sure that applies to Orv. When I read in the paper about Emil Ludwig, the German historian, naming him as one of the four greatest living Americans—in the company of Thomas Edison, Jane Addams, and John D. Rockefeller, no less—I couldn't keep from smiling, for all my pride. It wasn't Ludwig's recognition of Orv's accomplishment that tickled me so much as the words he chose to describe him: "The sublime quality in Wright is, after all, not lightning flash of genius; it is the immensity of perseverance, the sure faith in reaching the sought-for goal, and the courage to rise again and again." Bubbo's "immensity of perseverance"—ah yes, no one knows more about *that* than I do!

Orville

I might have foreseen that dispatching the flyer to England would solve none of my problems. Not only did it fail to put a damper on my dispute with the Smithsonian, it dragged the controversy right back out into the open. The papers retailed that stale old story for weeks, as if it were breaking news. First the secretary of the Smithsonian would put out an official statement, then the reporters would come around badgering me for a comment, which brought forth another statement from the Smithsonian, to which I felt obliged to respond. On and on it went, like an infernal merry-go-round that left us right back where we were when it all began.

I bear Dr. Abbot no ill will. He seems a thoroughly decent and fair-minded man, and naturally he bears no responsibility for the actions of his late, unlamented predecessor. Indeed, no sooner had Dr. Walcott died than Dr. Abbot let it be known that the Smithsonian was desirous of mending fences and bringing the flyer back to the United States as soon as possible. The resolution the Board of Regents adopted at his behest all but conceded that Will and I had been in the right from the very beginning. I had an amicable conversation with Dr. Abbot at the Carleton Hotel in Washington. He told me that the whole country was with me in the dispute, offered to change the label on the Langley machine, and agreed to sign any statement so long as it did not vilify the Smithsonian Institution.

While I am, of course, gratified that Dr. Abbot and his colleagues are prepared to let bygones be bygones, as far as I'm concerned it's a case of too little, too late. Unfortunately, the Regents' resolution did not touch upon a single point that has been at issue during the controversy and did not clear up any of the discussion as it has been waged through the years. The statement showed that there had been no change in the attitudes and methods consistently adopted by the Smithsonian ever since the Hammondsport trials in 1914. It was merely another clever use of words. It certainly did not correct the false propaganda that has been put forth in an attempt to take credit for what Will and I did and give it to Langley.

In my view, the misstatements that have been repeatedly promulgated in the Smithsonian's various publications are a much more serious matter than the wording of the label on the Langley machine. As I told Dr. Abbot, if one wishes to continue to believe that Langley's aerodrome was "capable" of flight in 1903, in spite of all evidence to the contrary, he has the privilege of doing so. But no one has a right to lead others to this belief through false and misleading statements, and through the suppression of important evidence. When last we spoke, I expressed regret that

the Smithsonian had not seen fit to make a full and unbiased statement of the controversy, and we left it at that.

We are thus no further along than we were four or five years
ago, when Kate was busy rallying the troops and Dr. Walcott's
minions were digging into the trenches in preparation for a long
siege. I don't know but that the only way of settling the issue is
through a congressional or some other impartial investigation.
But somebody else will have to lead the charge now that Swes has
taken herself out of action. I have neither the strength nor the will
to soldier on alone.

Harry

I gather Orville said about the same thing to Anne McCormick
that he did to me. There was nothing definite, but his feeling that
Katharine wanted to keep house for her brothers and did not want
them to marry deterred him from "going out with the girls" and so
prevented his forming any attachment that might have led to marriage. The fact is, I suppose, that his concentration on his work prevented any social activities on his part, and Katharine was making
them so comfortable that he was not driven out to find somebody
to make him a home. I suspect the idea that there was an implied
obligation on her part not to leave him because he did not set up
a home of his own has become an obsession with him. But I am
convinced not merely by Katharine's recollection but also by the
recollection of other members of her family that he is wrong.

On the other hand, Orville had every reason to reject
Dr. Abbot's overtures out of hand, well intentioned though they
undoubtedly were. I said so in an editorial I wrote at the time.

The Smithsonian's attitude is all too typical. It has long been fashionable in scientific circles to sneer at the Wright brothers as "two clever mechanics," the "bicycle repair men" who used the work of real scientists to construct a plane. The great difficulty seems to lie in the prejudice and class feeling of the professional scientific bunch. I fear they regard the Wrights as outsiders who had no business to invent the airplane and so *didn't* invent it. Where that feeling exists, evidence to the contrary is almost futile.

The facts are that the scientists working in aviation at the end of the last century were all in a blind alley. The Wrights had to sweep aside most of their work and start anew to solve the problems of flight. Not until Dr. Abbot is prepared to make a frank confession of the misleading reports put out by his predecessor will Orville consent to bringing the Kitty Hawk plane back from England. It seems little enough to ask, but clearly the Smithsonian considers the stakes unacceptably high.

I can't help feeling that there is a lesson in all this for Orville, if only he could see it. What miracle will it take for him to own up to his own mistakes and allow Katharine back into his life?

Katharine

Why should it be that I am so incurably interested in other people's weddings? I 'spect it's because my own wedding was such a letdown—not the ceremony itself, of course, that was perfectly lovely, but all the dear little things that *should* have led up to it. I spent months dreaming about being married and making plans—the way all women do, I imagine, regardless of their age or particular circumstances. There were guest lists to be drawn up, announcements and invitations to be engraved, gowns to be ordered, music and flowers and food to be arranged—and in the end everything fell by the wayside in our mad rush to get the ceremony over and done with. Harry didn't mind so much—or if he did, he didn't show it—but it was different for me, especially since I'd been waiting thirty years for the right man to pop the question!

I'd have given a good deal to be at my nephew Bus's wedding in Dayton last June. I was interested enough to go, for sure, but it wasn't possible, not with things as they are between Little Brother and me. So I stayed home and tried to picture Bus and Sue and the rest of the family, and how pretty the little church must have looked decorated with all those pink climbing roses. We heard from various sources about how Orv helped the newlyweds escape from the reception at her parents' house. A natural-born conspirator he is! Life is all a game to Little Brother. Some way he reminds me of Peter Pan, the boy who never grew up. No wonder he stayed a bachelor—he wasn't cut out to be a husband, and that's a fact. Even Griff says it was probably a good thing that Orv was stopped from marrying thirty years ago—Harry and I roared over that!

The plain truth is that Orv was free to marry any time he pleased. No one was standing in his way—certainly not sister Kate! He would have had his pick of the young ladies too. My friend Agnes was "Orv's girl" when we were young—at least we were all convinced *he* was sweet on *her*, even if she didn't necessarily return the favor. No doubt plenty of others were in the running, including a few I may never have known about. Why, there even was a rumor that he was once engaged to Mrs. Barney! Not much likelihood of that, I should say. According to Carrie, when that French "vidder" came to Hawthorn Hill last summer, prospecting for a husband, he and Miss Beck sent her packing as quick as a wink!

One way and another, I seem to be living in Dayton a good deal of the time these days. Here's a fine howdy-do! Before I was married, I could hardly wait to move to Kansas City and set up house with Harry. I actually used to worry over whether we could live through the happiness of being together! I imagined we would laugh a good deal and have long, serious talks and try to get the universe settled as it should be. And then we'd wind up not caring about anything but just each other, and we'd talk and talk endlessly about the dear little things that we both love to talk about. We'd mix in a lot of things that young people don't have and don't know about and can't appreciate as we can. The last of life *is* the best, I believe.

It all seemed like another dream waiting to come true, and now that it *has* come true, what do I do but fritter away my time worrying about Orv and wishing I could be with *him*—and be something to him—back at Hawthorn Hill. That never can be, of course, but home is such an ideal place when you are far from it—as I know from experience.

Orville

"The drapes of secrecy do not fit the captains and benefactors of mankind." So says the latest issue of *Popular Science Monthly*. "The Real Fathers of Flight" indeed! I ask you, who is Mr. John R. McMahon to decide what the public needs to know about our family's affairs? My private life is nobody's business but my own. To think that Kate and I actually welcomed that man under our roof, gave him the run of the house for two weeks, shared family intimacies and personal documents with him—and now, years later, over my protests, he abuses the privilege we extended to him by publishing trivial tittle-tattle. I scarcely know which is more despicable: the Smithsonian's lies and deceptions or these flagrant invasions of my privacy.

I sometimes wonder if Anne McCormick has any more scruples than the rest of that lot. The nerve of her, barging in here and lecturing me on my duty toward my own sister. I'll have to watch my tongue around her or she'll be spreading rumors too. Next thing you know the reporters will be fabricating stories about why Will and I never married. I can see the headlines now: "Extra! Extra! Inventors of Aeroplane Had Secret Love Lives! Our Special Correspondent Reveals the Human Heart That Beats Behind Mr. Orville Wright's Unruffled Exterior!" I wouldn't put it past the newspapers to concoct a fairy tale about a childhood sweetheart, or even about "goings on" between me and Miss Beck.

I hate to punch a hole in their balloon, but the real Orville Wright cuts a less romantic figure. The occasional family wedding is as close to the altar as I am likely to get. But just ask Bus and Sue what their Uncle Orv is made of. Organizing their getaway was one of my finest hours, if I say so myself. To begin with, I parked my Franklin alongside a vacant lot behind the bride's home. Then I left the wedding reception early and drove away with a posse of young scalawags from the party hot on my tail. I cut across a field to shake them off, the newlyweds following hard on my heels. When we reached Hawthorn Hill, Bus and Sue scampered through the hall to the back entrance and down the hill to catch a streetcar on Harmon Avenue. I waited until they had made their escape, then lit all the lights in the house and invited everyone in. That beats racing along Far Hills Avenue at forty miles an hour any day!

On the other hand, my latest brush with matrimony was no laughing matter. Last summer Carlotta Bollée and her daughter did me the "honor" of paying me a visit. I could hardly turn them away, seeing as how the late Mr. Bollée was so helpful to Will in France before the war. But I did take the precaution of asking my sister-in-law to stay in the house as a chaperone. Soon enough, Madame Bollée started making insinuations, which I managed to ignore. But when she let out that she looked forward to seeing Niagara Falls—presumably in the company of you know who—before returning to Europe, I realized I had better act quickly. I told her that train reservations to Niagara were hard to come by, but I would see what I could do. Then I had Miss Beck telephone the ticket office and book the Bollées berths on a train departing that very afternoon. After shooing them out of the house, I took off like a shot for Lambert Island—alone.

Katharine

It's good to know that Orv's friends are keeping up with him. I am always so glad to hear that Griff is coming to Dayton or to the bay—and yet sad too, because I know that my share in the enjoyment of his visits is past. Orv is at his best on the island, and Griff has been coming up so long that he feels completely at ease. If only they could find a way to spend more time there together. Still, Bob Hadeler must be a good companion for Little Brother. He was always such a nice boy and has had a very good upbringing. I imagine he sleeps in my old room in the big cabin. I wonder if old

Mr. France, George's father, is still living. And are the Williamses and McKenzies on their island, and does Orv still get milk down across from Tomahawk, at the Indian's? And is there still such a mess of children there? They were interesting and well behaved.

When I opened Griff's package last fall and saw his photograph, I nearly wept for joy. I always did want him to have a portrait taken, and I am as pleased as I could be to have one here in Kansas City to remind me of him. It is good of Griff not to drop me now that I am not in Dayton. I care so much to keep up every connection with our old friends—especially the ones who were associated with Will as well as Orv. And Griff is the most special of all. I can never think of him without thinking of the boys.

Some way I seem to need friends more than ever these days—even Stef, dear, disappointing, exasperating Stef. How queer it is, to be sure: I once had a feeling deep down in my heart that I would never see Stef again, that despite our special friendship we were too different to understand each other and were bound to go our separate ways sooner or later. There were long stretches when I didn't hear from him at all, and the few letters I got were not very informative. But he too has stayed in touch after his fashion and writes or cables us every time he happens to be passing through Kansas City. I expect he does the same with Orv. What a trump Stef is, for all his flaws!

It was only a few weeks ago that Stef paid us one of his flying visits. He phoned from the station and came out to the house for a few hours. Poor man—I'm afraid we rather overwhelmed him with stories of our newfound wealth and happiness. It really has been the most extraordinary experience. Mr. Seested, the *Star*'s top executive, died in October, and as a consequence Harry was named editor as well as first vice president of the company. He even had another increase in salary—his second in a little over a year. We still owe a quite respectable amount of money to the bank for the staff's purchase of the paper, but the stock is such a wonderful investment. The share value seems to grow and grow like a beanstalk. So we are getting rich quite unexpectedly—but, as Harry says, it keeps us poor while we are getting rich!

We always used to say that when we "got the *Star* bought" we would go on a trip to Europe, but I never dreamed that day would arrive as soon as this. Harry has fixed things so he can be away from the office for six whole weeks. It will be simply heavenly. We'll troop around everywhere hand in hand and have the gayest time. How unspeakably romantic it feels to be going on our *second* honeymoon—and the first one only two years behind us!

Orville

Talk about shades from the past—who should turn up the other day but Frank Lahm. He had just come over from Paris and was on his way to Texas to visit his son and daughter-in-law. It's always a pleasure to see Mr. Lahm. He was a good friend to us back when Will and I were dickering with the French over the flyer. He asked me to write the foreword to a book on aviation that he hopes to publish with one of the New York houses. I owe it to him, I reckon, though I don't relish the thought of writing such a piece without Kate to back me up. She always was fond of old Mr. Lahm. And young Lieutenant Lahm clearly carried a torch for her when I was in the hospital after my accident. In fact, it wouldn't surprise me a bit to learn that he made Swes a proposal of marriage. It must have been a temptation to them both—but she was still on my side in those days.

Hawthorn Hill isn't the crossroads it used to be when Kate was the lady of the house. Still, I get a respectable tally of visitors for an old retired man. A bunch of them turned up last month for the twenty-fifth anniversary of the first flight, including a number of delegates to the big Civil Aeronautics Conference in Washington who stopped off in Dayton to pay their respects. There were the usual banquets and ceremonies and hot-air speeches about Will and me belonging "to the immortals of all history"—as if we were *both* dead and gone to our rewards. The president said nice things about us at the opening of the conference, and afterward Congress finally got around to awarding Will and me the Distinguished Flying Cross. The Post Office Department even brought out a new two-cent stamp commemorating our flight at Kitty Hawk. That beats all!

On the seventeenth of December last, a group of us took the steamer from Washington to Norfolk, and from there we traveled overland to North Carolina for the laying of the cornerstone of the Wright brothers monument. Below Kill Devil Hills, near the spot where we got the flyer up into the air, there is a plaque stating that Will and I made "the first successful flight of an airplane." Short, sweet, and factual. I hadn't been back to Kitty Hawk since the year before Will died and was interested to observe how little the place has changed. There are the same scrub trees, the same wood-frame cabins, the same seamless expanse of sand, water, and sky stretching as far as the eye can see. The dunes have shifted about a good deal, but I reckon we were standing close to where Will and I pitched our camp that first summer. About the only things lacking to complete the picture were the wild pigs and marsh mosquitoes!

Meanwhile, over in merrie olde England, Griff was standing beneath the 1903 flyer at the Science Museum in London, addressing a meeting of the Royal Aeronautical Society. By all accounts, he gave an admirably full and succinct summary of our work. Dr. Abbot and his associates at the Smithsonian could learn a thing or two from it, if they took the trouble to read the press reports. In fact, so many articles on the first flight have come out in the past few weeks that a person would have to go out of his way to avoid them. The McCormicks came to the house for dinner over the holidays, and I showed Anne the big spread on the anniversary in *Airway Age*. She paused when she came to the picture of Kate, as if she expected me to say something. But I held my tongue. Swes walked out of my life two years ago, and it will take more than an old photograph in a magazine to bring her back.

Katharine

I have had my share of ups and downs these past few weeks, sure enough—the ride has been almost as bumpy as my maiden flight in an airplane! First thing after Thanksgiving I came down with the flu and kept to my bed for ten days with a blazing fever. By the time the big celebration for the boys rolled around on Wright Brothers Day, I was pretty much right as rain. Even so, I stayed away from the anniversary dinner in Kansas City for fear it would annoy Orv if anything was said about me—especially after one of the Cleveland newspapers dug up that old wives' tale about me chipping in my own money to help Will and Orv. "Without Kitty

Wright there might have been no Kitty Hawk"—what bosh and nonsense! I have written to the Associated Press to request that their members remove that old, worn-out *Hampton's Magazine* story from their morgues. It must be on its last legs by now, but it positively refuses to lie down and die!

I *did* write a letter to Mr. Kent Cooper of the AP—my recollection is quite clear on that point. But did I ever put it in the letter box? I s'pose it's just conceivable that it *might* have slipped my mind. My memory is getting to be awfully wobbly. I certainly mixed things up royally on Christmas morning. After we got through opening presents, I found that table runner, unaccountably, with no card near it. The only reason I am sure it came from Dayton is that it was in a Rike-Kumler Department Store box. For the life of me I still don't know *who* sent it to me. And for the longest time I couldn't think what my friend Irene had given me—though I opened the package myself and later *wore the apron*! Then all of a sudden when I went to get another apron to get dinner, on Ollie's night out, it came over me in a flash—the nice apron Irene made for me. Can you beat that? My only excuse is that I was terribly tired, and I'm always a perfect dunce when I get really exhausted.

It didn't do much to improve my performance to know that Harry wasn't feeling any too zippy himself. Fortunately, he is not as slow off the mark as Orv and I are when it comes to taking medical advice. When Dr. Bohan examined him and identified a kidney stone as the cause of his discomfort, he phoned the Mayo Clinic straight away and made an appointment to have it out at the end of January. Everyone in Minnesota was very nice to us, just as they were the time Orv was treated there for his sciatica.

The Mayos—Dr. Will and Dr. Charlie—stopped in to see Harry on their rounds every morning, and he got a lot of information from them on the early days of the clinic. I'll bet my last cent that sooner or later he'll turn it into an article or editorial. Newspapermen are almost as bad as scientists—never off the job for a minute!

It felt strange for me to be nursing Harry, instead of the other way around—but the tables were turned right back again soon enough. It's just my luck. I hadn't quite gotten over the flu that laid me low before Christmas, and the weather in Minnesota was bitter cold—anywhere from about ten to twenty-eight degrees below zero. Anyhow, the day after Harry left the hospital, I came down with a terrific cold—I was practically an invalid the whole time he was recuperating from his surgery at the hotel—and it has only gotten worse since we came home. Poor Charlie Taylor! He has never been one of my personal favorites, though Will and Orv were devoted to him, but we were pretty poor company the day he stopped off here on his way west. Anybody could see how he was dying to talk about the old days and working with the boys on the flyer—and there we sat, Harry and I, like a pair of thick-witted bumps on a log.

All I could think of the whole time Mr. Taylor was here was how we had to save up our strength for our big trip. I've been busy as anything—trying to get my clothes ready, my teeth fixed up, my passport photo taken, and any number of odds and ends that have been neglected. It has only been in the last two or three days that I could get out at all. There is so much to do—and less than two weeks left! Harry has taken care of all the arrangements. We sail from New York to Naples and plan to go straight on to Athens, if he feels equal to it. The Lords are living there this year—Louis is the annual professor at the School for Classical Studies—and this is the year of all years for us to see Athens. I 'spect we'll spend most of our time in Italy, though, and maybe come home by the North Atlantic, stopping in London to see Griff. Harry is so delighted over going to Italy. He says it takes the curse off his operation!

We'll visit Rome, of course—I wouldn't miss that for anything. I wonder if the Hotel Russie is still open for business. The boys and I stayed there in 1909. It backed up against the slope of the Pincian Hill and had a lovely garden with a fountain, where meals were served in mild weather. I fell for Italian cooking almost as hard as I fell for the fountains. Maybe we'll stop in France too, or maybe not—we don't know exactly. We'll see how strong Harry is. I used to dream that Orv, Harry, and I could get up a little party and take a cruise to that part of the world. I am bound and determined to see the South of France again before I die. It's my special place—my Carcassonne, you could say. *Tout le monde a son Carcassonne*—"Every man has his Carcassonne"—and every woman too!

> "My friend, come, go with me,
> Tomorrow then thine eyes shall see
> Those streets that seem so fair."

How sad it is to think that the peasant in the poem didn't get his wish—

> That night the church bell's solemn toll
> Echoed above his passing soul.
> He never saw fair Carcassonne.

But I will—*I will see Carcassonne!* Can it be that my wish is actually coming true, after all these years? How delightful it will be to go back to the dear old places with Harry by my side—to bury myself in his arms, without a care in the world, and sightsee to our hearts' content. My head spins like a top to think of it! It's like another dream—a tale of star-crossed lovers, only *this* time with a happy ending. We'll spoon and coo like a pair of lovebirds, the way we used to do in the "blue room" at Hawthorn Hill. We were bold and shameless, mister, I must say—with Little Brother asleep right down the hallway!

Harry, dearest, do you remember that magical Illumination Night at Oberlin? The campus was all aglow with Japanese lanterns, you were coming on to me, and I was growing sillier by the minute. An enchanted evening! It was all so unreal, almost as if we were suspended in time. One more breath and we would be sitting across from each other at dinner in Mrs. Morrison's boardinghouse—or walking back from chapel together the day I received the prize for my essay on the Monroe Doctrine. I do believe I would have agreed to marry you right then and there if you had asked me, Mr. Haskell! But I'm not sorry about the past. We could have been a good deal to each other, but we have each other now and that is so exquisite—and we have so much more to give each other than we would have had all those years ago. No, my own darling, we won't spend any vain regrets over those thirty-four years. We'll just make the most of the time that is left for us to be together.

Time—bless my soul, how it does fly! May I tell you a little secret, Harry dear, a very *secret* secret, something I have never told *anyone* before? Every now and again I feel as if I have slipped these mortal coils and am riding alone in my own personal flying machine. Up and up and up I climb, higher and higher and higher, until my head is poking above the clouds and I catch a little glimpse of heaven. If only my friends back home could see me now—little Katie Wright from Dayton, Ohio, doing the bird act! And who is that, way down below on the ground? Why, it's Orv, propped up on his crutches and gazing up at me with love in his eyes. If I bend down, I can practically touch him—but no, now he's gone, vanished behind a cloud. Where are you, my darling Little Brother? And Will? I hear your voice calling to me—"Swes! Swes!"—but you are nowhere to be seen. Won't you come back, come back to your Sterchens?

Ah, Lorin, here *you* are, at least. What a good brother you have been—sweet and thoughtful and true! Yes, it's Phiz, standing before my very eyes, large as life. Now, where can Orv be? Lost and gone forever, I fear. But wait! Someone is leaning over me, someone is whispering in my ear—whispering Orv's name—his blessed, blessed name. Here he is!—Little Brother, right by my side, smiling that sweet, crinkly smile of his. Of course I know him—how could I not? Or is this just another fairy tale, a dear, insubstantial fancy? Come to me, Orv! Come to me, Harry! My darling boys, come to me and let me release you. I can never have you both, I see that now—I can never go home again—but I can still dream. Yes, I still have my dreams! Truly, *tout le monde a son Carcassonne!*

Epilogue

Orville

First Will, then Reuch, and now Swes. Three of us gone before their times, and two left to tell the tale. Would I have done what I did if I had known Kate was going to die so soon? I guess I'll never know. In hindsight, that letter from Harry's sister should have tipped me off. He had written to her before Christmas to say that Swes was in bed with the flu and a 103-degree temperature. Mary Haskell was quite upset, understandably, but there was more behind her letter than that. I have a notion that Kate's illness gave her an excuse to ask me for something. She seemed to want me to grant Harry a kind of absolution. Here, let me read the letter and you can judge for yourself:

"I may be all wrong," Mary writes, "but I kept on wondering— You see when I have written to ask Harry whether he was forgiven for taking away Katharine, he did not answer, and I did not repeat the question, only wondered. When Harry called me to Kansas City in '26 to tell me of this prospect, I thought I had never seen him so happy—the only sorrow being that his gain was your loss.

211

But he said, 'Katharine will just have to commute between Dayton and Kansas City.' He also remarked, 'Of course, Katharine's being sorry for me has much to do with her marrying me.'

"Before our Mother died we spoke together of the possibility of that marriage and Mother said, 'She will never leave her brother!' But you see it is true that Harry was more alone than almost any man, because all the rest of the family were missionaries and our interests became so far apart—and our sympathies. Perhaps dear Katharine reasoned it out that if she married Harry she could spend lots of time in Dayton and so make you both happy, but of course if she were not married, she couldn't go freely to Kansas City and so couldn't help Harry much.

"Is not love blind sometimes in its reasoning? I felt dreadfully about the dilemma myself, but then I concluded that Harry too is a human being, and if God had pity on him in giving Katharine this love to him, would not the great Father in some way make up the loss to her brother—even tho it be to show him the difference between the finite and the infinite?"

Mary meant well, I expect, but she jumped to the wrong conclusion. She assumed my quarrel was with her brother and not with Kate. Harry is a good man, an honorable man. Anyone could see how broken up he was when his first wife passed away. God knows he is entitled to all the happiness he can find in this vale of tears. But I know of no law of man or nature that says his loneliness as a widower should rightfully take precedence over mine as a brother. Family comes first with the Wrights. That is why I never married. That is why I can never forgive Kate for leaving me. And that is why I had no choice but to shut the door behind her and get on with my own life.

Mary's letter was an omen. No sooner had I gotten back from Washington at the end of February than Lorin came over with the news that Swes had contracted pneumonia and her life was in danger. I knew then and there that I would have to swallow my pride and go to Kansas City. In fact, I went out and bought my train ticket that very day. Lorin pressed me to come with him immediately on the overnight train, but I froze up. I couldn't seem to make myself do what I knew had to be done sooner or later. Finally Lorin said nobody in the family would ever speak to me again if I didn't go to Kate's bedside, the way she came to mine after the accident at Fort Myer. That was no idle threat, you can be sure. I packed my bag and wired Harry to expect me the next afternoon.

By the time I arrived at the house, the death watch had already begun. There was nothing the doctor could do except keep Kate sedated and comfortable. And there was nothing any of the rest of us could do—Lorin and I, Harry and his boy—except gather around her bed and wait quietly for the end. Swes woke up for a moment or two before she died and recognized me, or so Harry said. Perhaps he was just being kind—that would be like him. Only then did it hit me that Kate and I never said good-bye.

Harry

We returned on February 13 from my operation at the Mayo Clinic and were planning a trip abroad for my recuperation. Katharine had a cold but had recovered and had started out shopping for her clothes. On Thursday, February 21, we engaged passage on the *Roma* sailing the ninth of March. On Friday morning, she had a severe chill without any warning—no cold, no head symptoms, no cough. I had her go to bed at once and sent for a doctor and nurse. Her temperature shot to 104 that day. Dr. Bohan suspected pneumonia, but could detect none of the characteristic symptoms—no coughing, shortness of breath, or pain in the chest.

Monday he was able with the stethoscope to get the localization of pneumonia in the bottom of the right lung. But she began Sunday night having chills, and Dr. Bohan told me he was disturbed because that indicated complications and infection outside the lung. Tuesday she almost collapsed, and we were thoroughly alarmed. After that she was out of her head most of the time and didn't realize how sick she was.

By Friday the pneumonia was clearing up. But the infection had entered the blood stream, and it was a general infection that over-whelmed her. That morning, though still irrational, she asked for Lorin, and I called him immediately on long distance. He arrived Saturday morning. Friday afternoon a telegram from Orville said he would arrive Saturday afternoon. When Lorin came we were able to rouse her for a moment. She smiled and said, "Why, it's Phiz," and then drifted off. When Orville arrived she was still weaker. I asked her if she knew him, and finally she aroused and said, "Of course I do." But that was all. She was unconscious until her death Sunday evening.

Bishop Spencer of Grace and Holy Trinity Cathedral conducted the Episcopalian service at the house on Monday afternoon, and we all left for Dayton that night. I felt that as Katharine had so long been identified with Dayton, she would like to be buried there. The funeral took place at Orville's on Wednesday. President Wilkins of Oberlin and Professor Stetson were there, as were various members of the Wright family, several of Katharine's old college friends, and the McCormicks. So she finally was reunited with her loved ones. The homecoming came too late, but Katharine would have enjoyed it, I feel.

Orville was cordial and sympathetic toward me and invited me to visit him. Before I left Dayton, he told me that Katharine had died for him three years earlier and that he had gone to Kansas City on my account, not hers. But I think he deceived himself. Obviously, he did not go on my account. He went because he could not bear not to—and his action is more significant than his own explanation of it. As I see it, in going to Kansas City he finally admitted defeat in one of the important attitudes of his life. His attitude had changed; he had been obliged under the tragic event to abandon his fixed position. So while he insists that he was not defeated, the facts are against him.

It is still hard to realize what has happened. But in accepting life we accept its dangers, and the only thing to do is to go on and do the best we can. I believe Katharine had two interesting and happy years in Kansas City. They were wonderful years for me. We had the same interests and tastes, and our home life was perfect. She was the most vital, radiant spirit I ever knew. Now she rests where she belongs, beside her father and mother and brother in the city she left under such unhappy circumstances. "Home is the sailor, home from the sea, and the hunter home from the hill."

Orville

In the end Sterchens did come home, though not in the way either of us would have wished. Harry and I escorted her body from Kansas City on the train, and she was buried the next day on top of the hill in Woodland Cemetery, between Will and the plot I've set aside for myself. Phil Porter, the rector of Christ Episcopal Church, conducted the service. The house was filled with floral tributes—that would have pleased Kate, with her love of flowers—and aeroplanes from Wright Field strewed roses over her grave as Reverend Porter read the last rites.

So many letters of condolence arrived over the next few weeks that I despaired of responding to each of them personally. It was easier to recite the conventional formula than to find words of my own: "Mr. Orville Wright acknowledges with grateful appreciation your kind expression of sympathy." Until then, I don't think I fully realized how many friends Kate had all over the world. Old Colonel Lahm wrote from Paris that he "never heard any woman more generally spoken well of, by those who knew her." The Oberlin trustees issued a citation praising her as "intelligent, devoted, unselfish, courageous, inspiring." The Kate I knew and loved was all of those things, and more. Griff was his usual tactful self. "Don't worry to write," he said. "I understand." Does he really understand, I wonder? For that matter, do I?

Harry passed through Dayton again on his way home from Europe in June. He and Kate had planned to travel together, but in the event, young Henry took her place. Harry had bounced back from his surgery and seemed in good spirits. He had lunch with Lorin and dinner with me at Hawthorn Hill. I made it clear that he would be welcome here at any time. By a curious coincidence, I ran into Stef a few days later at the St. Louis convention of the Aeronautical Section of the American Society of Mechanical Engineers. We had a good talk, and he seemed relieved to hear that, as far as I was concerned, there had never been any ice between us.

I often think back to the many times Harry and Stef stopped here, before I knew or even suspected anything about my sister's feelings for either of them. Life was a good deal less complicated in those days, or so it looks to me now. Of course, none of us can predict the paths our lives will take. I foolishly imagined that Kate and I were on a safe and steady course; the truth was we were flying straight into the eye of the storm. I have no one but myself to blame. Any man who has piloted an aeroplane as often as I have ought to know that human nature is no less fickle and treacherous than Mother Nature.

My big mistake was to assume that Kate was in control of her actions and emotions. I've always thought I was in control of mine, but now I'm not so sure. I guess Kate had to do what she had to do, the same as I did. Neither of us was wholly the master of his own fate. As a man of science, I have been guided all my life by the laws of physics. The phenomena I deal with in my work are measurable and predictable. In the laboratory I can set the parameters of an experiment and compute the results with a high degree of confidence. But if I have learned one thing over the years, it's that life contains too many variables for us to be absolutely certain about anything. In the last analysis, there is no accounting for the human factor. It is always easier to deal with things than with men, and no one can direct his life entirely as he would choose.

Orville Wright lived quietly in retirement at Hawthorn Hill for nearly two decades after Katharine's death. His housekeeper, Carrie Kayler Grumbach, and his secretary, Mabel Beck, continued to serve him faithfully. Family members say he never spoke of his sister, though he did refer to her on at least one occasion: in a letter written toward the end of his life, he once again denied that she had played any role in the invention of the airplane. Not for many years would the "Wright sister's" crucial contribution to her brothers' work, and to Orville's well-being, come to be widely recognized.

On October 24, 1942, the Smithsonian Institution published a brochure entitled The 1914 Tests of the Langley Aerodrome. *The document amounted to an official retraction of and apology for the Smithsonian's longstanding insistence on the precedence of*

Samuel Langley's ill-fated flying machine. Although he had finally been vindicated, the surviving Wright brother characteristically refused to gloat. In late 1948, eleven months after his death of a heart attack, the original Wright flyer was finally repatriated from London, in accordance with Orville's wishes. Today it occupies a place of honor in the Smithsonian's Air and Space Museum.

Harry Haskell sailed for Europe with his son in April 1929. Two years later, on a trip to Italy with his third wife, he commissioned a copy of a bronze statue by Andrea del Verrocchio for a fountain that he intended to donate to Oberlin College in Katharine Wright Haskell's memory. Depicting an angel boy cavorting with a dolphin, it graces the entrance to what is now the Allen Memorial Art Museum. Every year on Katharine's birthday Harry sent money for flowers to be placed on her grave, and every year on the anniversary of her death he reread her love letters.

In his remaining years, Harry wrote two books on Roman history and won two Pulitzer Prizes for his editorials in the Kansas City Star. *He stayed in touch with Orville and with younger members of the Wright clan, to whom he was fondly known as Uncle Harry. In 1948 the family asked him to write a book based on the brothers' scientific papers, but he reluctantly declined, pleading poor health. "I have a feeling that Katharine would have liked me to do it if I could," he wrote. "She was so proud of Wilbur and Orville and of their great achievements."*

Harry Haskell died in 1952. The Papers of Wilbur and Orville Wright, *a definitive record of the brothers' scientific work, appeared the following year under the editorship of Marvin W. MacFarland. Orville never got around to writing his own book about the invention of the airplane.*

Author's Note

In writing *Maiden Flight*, I wanted to let Katharine, Orville, and Harry tell their stories as far as possible in their own words. (Full disclosure: Henry J. Haskell was my grandfather and died two years before I was born.) No linear historical narrative, it seemed to me, could do justice to the tangled emotions, psychological complexities, and multiple perspectives of such a lovers' triangle. I opted instead for a contrapuntal medley of interlocking memoirs, whose notes and themes are drawn from letters and other contemporary documents. It is my hope that the resulting three-part invention will help others hear the voices of these three extraordinary individuals as vividly as I hear them.*

A few short extracts from the protagonists' many extant letters may serve to convey the distinctive flavor of their speech.

---

* Despite Katharine's and Orville's worldwide renown, no recordings of their voices are known to exist. (It's said that Orville and Wilbur sounded so much alike that people overhearing them in another room had trouble telling them apart.) To the best of my knowledge, Harry's speaking voice is preserved only on a short promotional film made by the *Kansas City Star* in 1929.

Listen, for example, to Katharine responding in 1925 to Harry's unexpected declaration of love in her characteristically breathless, unguarded voice, liberally punctuated with dashes, underlinings, and exclamation points:

> Harry, how can I tell where affection leaves off and love begins? I haven't thought [about] your loving me or my loving you until you overwhelm me. Give me a little chance, <u>please</u>, and let me talk to you. I don't <u>know</u> you, as you are now. I don't see that I could ever leave Orv but let me talk to you. It just <u>breaks my heart</u> to have you send such a telegram. "It's all right. Please don't worry" etc. Of course it <u>isn't</u> all right and, of course, I <u>will</u> worry. So I have sent you an answer and asked you to come—but I don't know myself to <u>what</u> I have asked you to come. Don't come if you will be more upset that way. Please, Harry, don't care so much—and please <u>do</u>! (Katharine Wright to Harry Haskell, June 15, 1925)

Katharine's epistolary style changed remarkably little over the years. Compare this passage from a letter she wrote to Wilbur in December 1908, leaping at his suggestion that she and Orville join him in France:

> I have been thumping off letters for brother [Orville] till I am black and blue in the face. We are hopelessly swamped with correspondence. What do you do with your letters? I am beginning to get interested in getting the letters out of the way 'cause Sister is thinking about hanging onto brother's coat-tails when he starts for "Yurp." In fact I made a visit to the dressmaker's today, prospecting a little. I suppose I shall have to have one good dress but I can't

go your pace on social functions. (Katharine Wright to
Wilbur Wright, December 7, 1908)

Orville, by contrast, expressed himself differently to various
correspondents at different times and under different circumstances. Like many famous people, he presented one persona to
the world and another to those close to him. Here is the folksy,
intimate, and occasionally petulant voice he used in writing to
Katharine (in this case, from Washington in 1908) and other family members:

> I haven't done a lick of work since I have been here. I have
> to give my time to answering the ten thousand fool ques-
> tions people ask about the machine. There are a number
> of people standing about the whole day long. . . . I find
> it more pleasant here at the Club than I expected. The
> trouble here is that you can't find a minute to be alone. . . .
> I have trouble in getting enough sleep. (Orville Wright to
> Katharine Wright, August 27, 1908)

And here is Orville's "public" voice—matter-of-fact, scientifically
precise, a shade impersonal (he's writing to a British friend about
the great Dayton flood of 1913):*

> The water covered over half the city. At our Third Street
> office the water was about ten to twelve feet deep in
> the street, but did not quite reach the second floor. On

---

* As Katharine repeatedly observed, Orville intensely disliked writing of any sort
and did his best to avoid it. In later years, including the period covered by this book,
much of his extensive correspondence was written either by Katharine or by his
longtime secretary, Mabel Beck.

> Hawthorn Street it was about eight or nine feet deep and
> stood six feet on the first floor. Most of the things down-
> stairs were ruined. We saved a few of our books and sev-
> eral small pieces of furniture. We might have saved almost
> everything had we had more notice, but Katharine and I
> overslept that morning and had to be out of the house
> within one half hour of the time we were up. (Orville
> Wright to Griffith Brewer, April 22, 1913)

Unlike Katharine and Orville, Harry was a professional word-
smith. As a newspaper reporter and editorial writer, he was trained
to express himself succinctly and directly. His epistolary voice was
straightforward, unpretentious, and often spiced with colloquial-
isms, as when he wrote to thank Orville after a visit to the Wrights'
summer home in Canada:

> Since I got back from Lambert I have felt my handicap
> in not having Dr. Dick's [a mutual friend in Kansas City]
> gift for description. If I had, Kansas City would know by
> this time that we went out sailing in a launch with an
> aviation motor so powerful that occasionally the boat left
> the water and took to the air, skimming over the tops of
> the islands. Ah, them were the days! I hope your busted
> back isn't going to keep you and Katharine from making
> that Western voyage this fall. (Harry Haskell to Orville
> Wright, September 25, 1925)

And here is Harry the ardent but ever-considerate lover, pouring
out his soul in a telegram to Katharine, who is (as usual) agonizing
over the prospect of leaving Orville:

When I went to D[ayton] last June, do you remember I told you I wanted to help you find out what was in your heart. I haven't changed since and I couldn't possibly ask you to do what you thought you shouldn't. You know that you don't have to decide right away. There is plenty of time to think it over. I know your feeling for Orv, dear. If you finally decide you can't leave him—even for the part of the time I have talked about, it will be all right dear. I'll do my best. I love you, K whatever happens. (Harry Haskell to Katharine Wright, undated telegram)

Allowing Katharine, Orville, and Harry to "speak for themselves," without playing overly fast and loose with the sources, involved setting a few basic ground rules. First: use the characters' own words whenever possible, with only minor adjustments for grammar, clarity, consistency, or flow. Second: never sacrifice factual accuracy for color or dramatic effect. Third: respect chronology. As Katharine's biographer Richard Maurer observes, the day-to-day unfolding of her romance with Harry "is as exquisitely timed as a Samuel Richardson novel."

Throughout this book I have occasionally put Katharine's words into Orville's mouth and vice versa. (They often used the same or similar language to express themselves, and Katharine's letters to Harry quote or paraphrase many conversations with Orville.) I have not hesitated to stitch together passages from letters written at different times or even to different people, provided I could satisfy myself that they were of a piece. In supplying the connective tissue necessary to construct a narrative, I have endeavored to mimic the memoirists' characteristic word choices and turns of phrase—for example, Katharine's fondness for up-to-date expressions like "bunk," "corker," and "nuff said," and Orville's preference for the old-fashioned "aeroplane" rather than "airplane."

Maiden Flight, then, is best described as an exercise in imaginative reconstruction. As such, it straddles the line between traditional historical fiction and the comparatively new genre known as creative nonfiction, which the Library of Congress defines as "works that use literary styles and techniques to present factually accurate narratives in a compelling, vivid manner." For the record, every incident, fact, and emotion that the three protagonists describe is either explicitly documented or can be plausibly inferred from the historical record. Readers who are acquainted with the voluminous literature on the Wright brothers will recognize many of the events and anecdotes related in this book, and at least some of the primary sources upon which I have drawn. In allowing the "Wright sister" to step outside Wilbur and Orville's shadow, I have endeavored to shed new light on the role she played in their private lives, as well as on her often misunderstood contribution to their scientific work. But Katharine's abundant store of "human nature"—her lively and perceptive outlook on life, her great capacity for both love and indignation, her acute and sometimes crippling self-awareness—is worth recording and celebrating in its own right.

Sources and Acknowledgments

Katharine and Harry stayed in touch with each other after graduating from Oberlin in 1898 and 1896, respectively. How often they corresponded in the early years is unclear, in part because his letters to her were destroyed in the 1913 Miami River flood. After Harry's first wife died in September 1923, however, they wrote to each other with increasing frequency and intimacy. Although Harry's side of this later correspondence has unaccountably disappeared, he kept virtually all of Katharine's many letters, spanning the period from early 1924 to a few days before their wedding in November 1926. The Katharine Wright Haskell Papers remain in our family's possession but are available on microfilm at the State Historical Society of Missouri Research Center–Kansas City (formerly the Western Historical Manuscript Collection, University of Missouri–Kansas City), Special Collections and Archives, Wright State University Libraries in Dayton, and other repositories. It was this epistolary treasure trove that inspired me to tell Katharine's story and that made its telling possible.

The other principal manuscript sources on which *Maiden Flight* is based include the cornucopia of Wright family papers held by Wright State University and the Library of Congress, supplemented by a smaller Wright brothers collection at the Royal Aeronautical Society in London; and the extensive correspondence of the Arctic explorer and author Vilhjalmur Stefansson, which is divided between the Rauner Special Collections Library at Dartmouth College and the National Archives. I have also drawn freely on letters, academic records, and other material in the Oberlin College Archives, as well as on a small collection of Henry J. Haskell's papers that I assembled while writing a book about my grandfather's career at the *Kansas City Star*.

For those seeking a straightforward historical account of the events chronicled in this book, I highly recommend the late Ian Mackersey's *The Wright Brothers: The Remarkable Story of the Aviation Pioneers Who Changed the World* (London: Little Brown, 2003). Alone among the Wrights' biographers, he devotes two full chapters to Katharine's love affair with Harry, her subsequent estrangement from Orville, and the sad coda to his illustrious career. Richard Maurer covers the ground more concisely in a meticulously researched biography for younger readers, *The Wright Sister: Katharine Wright and Her Famous Brothers* (2003; rpt. New York: Square Fish Books, 2016). I owe each of these authors a debt of thanks for sharing their knowledge and insights, and for encouraging me to relate the story of Katharine, Orville, and Harry in my own way.

For much-appreciated assistance of various kinds, I am happy to express my gratitude to Tracy Barrett, whose vividly fictionalized autobiography of Anna of Byzantium was an inspiration for my work; Dawne Dewey, head of Special Collections and Archives at Wright State University Libraries, who graciously fielded my questions and guided me through the Wright family materials in her care; John Dizikes, historian extraordinaire, whose comments and insights improved a preliminary draft of *Maiden Flight*; Sarah H. Heald, staff curator at the National Park Service, who shared her painstakingly researched historic furnishings report on Hawthorn Hill, the Wright family home in Dayton; Susan Marsh, whose valuable perspective as a sympathetic nonspecialist reader helped me tailor the book for a general audience; Lester Reingold, longtime friend, aviation writer, and avid Wright brothers enthusiast, who likewise commented on an early draft of the manuscript; and Paul Royster of the University of Nebraska–Lincoln, who generously placed his publishing expertise and scholarly acumen at my disposal. Jordan and Anita Miller, my unflaggingly supportive acquiring editors at Academy Chicago, and their colleagues at Chicago Review Press, notably Jerome Pohlen and Ellen Hornor, brought the book to fruition with courtesy and professionalism.

Special thank-yous go to my beloved wife, Ellen Rose Cordes, whose unflagging enthusiasm for the project sustained me over many years; and Amanda Wright Lane, Katharine and Orville's great-grandniece and trustee of the Wright Brothers Family Foundation, who welcomed me and my sister to a Wright-Haskell family reunion in Dayton long before *Maiden Flight* was airborne.

Explanatory Notes

6   *I told the boys there was at least one person outside the family who would know it wasn't so:* Harry wrote about his first meeting with the Wright brothers many times in later years. Katharine, to the best of my knowledge, recorded her early memories of Harry only once, in a long letter to Vilhjalmur Stefansson dated December 2, 1923. I am indebted to Ann Honious and Edward Roach of the National Park Service for providing photocopies of this and many other letters to and from Katharine in the Vilhjalmur Stefansson and Evelyn Stefansson Nef Papers at the National Archives.

8   *I was detained after breakfast three times a week to give aid and advice:* Although Katharine was at pains to rebut news reports that she had assisted her brothers with their mathematical computations, she bristled at Harry's suggestion that she needed help in math. In a letter dated November 13, 1925, she twitted him gently about his claim to have tutored her in freshman Math Review, saying, "I don't think you ever did help me with that but maybe you did."

11 *Sterchens, we called her, or Swes for short:* The Wright children went by a variety of nicknames that constituted a sort of private family code. Katharine was Kate or Katie to her friends, but her brothers called her Swes or Sterchens (from the German for "little sister," *Schwesterchens*), while her father used the more formal German *Tochter* (daughter). Lorin was affectionately known as Phiz, Reuchlin as Reuch (pronounced "Roosh"), Wilbur as Ullam, and Orville as Bubbo, Bubs, or Bubbies. Katharine habitually referred to Orville as Little Brother, despite the fact that he was her senior by three years.

13 *My college roommate:* Margaret Goodwin and Katharine were charter members of the lovelorn Order of the Empty Heart, to which Katharine refers later. They remained close friends after college and visited the St. Louis World's Fair together in 1904. Two years later, Margaret died of tuberculosis. Shortly before her own death, Katharine endowed a scholarship at Oberlin in her roommate's memory.

14 *if it hadn't been for his ice hockey accident:* The "accident" that changed the course of Wilbur's life may in fact have been a malicious attack by the neighborhood bully. As David McCullough writes in *The Wright Brothers* (New York: Simon and Schuster, 2015), a young tough named Oliver Crook Haugh, deliberately or otherwise, "smashed [Wilbur] in the face with a stick, knocking out most of his upper teeth." Years later Haugh would be executed for murdering three members of his own family.

16 *I never did anything so well as the teaching I did at the high school:* A classics scholar at Oberlin, Katharine taught Latin

and history at Dayton's newly opened Steele High School from 1899, a year after her graduation, until 1908. Although she chafed at women's second-class status on the faculty, by 1902 she was earning twenty-five dollars a week, 10 percent more than Harry was paid at the *Kansas City Star*.

19 *It was Kate who insisted that we had outgrown the house on Hawthorn Street and needed a bigger place:* The Wrights' seven-room house at 7 Hawthorn Street, on Dayton's low-lying West Side, was badly damaged in the 1913 Miami River flood. But Katharine and her brothers had begun planning their new mansion in suburban Oakwood several years earlier. The old house remained on its original site until 1937, when Henry Ford moved it to Greenfield Village in Dearborn, Michigan. After Orville's death in 1948, Hawthorn Hill passed to the National Cash Register Company, which maintained it as a guest house. Today it is open to the public as a national historic site, jointly administered by Dayton History and the Wright Brothers Family Foundation.

20 *She called his room the "blue room," on account of the blue wallpaper:* As Harry tells us later, the "blue room" was where he and Katharine secretly kissed and petted after Orville had retired for the night. It was the bedroom at the southeast corner of the second floor, just across the hall from the guest room where Harry slept, and linked to Katharine's room by a shared bath. Orville's bedroom was at the far end of the house, some forty feet down the corridor. In April 1926 Katharine wrote to Harry that "we really need the blue room, dear, when you come for a visit. It was such a sweet place to love you, with the lovely moonlight

for our only light." Although no trace remains of the original wall color, Sarah Heald of the National Park Service has identified the "blue room" through a historical analysis of Hawthorn Hill's furnishings.

21   *Certain high-ranking Smithsonian officials pursued Curtiss's campaign of misrepresentation for their own ends:* The story of the bruising competition between Curtiss and the Wrights—of which the characters in this book naturally present a one-sided view—is told in Lawrence Goldstone, *Birdmen: The Wright Brothers, Glenn Curtiss, and the Battle to Control the Skies* (New York: Ballantine Books, 2014) and Edward J. Roach, *The Wright Company: From Invention to Industry* (Athens: Ohio University Press, 2014). On Orville and Katharine's long-running feud with the Smithsonian, see Tom Crouch, *The Bishop's Boys: A Life of Wilbur and Orville Wright* (New York: Norton, 1989) and Ian Mackersey, *The Wright Brothers: The Remarkable Story of the Aviation Pioneers Who Changed the World* (London: Little, Brown, 2003). Ironically, the Wright and Curtiss companies merged in 1929, long after Orville sold the business, to form the Curtiss-Wright Corporation, which still exists today.

23   *the Bishop, whose lonely crusade against the forces of darkness in the church had consumed so much of his and his children's lives:* Milton Wright first crossed swords with his ecclesiastical brethren in the 1880s over the issue of admitting members of secret societies into the church. In 1901 he discovered that Rev. Millard Keiter had embezzled thousands of dollars of church funds, but the elders refused to take action. When the Bishop, ably seconded by Wilbur, pressed

his case, he was forced to stand trial, ostracized, and briefly expelled from the church before finally being vindicated in 1905. Ian Mackersey recounts the Wrights' ordeal in fascinating detail in *The Wright Brothers* (see preceding note).

24 *a special Justice Department investigation issued a report*: Government investigators found Edward Deeds guilty of favoritism in steering lucrative contracts to the Dayton-Wright Company, which he had founded in 1917, and recommended that he be prosecuted. Orville served as a consultant to Dayton-Wright after selling the original Wright Company in 1915; he testified at the hearings of the Hughes commission but was not implicated in any wrongdoing. Upon receiving the commission's report, Secretary of War Newton Baker dumped the political hot potato into the lap of a US Army board of review, which declined to press charges against Deeds.

29 *his real name, Vilhjalmur Stefansson, is such a mouthful*: In fact, Stefansson's birth name was William Stephenson. Born in Manitoba, Canada, he grew up in South Dakota and changed his name in 1899 in acknowledgment of his Icelandic parentage.

30 *there has been talk about him and that lady novelist*: Stefansson's dalliances with Hurst and sundry other women are documented in letters preserved in the Rauner Special Collections Library at Dartmouth College, many of which date from the same period in which he and Katharine were becoming emotionally involved. If Katharine was aware of Stef's philandering, she never spoke of it in her own letters, but it was an open secret among his artist and writer friends.

42   *neither Carrie nor Kate has ever had a good word to say
       about Miss Beck:* Fourteen-year-old Carrie Kayler came
       to work for the Wrights in 1900 and remained in Orville's
       employ until his death in 1948. After Katharine's marriage,
       Carrie and her husband moved into a suite of rooms at
       Hawthorn Hill to look after Orville. Both Carrie and Katha-
       rine resented the protective cocoon woven around Orville
       by the strong-willed Mabel Beck, whom he had "inherited"
       from Wilbur as his private secretary.

42   *Kate and I used to hole up on Lambert Island for weeks
       on end:* The Wrights first visited their future summer
       home in 1916 while vacationing on Georgian Bay, on the
       northeastern shore of Lake Huron. Lambert Island was a
       twenty-six-acre expanse of exposed granite on which the
       owner had started building and then abandoned a vacation
       compound for his wife. Orville was so taken with the set-
       ting that he purchased the island a few months later. From
       1918 to 1926, he and Katharine spent up to two months
       there every summer. The rustic simplicity and privacy of
       their summer "camp" afforded a welcome respite from the
       fishbowl formality of Hawthorn Hill. Orville continued to
       vacation on the island with various family members and
       friends until World War II.

45   *I had no idea how reckless Stef's ambition was until the
       Wrangel Island episode flared up in the newspapers that
       fall:* A footnote in history books today, the ill-fated scien-
       tific expedition to Wrangel Island—an Arctic wilderness
       off the coast of northeastern Siberia that has been called
       "the Galápagos of the far north," successively claimed by

the American, Canadian, and Russian governments—that Stefansson organized in the early 1920s temporarily soured his relations with the Wrights. The essential details are presented piecemeal in the narrative that follows, as they gradually became known to Katharine, Orville, and Harry. Although Stef emerged from the fiasco with his reputation largely unscathed, criticism of his conduct was so intense that he felt compelled to plead his case in a book titled *The Adventure of Wrangel Island* (1926).

49 *President King intended to appoint her to Oberlin's board of trustees:* Katharine served as an Oberlin trustee from 1924 until her death. Keenly aware of her special status as only the second woman to hold such an appointment, she reveled in locking horns with her male colleagues and the college administration, making her influence felt in such areas as faculty appointments, gender discrimination, and building plans. She may have inspired the $300,000 bequest that Orville made to Oberlin in his will, which was used to offset the cost of building the Wilbur and Orville Wright Laboratory of Physics.

49 *I was so taken with it that I went back the following day and purchased another copy for myself:* The Wrights hung their copy of the Rouen Cathedral print in what Katharine called the "cold-storage room" or "trophy room"—the front parlor at Hawthorn Hill—where it was photographed after Orville's death in 1948. A snapshot that Harry sent to Katharine during their courtship shows the identical image on display in the dining room of the house in Kansas City.

52   *It was absolutely the first time that anything pro-French had been so much as* mentioned *in that setting:* Katharine returned from her first visit to France in 1909 a confirmed Francophile. Among the few possessions she brought to Kansas City was an autographed photo of Marshal Ferdinand Foch, the Allied commander in World War I. She laced her correspondence with French phrases and once wrote Harry a note in French, thanking him for sending her flowers. But her command of the language was imperfect. "I would like to do something with French but I have a curious feeling that it's no use," she replied when Harry suggested they take French lessons together in Kansas City. "I can't remember anything long enough to build up any kind of a knowledge."

95   *Western Union was on the line with a telegram for Katharine:* Telegrams such as the ones between Katharine and Harry were taken down in Morse code, transmitted over dedicated wires, decoded and printed out at the receiving end, and delivered by special messengers. To ensure the message arrived promptly, a Western Union employee telephoned the recipient while the paper telegram was en route. Katharine would have taken such a call in the phone closet located at the far end of the central hall at Hawthorn Hill, safely out of earshot of Orville in the dining room.

97   *Then I tried the Postal:* Katharine is referring to the Postal Telegraph Company, Western Union's principal competitor until the two companies merged in 1943.

112   *Sinclair Lewis's so-called Sunday school class:* Sinclair Lewis spent several months in Kansas City in 1926–27 researching

and writing his bestselling novel *Elmer Gantry*, an unflattering portrait of a loose-living fundamentalist preacher. Katharine, who took a dim view of Harry's Unitarianism, was shocked when he told her about attending one of Lewis's irreverent "Sunday school classes" at a local hotel. "Maybe I'd better darn stockings on Sunday mornings," she wrote. "It may be better for my soul—and yours, too, dear!"

120   *a sort of wild John Gilpin ride:* Orville is referring to a character in a popular eighteenth-century ballad by William Cowper who careened comically through the British countryside after losing control of his horse.

122   *our tastes in literature run pretty much along the same lines:* When Harry graduated from Oberlin in 1896, Katharine gave him a collection of essays by James Russell Lowell; two years later he reciprocated by presenting her with a prized edition of Robert Louis Stevenson's *Vailima Letters*. Their correspondence is strewn with comments on books they were reading. They shared a love of Romantic poetry—Keats, Shelley, Wordsworth, and especially Stevenson. Katharine was initially bemused by Harry's interest in modern drama and philosophy, but eventually conceded that Shaw "has a lot of sense." Her own taste in fiction was decidedly middle-brow; among her favorite contemporary authors were Hamlin Garland, Josephine Bacon, and Dorothy Canfield. She couldn't abide Sinclair Lewis or H. L. Mencken, whose work Harry admired, and when he sent her Philip Gibbs's mildly antiwar novel *The Middle of the Road*, she dismissed it as "parlor pacifist nonsense."

127   *he slipped his hand down where I love to have it and held it
      against me:* This is the closest Katharine comes in her let-
      ters to describing the physical act of lovemaking, but the
      passion that her relationship with Harry unleashed in her
      is never far below the surface. Until her side of their cor-
      respondence was made public in the early 1990s, Wright
      biographers naturally assumed that Katharine had little
      interest in sex. Adrian Kinnane, whose unpublished psy-
      chological study of the Wright family called "The Crucible
      of Flight" (1982) has provided rich insights for histori-
      cal accounts (including this one), states categorically that
      "there is no sign that Katharine allowed herself romantic
      involvement with anyone," either before or—surprisingly
      enough—after her marriage. The portrayal of Katharine as
      fundamentally asexual accorded with the well-established
      image of her brothers as lifelong celibates. One senses that
      the sensuality Katharine expressed to Harry in her love
      letters was as much a revelation to her as it was to him.

134   *not letting them have any credit before the public:* Bylines
      almost never appeared in the *Star* in the Nelson era, or for
      some years afterward. As an editorial writer, Harry was
      so accustomed to anonymity that it became an ingrained
      habit; even when he started writing a weekly column in the
      1930s, titled Random Thoughts, he signed it only with his
      initials. Not until he won a Pulitzer Prize for his editorials
      in 1944 was his individual contribution to the paper pub-
      licly recognized.

155   *Mr. Akeley's bronze elephants:* Carl Akeley's miniature
      sculpture of two African elephants supporting a wounded

comrade had a double significance for Katharine as a memento of both Hawthorn Hill and Akeley's close friend Vilhjalmur Stefansson. According to Lorin Wright's grandson Wilkinson Wright, Katharine asked Carrie Kayler Grumbach—with whom she stayed in touch after her marriage—to pack the sculpture up and ship it to Kansas City. Carrie stood firm, however, explaining that she "couldn't take those things out of the house without Mr. Orv's permission."

167 *my new stationery, with the initials K.W.H. woven into a neat little circle at the top:* The letterhead on the stationery Katharine used in the mid-1920s, while she was living with her brother, read simply "HAWTHORN HILL / OAKWOOD / DAYTON . . OHIO." She reported to Harry that although Orville was "inclined to be critical of my buying," he "likes my new stationery so well that he wants to get some for himself." The fact that she waited a full year after moving to Kansas City to order new letterhead under her married name suggests that she was in no hurry to shed her old family and home ties.

167 *I can be of little help to her in talking about aviation developments:* Despite Harry's close ties to the "fathers of flight," trains remained his preferred mode of travel; not until 1947 did he take his first ride in a private airplane. Katharine, likewise, rarely had occasion to fly after her much-publicized early sorties with Wilbur and Orville.

178 *we had a visit from the Bulgarian Haskells:* Harry's older brother Edward, a missionary stationed in Bulgaria, brought his Swiss wife and three of their children to Kansas

City in June 1927. His twelve-year-old daughter recorded in her diary the dressing-down her younger brother received from Katharine. Eldora found her new aunt "very nice although she would be nicer if she did something worth while. A person who lives as idle a life as she does has no right not to be nice." Ironically, Katharine was even harder on herself: while still living in Dayton as Orville's helpmate, she confided to Harry that "there is no excuse for my doing nothing. If a man did that, I'd have my opinion of him."

178–79   *I'd say the children of missionaries were no less inclined to Goopish behavior than the common garden variety:* Gelett Burgess's humorous cautionary tales about the "Goops"— children who "lick their fingers . . . lick their knives . . . spill broth on the tablecloth . . . [and] lead disgusting lives"— were among Katharine's favorite readings for her young nieces and nephews.

182   *he sat down at his desk and turned out a column for his news-paper:* William Allen White's moving eulogy to his teenage daughter Mary, which appeared in the *Emporia Gazette* on May 17, 1921, is justly famous and widely anthologized. Among Harry's papers is a galley proof of the essay that White apparently gave him at the time of her death.

183   *Writing, which used to be my delight, has become an almost forgotten art with me:* Katharine's hundreds of surviving letters—surely a mere fraction of the actual total—show that she treated letter writing as both an art form and a social obligation. At the height of her quandary over leaving Orville, it was not uncommon for her to write Harry two or even three letters in a single day, typically in beautifully

formed longhand. When Orville gave her a Hammond typewriter for Christmas in 1921, she enthused to a friend that she "took to it as a duck does to water. . . . It saves so much wear and tear. I have a large correspondence which otherwise would be a burden." A sampling of her correspondence has been digitized and is available on the Library of Congress website.

183   *I left him my entire estate free and clear—apart from a few small bequests to Carrie, Lorin, and other special people:* The $50,000 that Wilbur left Katharine in 1912 made her a woman of means. In her own will, executed on August 5, 1927, she made several small bequests and left her residuary estate to Harry, stipulating that certain additional legacies be paid to family and friends after his death. However, Harry elected to fulfill her wishes as soon as his finances permitted. On January 1, 1931, he mailed a $1,000 check to Orville and disclosed that he also intended to distribute bequests early to Katharine's other heirs. How Orville felt about his sister's posthumous gesture of reconciliation is unknown. In acknowledging receipt of the money, he wrote to Harry, "If you should ever need the use of it, don't hesitate to let me know and it shall be yours."

186   *as soon as we get the mortgage paid off:* As recounted in my book *Boss-Busters and Sin Hounds: Kansas City and Its "Star"* (Columbia: University of Missouri Press, 2009), the newspaper remained so profitable throughout the Great Depression that the employee owners were able to retire all outstanding debt in the early 1930s, several years ahead

of schedule. As a major stockholder in the Star Company, Harry eventually amassed a considerable fortune.

189   *I fear it would be like rubbing salt in the wound for Orv to see my name in print:* Apart from a flurry of news reports, mostly in the society pages, that appeared soon after her move to Kansas City, Katharine—once among the most visible women in the world—all but vanished from the public eye in the last two years of her life. Fortunately, she continued to correspond with Vilhjalmur Stefansson, Agnes Beck, Griffith Brewer, and a handful of other friends. It seems probable that her decision to maintain a low profile after her marriage reflects an instinct for self-protection as much as sensitivity to her brother's feelings.

193   *He always complained that McMahon's approach was too personal and chatty:* In 1915 Orville agreed to collaborate with two would-be biographers, John McMahon and Earl Findley, but he disapproved of the manuscript they produced and refused to endorse it. Fourteen years later, McMahon resurrected the material for a series of articles published in *Popular Science Monthly.* When Orville learned that Little, Brown planned to bring the serialized biography out in book form, he unsuccessfully attempted to quash it and was incensed when McMahon's *The Wright Brothers: Fathers of Flight* appeared in 1930.

198   *My friend Agnes was "Orv's girl" when we were young:* Tom Crouch (see note to p. 21 on p. 232) writes of Agnes Osborn Beck that "tradition in the Osborn family has it that Orville actually proposed marriage" to her, but, for whatever reason, "the romance came to nothing." In an

unpublished memoir, Agnes's daughter, Becky Rehling, recalls that Orville "developed the habit of calling on Agnes" while Katharine was at Oberlin and often took her to lectures and concerts. Although Orville "seemed a most persistent suitor," however, "things never progressed to the point of tackling her Victorian father."

209   *Illumination Night at Oberlin:* The ongoing tradition of festooning the Oberlin campus with thousands of multicolored Japanese lanterns during commencement weekend began with the inauguration of President Henry C. King in 1903.

213   *We returned on February 13 from my operation at the Mayo Clinic:* Harry's account of Katharine's last days is taken, nearly verbatim, from two letters he wrote shortly after her death, one to his brother Edward, the other to Griffith Brewer. The Wrights' biographer Ian Mackersey and I, working independently, discovered these previously unknown sources among photocopies of Edward Haskell's papers at the Ohio State University in Columbus (the originals are now at Harvard's Houghton Library) and the papers of Charles Gibbs-Smith at the Science Museum in London.

215   *beside her father and mother and brother:* Until Katharine's death in 1929, Wilbur was the only one of the five Wright siblings buried beside their parents in Woodland Cemetery. (Orville would join them in 1948.) Reuchlin Wright, Katharine's oldest brother, is buried in Kansas City's Forest Hills Cemetery. Lorin and his wife, Netta, attended Reuch's funeral in 1920, but Orville's illness prevented him and Katharine from making the trip. Lorin, who died in 1939, was buried in his wife's family plot in Woodland Cemetery.

218   *the original Wright flyer was finally repatriated from London, in accordance with Orville's wishes:* Upon resolution of his dispute with the Smithsonian in 1942, Orville confidentially notified the Science Museum of his desire to bring the 1903 flyer home from London as soon as it could be safely transported. In the event, the Wright flyer was not restored to its rightful place in the North Hall of the Smithsonian's Arts and Industries Building until December 1948. Harry came out from Kansas City for the installation and hosted a dinner for the Wright family at the Statler Hotel; it was the last time they were to see him. As Tom Crouch writes in his biography of the Wright brothers (see note to p. 21 on p. 232), the family's agreement with the Smithsonian stipulated that "if the Smithsonian ever recognized any other aircraft as having been capable of powered, sustained, and controlled flight with a man on board before December 17, 1903, the executors of the estate would have the right to take possession of the machine once again."

218   *a fountain that he intended to donate to Oberlin College in Katharine Wright Haskell's memory:* Harry served on Oberlin's Board of Trustees from 1930 to 1947. Through the generosity of members of the Wright family, the Wright Brothers Family Foundation, and other donors, the Katharine Wright Haskell Fountain was restored in 2007 by sculptor Nicholas Fairplay.

Glossary of Names

Charles G. Abbot Secretary of the Smithsonian Institution from 1928 to 1944. Despite his amicable relations with Orville, institutional loyalty inhibited him from resolving their dispute over the Langley aerodrome until long after Katharine's death.

Carl E. Akeley Prominent naturalist, taxidermist, and friend of Vilhjalmur Stefansson. *The Wounded Comrade* (1913), his small bronze sculpture of two elephants supporting an injured companion, was one of the treasured possessions that Katharine left behind at Hawthorn Hill.

Josephine Bacon Prolific fiction writer known for her treatment of female themes. Katharine recommended her *Middle Aged Love Stories* to Harry early in their courtship.

Agnes (Osborn) Beck Katharine's closest woman friend after her move to Kansas City. A neighbor of the Wrights when they lived on Hawthorn Street, she was rumored to have been Orville's girlfriend.

Mabel Beck Orville's longtime and fiercely protective private secretary (no relation to Agnes). Katharine and Carrie Kayler Grumbach resented her influence over him.

Hiram Bingham US senator from 1924 to 1933. Famed for discovering the Inca city of Machu Picchu in Peru, he served as an aviator during World War I.

Dr. Peter Bohan Katharine's attending physician in Kansas City during her final illness.

Carlotta Bollée Widow of Léon Bollée, French car manufacturer and flying enthusiast, who gave the Wrights facilities to repair their damaged flyer in Le Mans in 1908.

Griffith (Griff) Brewer British patent attorney and longtime friend and business associate of Orville and Katharine. He served as an emissary between them after Katharine moved to Kansas City.

Frank Hedges Butler English wine merchant, balloonist, flying enthusiast, and founder of the Aero Club of Great Britain.

Frank and Bertha Canby Friends of the Wrights from Dayton.

Octave Chanute Distinguished French American railroad engineer and aviation pioneer. His generously shared expertise was crucial to the Wright brothers' successful solution of the problem of flight.

Frank M. Chapman Renowned ornithologist and author of numerous field guides, several of which he autographed for Katharine. She and her brothers were avid bird watchers.

Calvin Coolidge President of the United States from 1923 to 1929. Katharine told Harry that she "didn't have much admiration for him until the intellectuals? brought out his virtues and superiority by their silly criticism."

James Cox Publisher of the *Dayton Daily News*. He served as governor of Ohio from 1913 to 1915 and again from 1917 to 1921.

Arthur Cunningham Katharine's college fiancé, captain of the Oberlin football team, and later a surgeon. She broke off their secret engagement when she realized she wasn't in love.

Glenn Curtiss Motorcycle racer, aviation pioneer, and the Wrights' most redoubtable business competitor. They accused him of stealing their patents, embroiling Orville in a prolonged series of bitterly contested lawsuits.

Edward Deeds Dayton engineer, wealthy industrialist, and friend and business associate of Orville. His wife encouraged Katharine to accept Harry's proposal of marriage.

Geneva Farmer Sick nurse to Harry's first wife, Isabel. Her attempts to snare the grieving widower provoked a concerned letter from Katharine, which in turn set off Harry's fateful "explosion."

Earl N. Findley Aviation editor of the *New York Times* and, along with Harry, one of the few journalists who enjoyed the Wrights' good graces.

Margaret Goodwin Katharine's Oberlin College roommate from Chicago.

Carrie Kayler Grumbach The Wrights' longtime housekeeper, with whom Katharine had a warm but competitive relationship. Carrie and her husband moved in with Orville after Katharine's marriage.

Bob Hadeler The Wrights' young friend and neighbor who spent several summers with Orville on Lambert Island in Canada after Katharine moved to Kansas City.

Edward Haskell Harry's older brother, a missionary stationed in Bulgaria.

Harry (Henry J.) Haskell Editor of the *Kansas City Star*, Katharine's middle-aged lover and later husband. She considered him "all head" when they were students together at Oberlin.

Henry ("young Henry") Haskell Harry and Isabel's only son, who graduated from Harvard in 1924. Katharine and Harry both tried to hide their growing interest in each other from him.

Isabel Haskell Harry's first wife, who succumbed to breast cancer in 1923. Katharine idealized them as a married couple and worried that Harry would rush into another woman's arms after Isabel's death.

Katharine Wright Haskell The Wright brothers' younger sister, who hesitated for months before agreeing to marry Harry in November 1926. Her relationship with Orville was so close that strangers often mistook them for husband and wife.

Mary Haskell Harry's missionary sister, who lived in Oberlin and cared for their aged mother. She begged Orville to forgive Harry for taking Katharine away from him.

Mrs. Tyler (Arabell) Hemingway Ernest Hemingway's aunt and one of the Kansas City widows suspected by Katharine of showing an unhealthy interest in Harry after his first wife died.

Burton Hendrick Noted American journalist and biographer. Orville designated him as his preferred collaborator on a never-to-be-written book about the invention of the airplane.

Charles Evans Hughes Former associate justice and future chief justice of the Supreme Court. Hughes led a Justice Department investigation into corruption and mismanagement in the wartime aircraft production program headed by Orville's friend Edward Deeds.

Fannie Hurst Author of *Back Street, Star Dust, Lummox,* and other bestselling but now forgotten novels; also, unbeknownst to Katharine, one of Vilhjalmur Stefansson's far-flung love interests.

Leontine and John Jameson Lorin Wright's daughter and son-in-law. Married at Hawthorn Hill in 1923, they were the only members of the Wright family who attended Katharine and Harry's wedding three years later.

Rev. Millard Keiter Milton Wright's antagonist in the Church of the United Brethren. Their fierce hand-to-hand combat hardened the Wrights for their later battles with Glenn Curtiss and the Smithsonian Institution.

Henry C. King Prominent theologian and longtime president of Oberlin College. He appointed Katharine to the board of trustees and presided over her marriage to Harry after Orville refused to hold the wedding at Hawthorn Hill.

Mella King and Katharine Wright King Mother and daughter (no relation to Henry C. King) who were Katharine's friends in Geneva, Ohio. Katharine's ears pricked up when she learned that Harry had given her namesake a high school graduation present.

Laura and Irwin Kirkwood Owners of the *Kansas City Star*. After Laura's death in 1926, Irwin and members of the staff bought the newspaper from her estate. Harry subsequently became editor.

Frank Lahm ("old Mr. Lahm") Expatriate American businessman living in Paris, and one of the Wrights' early champions. The sympathetic letter he wrote to Katharine after her marriage reminded her of the old days.

Lt. Frank Lahm ("young Frank") The Wright brothers' liaison in their business dealings with the US Army. Orville suspected him of being sweet on Katharine.

Samuel P. Langley First secretary of the Smithsonian Institution. A distinguished scientist respected by the Wright brothers, he designed the ill-fated "aerodrome," which plunged into the Potomac River shortly before the Wrights made their first flight at Kitty Hawk.

Kate Leonard A college classmate of Katharine's who lived in Oberlin. They remained close friends after graduating and saw each other regularly.

Otto Lilienthal German engineer and aviation pioneer whose experiments with gliders inspired the Wright brothers to build their own flying machine. He died as a result of a glider crash in 1896.

Charles Lindbergh World-famous American aviator who made the first solo flight across the Atlantic Ocean in 1927. His penchant for generating publicity made "Lindy" the antithesis of the modest, reclusive Orville.

George Longan The *Kansas City Star*'s managing editor whom Katharine and Harry saw socially.

Louis and Frances (Frannie) Lord Katharine and Harry's friends and confidants in Oberlin. A professor of classics, Louis sided with the lovers but failed to persuade Orville to attend their wedding.

Anne and Frank McCormick The Wrights' close friends and neighbors in suburban Oakwood. A well-known journalist, Anne spoke her mind to Orville in a fruitless effort to shame him into reconciling with Katharine.

John R. McMahon Journalist and author of an early biography of the Wright brothers, which Orville considered invasively personal and attempted unsuccessfully to suppress.

H. L. Mencken Brilliantly iconoclastic journalist and magazine editor who cofounded the *American Mercury* in 1924. Harry admired his writing, but Katharine considered him a self-promoting "smarty-pants."

Ivonette and Harold ("Scribze") Miller Daughter and son-in-law of Lorin and Ivonette Wright. They were married at Hawthorn Hill in 1919.

William Rockhill Nelson Laura Kirkwood's father and the *Kansas City Star*'s cofounder, who died in 1915. Katharine accused the Nelson clan of thinking only of their own family.

George W. Norris Influential progressive politician. He represented Nebraska in the US House of Representatives and Senate from 1903 to 1943.

Alec (Alexander) Ogilvie English pilot who founded the British Wright Company with Griffith Brewer and Orville. The set of red-and-gold coffee cups that he gave to Katharine may have been a sign of deeper admiration.

Arthur Page Editor of the *World's Work*, a widely respected magazine of news and commentary. The Wrights considered him a trusted ally, despite his persistent attempts to persuade Orville to write "the book."

Roy Roberts Washington correspondent and later managing editor of the *Kansas City Star*. He succeeded Harry as the paper's top editor in 1952.

August Seested Chief executive of the *Kansas City Star* in succession to Irwin Kirkwood. After his death in October 1928, Harry was promoted to editor.

Lt. Thomas Selfridge US Army officer and aviator who was killed in the crash of an airplane piloted by Orville at Fort Myer, Virginia, in 1908.

Vilhjalmur Stefansson (Stef) Dashing Canadian explorer of the Arctic, lecturer, and prolific author of Icelandic extraction. His emotionally unsatisfying "friendship" with Katharine, coupled with his questionable professional ethics, helped propel her into Harry's arms.

Raymond H. Stetson ("the Prof") Professor of psychology at Oberlin, to whom Harry turned for advice on wooing Katharine.

Richard Sutton ("Doctor Dick") Socially prominent Kansas City dermatologist, big-game hunter, and author. One of Harry's closest friends, Sutton urged him to "camp on the trail" and bag Katharine before it was too late.

William Howard Taft Former president of the United States, chief justice of the Supreme Court, and chancellor of the Smithsonian Institution.

Booth Tarkington Popular American novelist, best known for *The Magnificent Ambersons*. *Seventeen*, a mild-mannered satire of Willie Baxter's puppy love for the worldly Lola Pratt, was a favorite of Orville's.

Charles Taylor A mechanic, whom Katharine disliked, in the Wright brothers' bicycle shop. He built the engine for the original Wright flyer and rescued Orville from the wreckage of his airplane at Fort Myer in 1908.

Charles D. Walcott Secretary of the Smithsonian Institution from 1907 until his death in 1927. His refusal to retract the Smithsonian's claim that Samuel Langley's aerodrome was the first powered aircraft capable of flight made him the Wrights' enemy.

William Allen White Editor of the *Emporia Gazette* and Harry's closest male friend. A folk hero of American journalism, the "Sage of Emporia" accused the disconsolate widower of nursing a "grouch on God."

Ernest H. Wilkins Henry C. King's successor as president of Oberlin, serving from 1927 to 1946. Katharine served on the committee that selected him.

Horace ("Bus") and Susan (Sue) Wright Katharine's nephew and his fiancée. After moving to Kansas City, Katharine turned down an invitation to their wedding in Dayton on account of Orville.

Lorin ("Phiz") and Ivonette (Netta) Wright Katharine and Orville's easygoing older brother and his wife. Katharine looked to them both for support and advice throughout her ordeal.

Milton Wright ("the Bishop") Katharine and Orville's strong-willed but loving father and a bishop in the Church of the United Brethren. He died in 1917, three years after the threesome moved to suburban Oakwood from downtown Dayton.

Orville (Orv) Wright Brother of Wilbur and Katharine and elder statesman of American aviation. He considered Katharine's marriage to Harry Haskell a betrayal of a family pact and refused to attend the wedding.

Reuchlin (Reuch) and Lulu (Lou) Wright The eldest Wright brother and his wife. Reuch plied a variety of trades in and near Kansas City before his death in 1920.

Susan Wright Katharine and Orville's mother. She died in 1889, leaving fifteen-year-old Katharine to take her place in the family.

Wilbur Wright Katharine's beloved "Ullam," who was coinventor of the flying machine with Orville and died in 1912 of typhoid fever. It was in the "blue room" intended for Wilbur at Hawthorn Hill that Katharine and Harry secretly made love.